GOD SAVE THE KING

ALICE DOLMAN

ISBN 978-0-6451497-2-2 (print)

ISBN 978-0-6451497-3-9 (eBook)

Cover by www.yummybookcovers.com

Editing by www.loptandcropt.com

Proofreading by www.efcservicesllc.com

❀ Created with Vellum

For the real (and best) Emma and Lucy

House of Huntington

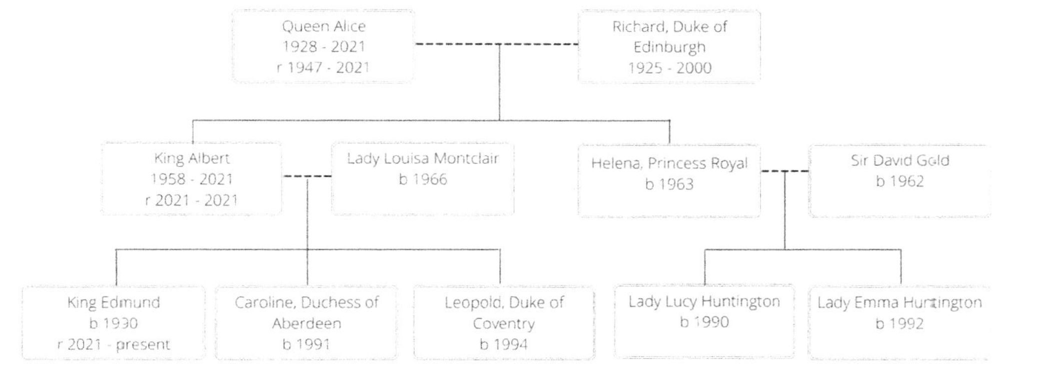

GOD SAVE THE KING

ALICE DOLMAN

GOD SAVE THE KING

Alice Dolman

CHAPTER 1

"So, are you engaged or not?"

"No, I'm not engaged. At least, I don't think I am," I say, wrinkling my nose.

My best friend, Penny, puts her hands on her hips and fixes me with a stare. "This is not something you want to be unsure about. Think, Amelia. What *exactly* did he say?"

"He said he loves me, and he wants to spend the rest of his life with me. And then he pulled out what looked like a ring box."

"Sounds an awful lot like a proposal to me. What did he say next?"

I shrug and shake my head. "He didn't say anything. That's when Henry arrived and told him his father had died."

I tell you what, nothing ruins a romantic mood faster than being told that one of your parents has died. Even if you were fighting with them. *Especially* if you were fighting with them.

Penny lets out a low whistle. "Talk about bad timing. He hasn't mentioned it since?"

"No, we've barely spoken. After we heard the news, we had a bit of time alone, but Eddie was devastated, and I was trying to be there for him, so I couldn't exactly spend the time peppering him with follow-up questions. After about half an hour, Henry came back and herded us onto a plane. They spent the entire flight talking about logistics and making dozens of phone calls."

"Why didn't you go back to KP when you landed?"

"I offered to, but Eddie said I should come back here and get some rest. Apparently, he's going to be in meetings most of the night. So I hopped in a car and called you instead."

"Right," Penny says with a sigh. "So to be clear—you flew to Kenya with your boyfriend yesterday, and while you were there, he told you he wants to spend the rest of his life with you, and then his father died."

I nod.

"And now your boyfriend is the king of England."

I inhale sharply. He is, isn't he? My boyfriend, Eddie—or Prince Edmund, Duke of Southampton, to be more precise—who makes cheesy jokes and bakes me pastries, has just become the king of England. My boyfriend is the king of an actual country. Several countries! Actually, I don't even know how many countries are in the Commonwealth—fifteen? Twenty? More? This is all too much.

Penny sits down next to me on the sofa. "Are you okay, Mils?" she asks, wrapping her arm around me. "You're so pale, and I'm pretty sure you're actually shaking."

I lean my head on her shoulder. "I'll be okay. It's just a lot to process."

Less than twelve hours ago, Eddie and I were in a lodge in Kenya planning our lives together, and now everything has changed. Last night he was ready to pack up and move home to Australia with me to enjoy a quiet life of charity work for the next thirty years while his father, King Albert, took care of the whole "ruling the kingdom" thing. Now I have no idea how my life is going to change, or if it's going to change at all. Eddie has a new life now, and there may not even be a place for me in it.

"Hey, Pen," I say, letting my heavy eyes droop shut, "thanks for being here for me."

"Amelia, I love you, and I'm always going to be here for you. You couldn't get rid of me if you tried."

"Not even if I stole your phone while you were sleeping and sent messages to all your exes begging them to take you back?"

She sniggers. "Please. They should be the ones begging me."

"True. You're pretty fabulous."

Penny pats my shoulder. "I am. Enough about me, though. It's late, and you should get some rest. Who knows what's going to happen in the morning."

I yawn. "You're right. The adrenaline has kept me up, but I'm crashing now. Will you stay in my room? I know it's weird, but I don't want to be alone."

"Of course I will. I'm not leaving your side until Edmund calls and I get to eavesdrop while you get the inside word on what's happening at the palace."

A FEW HOURS LATER, I'm woken up by Penny shaking me. I rub my eyes and try to pull the blanket back over my head, but she rips it away. "What time is it?"

"It's quarter past nine."

"Nine! Why are you waking me up? Why are *you* even awake? We went to bed less than five hours ago."

"I'm awake because my phone has been ringing non-stop for the last fifteen minutes."

I scrunch my face up, and my tired, blurry thoughts slide into focus.

"They made the announcement."

"They did. I thought you'd want to watch some of the news."

I rub my eyes. "Thanks, Pen, I do."

I wrap a blanket around myself and pad out into the tiny

living room of our flat, where Penny and I huddle together on the fraying sofa. While Penny searches for the remote, I check my phone—twenty-seven missed calls in the last hour, but none of them are from Eddie. Four of them are from my mum, so clearly the news has made it to Australia. I only told her yesterday that Eddie and I had gotten back together. She must be losing her mind that her daughter is suddenly dating the king.

Penny switches on BBC News, and we're confronted by an image of Buckingham Palace. Flags are flying at half-mast, and a small, golden easel sits at the front gates. The camera zooms in on a piece of cream paper in a black frame.

"Here, Elizabeth, we see the official announcement displayed in the Buckingham Palace forecourt," BBC special royal correspondent Cyril Bingham narrates.

"That's right, Cyril. For those just tuning in, the palace confirmed in a shocking statement this morning that His Majesty, King Albert, has died at age sixty-three after less than three months on the throne."

"His death so soon after the passing of his mother, Queen Alice, has plunged the country into mourning for the second time in less than a year," Cyril adds. "Stay tuned. As your senior royal correspondents, we'll be keeping you up to date throughout the day as more details come to light regarding this untimely tragedy."

The presenters disappear, and the screen fades to black before transitioning to an obituary package detailing King Albert's life. They've probably had it ready to go for at least thirty years.

I hug my knees to my chest and start checking messages.

Mum: *Hi Amelia, I heard the news. I can't believe it! He was so young, basically a spring chicken! Look after yourself and Edmund. Love Mum.*

Mum: *P.S. Let me know if there's anything we can do from here. Should we send a casserole to the palace? He'll need to eat and you've never been the best cook.*

Mum: *Oops, realised he's probably got people at the palace to buy food. Still, if there's anything you need, let us know. Send Edmund our love, and Leo, I've always been quite fond of him xx*

Sometimes I wish my parents were here, and sometimes I thank my lucky stars that they're not. If they lived within driving distance, they'd be here trying to barge into Kensington Palace with a lasagne for the king whom they've never met. The guards wouldn't have a clue what to make of them.

"I can't get over the fact that he waited over sixty years to be king and then didn't even last a year," Penny says.

I shake my head. "It doesn't seem real, does it?"

As the obituary reel hits Albert's teen years, my phone rings.

"Is it him?" Penny asks.

I check my phone and give her a thumbs-up as I answer. "Eddie? How are you?"

"Amelia! It's so good to hear your voice. I'm sorry I didn't reply to any of your messages last night. Henry took my phone and had me locked in my office all night."

"It's fine, I knew you'd be busy. I was just worried about you and wanted to see how you were coping."

Eddie gives a deep yawn. "I honestly don't know. I haven't had a chance to come to terms with any of it. The last time I slept was on the plane to Kenya almost thirty-six hours ago. I've been in back-to-back meetings since we landed, and I haven't the foggiest what half of them were even about."

"Oh, Eddie, it all sounds so stressful. What can I do to help?"

"Can you come over here? I'm going to try to give Henry the slip and sneak off to bed now, but I'd appreciate some company when I wake up."

"Of course. You get some sleep, and I'll be there as soon as I can. I love you."

There's silence, followed by another cavernous yawn. "I love you too."

When I hang up, Penny is staring at me, eyes wide. "What did he say?"

"Not much. He asked me to come over. He sounds so exhausted. I can't even imagine how hard this is for him. His father has died, and he's being pulled from meeting to meeting, trying to deal with logistics. I know the palace has plans in place for these kinds of things, but they can't have been expecting to deal with two monarchs dying within three months of each other."

She presses her lips together and frowns. "Did he happen to mention whether or not he thinks he proposed last night?"

"He did not."

"And you didn't ask him?"

"Pen," I say, shaking my head, "he's got enough going on at the moment."

"Well, make sure you ask soon. I want to know if I've been sharing a bathroom with the future queen for the last four years."

I feel like someone has slapped me in the face. I hadn't even considered that Eddie being king means if we get married, I'll become queen. Me. Queen.

The idea shouldn't come as a shock. I knew I was dating the first in line to the throne and was vaguely aware if we ever got married, I would technically be a princess, but I'd never stopped to seriously consider what that would mean. We'd only been together for a few months, and besides, we were talking about moving overseas and living as normal a life as possible for the next few decades. When I pictured life with Eddie, I always imagined us hanging out together in his little garden at Kensington Palace or a cosy house on the coast in Australia—cooking and watching terrible reality TV or planning a charity project together. Eddie becoming king seemed like such a distant prospect, I'd never given it any real thought.

I am not at all prepared for this—I can barely make it through a meal without spilling food on myself, I can never figure out how to do that thing where you cross one ankle behind the other gracefully, and my hair is way too frizzy for a princess's, let alone a queen's!

No point thinking about it now, though, when I don't even know if we're engaged. I should probably figure that out before I end up in a stress spiral about my non-regal hair. So I'm going to ignore it and leave future-Amelia to deal with the whole queen business.

I walk over to the front door of the flat and peer out the window next to the door. Thankfully, there's no sign of any photographers outside. Three weeks ago, I couldn't step out onto the footpath without dozens of paparazzi snapping away and shouting questions and sleazy comments at me. I'm not a centre-of-attention kind of girl, so the constant news articles and people staring and pointing at me in the streets were a total nightmare. There was nowhere to hide, and it made me feel like I was suffocating. It was so overwhelming that, for a little while, I thought it meant life with Eddie wasn't worth the pain. That he wasn't worth it. I came to my senses, obviously, and learned to deal with the attention, but I'd rather not have to.

"Anyone camped outside?" Penny asks.

"No, thank god. Turns out there are some advantages to people still thinking Eddie's engaged to Sibella."

Oh yeah, as far as the palace and public are concerned, my boyfriend is currently engaged to someone else. Long story.

"Maybe Albert did you a favour forcing the engagement on them."

"I'd still prefer not to have gone through the pain of thinking it had only taken Eddie three days after our break-up to decide he'd rather marry someone who'd already left him at the altar once than be with me."

Penny waves her hand in the air. "Details, details! Right now it's working out for you, so open that door and get your butt over to Kensington."

CHAPTER 2

I PULL on my coat and walk out into the street. When I was officially dating Eddie and the paparazzi were hounding me, he organised security and a car for me—privately funded, of course. After his re-engagement to Sibella was announced, public interest in me dropped right off, and the palace quickly deemed me safe to continue my normal life without protection. It was a welcome change at the time, but it means I'm back to having to make my own way around London. I'd normally take the Tube, but I don't want to be trapped on a train with a bunch of strangers who might recognise me, so Uber it is.

The driver does a double take when I get into the car and gives me a funny look when he sees that I'm going to Kensington Palace—affectionately known as KP—but thankfully, he doesn't say anything. Keeping my eyes glued to my phone and pretending to listen to something on my headphones probably helps. The trip across the city from Camden is mercifully quiet. I can't stand when drivers want to talk the whole drive. It's almost worth paying the extra for a taxi just to have a driver who can't give you a bad rating for ignoring them.

As we approach the palace, there are crowds of people lining the street. Flags are waving, and there are mounds of flowers piled on the ground. About a hundred metres from the gates, we get stuck in traffic. Guards are walking from car to car in front of us and turning everyone around. After a few minutes, one of them approaches the car and gestures for us to go back the way we came. I tell the driver to wait and roll down the window.

"Ma'am, we'll need you to turn around, please. No visitor access to the palace today."

"Prince Ed . . . sorry, the king is expecting me."

The guard raises an eyebrow. "Name?"

"Amelia Glendale. I should be on his list."

He taps away on the iPad he's holding and looks up at me again. "I'm sorry, ma'am, you're not on the list."

Ugh, I must have been taken off the permanently approved visitor list when Eddie and I broke up. "Would you mind calling him? He *is* expecting me."

The guard looks down his nose at me. "I'm sorry, ma'am, I'm going to have to ask you to leave."

He either doesn't know who I am or is doing an outstanding job of feigning ignorance. "I promise I'm not some kind of crackpot stalker trying to break in. If you can call him, he'll tell you. Or you could call his private secretary—Henry will vouch for me."

"As I said, ma'am, I'm going to have to ask you to leave."

I grab my phone and try to call Eddie, but there's no answer. "Give me a minute, please—he's not answering. Maybe you could escort me to his house and leave once he answers the door?"

The guard looks at me, stony-faced, and pulls out his radio. "Walker here. Can I have backup at the main gate, please?"

This isn't going well, is it? Oh, I know! I scroll through my contacts and hit call. As the phone rings, I see another two palace guards approaching the car.

"Amelia!"

Oh, thank god.

"Emma! Are you at home? I'm stuck on the road outside in an Uber, and I'm about to be forced to leave by several heavily armed guards."

She titters. "Give me a sec," she says and promptly hangs up on me.

The backup guards are walking towards my car when I hear a phone ringing outside. The guard who had been so intent on sending me on my way unclips a phone from his utility belt and answers it. "Good morning, Your Highness. Uh, yes . . . we do. Right, of course. Straight away, Your Highness." He turns and walks back to the window. "Go right through, ma'am. Princess Emma is expecting you."

We're waved down the road and through the gates, past the crowd of mourners. I direct my Uber up the drive and past the palace to the row of little cottages behind the main building. When I say "little cottages," I mean two- and three-storey houses. "Cottage" is palace-speak for a house with less than seventeen bedrooms. We park at the far end of the row, in front of Ivy Cottage—home to Eddie's cousins, Princesses Emma and Lucy.

I walk up the cobblestone path to the door of the ivy-covered red-brick house and ring the doorbell. Straight away, the door swings open, and I'm enveloped in an enormous hug.

"Amelia, it's so good to see you, darling. Come in."

"It's good to see you too, Em. It feels like it's been months since I was here, not less than two days."

"So much has happened since we saw each other. I can hardly believe it. Come in and sit down. We've got so much to discuss."

We walk through the modest foyer and into the princesses' living room. Lucy is curled up in a cream linen armchair next to the fireplace, her eyes puffy and her face stained with tears.

"Oh, Lucy," I say, running across the room to give her a hug. "I'm so sorry."

Lucy sniffs. "Thank you, darling."

"How are you feeling?"

"Oh, I'll bounce back," she says with a shrug. "It's hard to believe it's been twenty years since the first movie was released, though, isn't it?"

I stop in my tracks. I'm so confused. "Sorry, what movie?"

"*Harry Potter,* darling. I've been watching the reunion show. The nostalgia really got to me—when Emma Watson and Rupert Grint started talking about how much they love each other, I lost it." She plucks a tissue from a box next to her and wipes away more tears.

I try to keep my expression sympathetic and not roll my eyes. I should have known she was crying about something ridiculous. I can't lie, though—that reunion had me welling up too.

"They were only tiny children when they started! And look at them now—Dan Radcliffe is a fully grown man with an overgrown beard and, from what I've seen in Monaco recently, absolutely no luck at all when it comes to roulette. Anyway, enough about me," she says. "How's Eddie holding up after Uncle Albert died? What happened in Kenya? We haven't even been able to speak to him since it all happened. The palace grey-suit brigade have had him locked away in emergency summits and are screening all his calls."

"I've only spoken to him for a couple of minutes this morning—he snuck out of a meeting and called me on his way to bed. He was devastated when he heard the news, obviously. He seemed quite overwhelmed too, but I don't really know because he and Henry were in talks the whole flight home, and then they sent me back to my flat when we landed."

"Typical courtier. All business and no regard for how difficult this must be for poor Eddie. Are you going to see him now?"

"I was planning to, but I think he's asleep, and I didn't realise until I was being interrogated at the gates that I don't have any way to get into Wren House. Based on the not-so-warm reception I got out the front, I can't imagine his staff will let me in if I ring the bell. Can I hang out here until he's awake?"

"You're welcome to stay here if you like, but we could let you into his place? One perk of being the king's favourite cousins is that we have a key and can let ourselves in whenever we like."

"We could make a fortune breaking in and stealing things to sell on eBay," Emma says. "Shame he'd know it was us straight away."

"How would he know it was you?"

A smile twitches on Lucy's lips. "She has priors."

I startle. "You've stolen things from Eddie before?"

"One time!" Emma says, rolling her eyes. "Once, when I was sixteen, I took a T-shirt from his wardrobe to give to a friend who was mad for him. Is that really such a crime?"

"Well," I say, "technically, yes."

Emma huffs. "Don't we have some sort of crown immunity? If not, Eddie should look into that as soon as possible."

"I'll be sure to mention it to him."

"Please do, dear. In the meantime, do you want to borrow our key? We should go out and check on Mummy anyway. She was a total wreck earlier."

"I might take you up on that offer, then."

Emma walks across the room to a sideboard inlaid with a delicate ivory pattern and takes a key from the top drawer. She strides back over and drops it in my hand. When I look down, I burst out laughing. There, sitting in my palm, is a single key hanging on the end of a chain attached to a plastic frog wearing a crown. The frog has a strangely familiar expression on its face.

"Is that a model of Eddie as a frog?"

"It certainly is," she says, puffing out her chest proudly.

"Where on earth did you get it?"

"I had it made for him for Christmas a few years ago."

"What a gift!"

"We always give each other gag gifts, but I was particularly proud of this one. It was easily the best gift of the day. Gran thought it was hilarious." Emma gives a tight smile and gazes into the distance. "I suppose Christmas is going to be very different this year. No Gran, no Uncle Albert."

"Oh, Em, it's going to be okay," I say, putting my arm around her.

She sniffs and wipes at her eyes. "I'm sure we'll be okay. It's just a lot to deal with. Don't waste your condolences on me, though. Head next door and make sure Eddie is doing all right."

"Thanks. I'll see you both soon."

I pick up my handbag and walk with Emma out of the living room and back to the small entrance foyer. I give her a big bear hug before opening the door of Ivy Cottage and stepping out onto the narrow path that runs along the front of the row of houses. Next door is Wren House, a three-storey red-brick house with dormer windows and a generous smattering of ivy, where Eddie lives. A little way farther down the path is the much smaller, two-bedroom Nottingham Cottage, where Eddie's brother, Prince Leo, lives. If you keep walking around the corner, you come to the main palace building, which is divided up into apartments of various sizes, mainly occupied by Eddie's extended family.

When I get to the door, I knock lightly in case Eddie is awake or there's a maid inside who might be startled by me strolling in unannounced. My knock is met by silence, so I slip the key into the lock and let myself in.

When I cross through into the foyer, everything is quiet—I assume Eddie is upstairs having a nap after Henry kept him up all night. I trek down the hall and past the kitchen towards his private den. It's a small room at the far end of the house with a cosy sectional, an enormous television, and a view out into the large walled garden hidden behind Wren House. The garden, with its ancient oak tree in the centre and the row of fruit trees along the back wall, feels like a complete escape from the city. It may surprise the public to learn that this room is where Eddie spends most of his time at home—watching reality TV with his fluffy poodle-cross named Poppy curled up at his feet and scrolling through celebrity Instagram feeds.

I round the corner into the room and stop in my tracks. There, lying on the sofa with his arm flung over his dog, is His Majesty King Edmund Louis Albert George the First, fast asleep with his mouth hanging open and a stream of drool running down his cheek.

An hour later, I'm back in the den, perched on the end of the sofa and watching my boyfriend sleep. Not in a creepy way. More in a concerned, loving way. I swear.

I lean over and wave the plate I'm holding in Eddie's direction.

"Mm," he murmurs, sniffing in his sleep. Suddenly, he jerks awake. "Ah! Who's there?"

"Eddie, it's me."

He relaxes back onto the sofa and rubs his eyes sleepily. "Mils. I'm so glad you're here. I've had such a long day."

"I can't even imagine."

"Do I smell pancakes, by the way?"

"You do. I thought you probably hadn't had time to eat, and wanted to make something for you, but my cooking repertoire is pretty limited. So pancakes it is."

Eddie props himself up on his elbows. "Thank you, pancakes are perfect."

He reaches up to give me a quick kiss, then looks across at the plate I've put down on the coffee table. "Er . . . are you sure those are pancakes?"

Okay, so when I said my cooking repertoire is limited, I meant limited both in terms of quantity and quality.

"They are definitely pancakes. I googled a recipe and everything."

"They're quite, uh, black. And I'm not sure I've ever seen pancakes in that shape before. It's rather . . . original."

I hit Eddie playfully on the arm. "Okay, they're not great. I think maybe we should stick to you being the chef in this relationship."

"Agreed," says Eddie far too quickly. "On second thoughts, I'm not particularly hungry after all. Thank you for coming over and for the thought, though—you've made me feel miles better already."

I smile sadly. Although he says he feels better, he doesn't look it—he looks like he's been hit by a truck. Or like his father just died and he hasn't slept in forty-eight hours.

"What were all the meetings last night about?" I ask, sitting at the island bench in Eddie's kitchen watching him flip something that—unlike my earlier attempt—is actually recognisable as a pancake. "What's so important that it couldn't wait a day?"

"Everything. We started with changes to my security arrangements, then there were awkward calls with various heads of state who didn't know whether to congratulate or console me. Afterwards, we started on the political briefings. I like to think I always keep abreast of what's going on in the country, but I never truly appreciated how much Gran and Dad had to be across."

"Sounds overwhelming."

"Incredibly."

"Do you have today off to get some rest and spend time with your family?"

Eddie gives a hollow laugh. "I wish. Henry has permitted me until eleven o'clock to 'collect myself,' and then I'm due in a senior royals summit to finalise funeral arrangements. At least

Mum will be there, so I'll finally get to see her—I had to fight Henry to find time in my schedule to call her last night. He let me speak to her for exactly four minutes between talking to the US President and the German Prime Minister."

"That's awful! I know there must be a lot of logistical issues to sort out, but your father died less than twenty-four hours ago. Surely you could have one day to spend with your family."

"Apparently not," Eddie says, flinching.

"Can't you say no to the schedule? Henry and the others work for you, not the other way round."

"Technically, that's true, but Henry has been working for the palace for years. He and the other senior staff know far more than I ever will about how the business of the monarchy runs. I wasn't anywhere near ready to step up—I need to take their advice."

"I understand, but you're still human. You need time to process and to grieve."

He closes his eyes and sighs. "Believe me, I would love nothing more than to have more time and be able to hide out here with you and bake depression cookies. But there's so much to do and so much to learn, and right now, my job is more important than how I feel."

"Well," I say, squeezing his arm, "I love you, so how you feel is the most important thing to me." I check the time on my phone. "Quarter past ten. By my count, that gives me forty-five minutes to cheer you up."

"What exactly did you have in mind?"

I pull him wordlessly towards the den and push him down on the sofa. "Oh, I think you can guess," I say with a conspiratorial grin.

I drape my arm across his chest and pause for a moment before leaning further and grabbing the remote from the end table next to him. I click the button, and the TV across the room lights up and soon fills with the colour explosion that is *RuPaul's Drag Race*.

For the first time since we got the news, Eddie smiles. His smile doesn't have all of its usual warmth, but it's better than nothing. "How do you always know just what I need?"

"It's because you're extremely predictable."

He arches his brow. "Is that so?"

"You're predictable to me," I say, crinkling my nose. "In the best possible way."

Eddie takes my hand in his and looks me in the eye. "I love you, Amelia. I don't know what I'd do without you."

I nestle my head into his chest and look up at him. "Who knows? Probably be hideously out of date on drag make-up trends. Luckily, you're never going to have to find out."

CHAPTER 3

Beep. Beep. Beep.

Eddie groans. "Ugh, it's time. I'd best be going."

"Who's going to be at the summit?"

"Mum, Aunt Helena, Leo, and me. And the aides, of course."

"No Caroline?"

"No, she's still up in Scotland—not due back until this afternoon."

I've never met Eddie's sister—and now first in line for the throne—Princess Caroline. She's spent most of her adult life living in Scotland. After going to university in Edinburgh, she put in a couple of years of face time back in London before convincing her parents to let her move north permanently. These days, I understand she lives in the Highlands, trying to keep as far away from royal life as possible. Other than the living in a castle bit, but you can't expect her to abandon her standards entirely.

"How long do you think you'll be?"

"Henry has it booked in for three hours, so I won't be back for lunch."

"Okay, I might head home then and try to get some work

done. My emails have been blowing up since the announcement came out."

Eddie looks at me, his eyes weary. "Would you mind staying? I don't want to be alone later."

I wrap my arms around him, and he collapses onto my shoulder. "Of course I'll stay. I can make calls and send emails from anywhere. Whatever you need, I'm here. If you need comfort food, maybe I should order in, though."

"Probably for the best," he says, grimacing. After a long breath, he draws back from me and shakes his head sadly. "Time to go and face reality."

THE HOUSE IS STRANGELY quiet with Eddie gone. In the shadow of his father's death, it seems to have lost its warmth and comfort. The awful London weather isn't helping—the normally bright living room is as grey and cold as the sky outside.

I put on some music to drown out the gloom and then glare at my phone. There's been a constant stream of calls and notifications this morning, all of which I've ignored, though I can't do that forever. Given I'm the Head of Legal at the Princes' Charitable Foundation, and one of said princes has suddenly become king, there are probably some things I need to deal with.

Half an hour later, I'm still triaging emails when the front door creaks open.

A voice that I don't recognise rings out. "Hello! Ed? Sib?"

Before I can figure out what to do, a woman appears in the doorway. Princess Caroline. I jump to my feet and curtsy, almost gracefully—looks like spending all this time around the royal family has finally taught me something.

"Good morning, Your Highness. We weren't expecting you to arrive until later today."

"Who are you? Where are Ed and Sib and the others?"

Eddie told me once that Caroline doesn't read tabloids or any other news about the family, but she's way more out of the loop than I realised. Sib—Lady Sibella Cavendish—was Eddie's fiancée until she dumped him in spectacular fashion earlier in the year when she left him at the altar in front of a live TV audience of more than a billion people. They were also technically engaged again until a few days ago when Eddie and I got back together.

"I'm Amelia," I say carefully. Caroline stares at me in silence, her eyebrow raised. So awkward. How do I explain this one? I clear my throat and try again. "I'm Eddie's girlfriend."

Caroline blinks. "Oh, that Amelia. Well, sounds like I've missed some news."

I giggle nervously. "It looks that way."

"Care to fill me in?"

"Of course, sorry. Ah, where do I start? I take it you knew Eddie and I were seeing each other for a while after his wedding?"

"Yes, I heard some talk about that. I'm surprised to see you here, though. I understood you had ended things."

"I did, but we got back together a couple of days ago."

She regards me curiously. "So Ed definitely isn't going to marry Sib then?"

"No, he's not. Eddie and I are . . ." I drift off. Are we getting married? I didn't find an opportunity to ask him earlier. Turns out there's not really a smooth way to ask your boyfriend to clarify if he was in the middle of proposing when his father crashed a helicopter into a mountain.

Caroline purses her lips. "You and Ed are *what* exactly?"

Best keep this simple. "We're together again now."

"I see. Next time I see my brother, I'll have to give him quite a talking-to—it's criminal for him to leave me so far out of the loop. Speaking of Ed, where is he?"

"He's in a meeting at his office with your mother, Leo, and your aunt Helena to talk about funeral arrangements."

"*Prince* Leo and *Princess* Helena, you mean?"

"Yes," I stammer.

"Always best to be on your best behaviour around here, Amelia. A palace is no place to let your guard down. They'll crucify you for it."

Who does she mean by "they"? Eddie and Caroline's younger brother Leo isn't exactly what you'd call an Amelia fan, but I hardly think he'd get upset about me calling him by his first name. Then again, he can be rather taciturn, so who knows.

"Apologies, Your Highness. I wasn't thinking. I'm really tired."

"No apologies necessary. It has been a singularly long day, and it isn't going to end any time soon. Speaking of, it sounds like Ed's meeting is one I should be a part of." With that, she gives a nod, turns on her heel, and walks out of the living room.

LATER, I'm sitting in a vintage Eames recliner, leafing through an album of old family portraits I found on a shelf by the fireplace when I hear the front door open again. This time—thankfully—it's Eddie. He strolls into the living room and drops onto a chair across from me. "Mils, I'm so sorry. That took much longer than I anticipated."

"Don't apologise, you have a lot going on. How did everything go?"

"Exhausting."

I walk over and lean over to kiss him on the cheek. "Did you get all the funeral details figured out?"

"More or less. The team has had most of it planned for years. It's macabre, but the palace keeps funeral plans and obituaries on file for all of us. There were several issues to address, though—Dad had only been king for three months, and everything was so sudden that the plans hadn't been fully updated."

"So what happens next?"

Eddie exhales slowly. "It will be a lot like after Gran died, an awful kind of déjà vu. There'll be another eleven days of national mourning after today. Tomorrow morning his casket will be set up at Westminster so the public can pay their respects during the mourning period. Then we have the funeral." His shoulders crumple, and he drops his head into his hands. "Mils, I don't know that I can do it all again so soon. I'm going to be under so much scrutiny through it all too."

"Oh, honey, I know it's awful and unfair, but you'll get through it. I'm here this time, and I promise I'm going to do everything I can to make this easier for you."

"That means so much to me. I still haven't a clue what I did to deserve you, but whatever it is, I'm bloody glad I did it."

"Remember that feeling next time I get a parking fine and need someone from the palace to make it disappear."

Eddie grins, a genuine smile this time. "Amelia, do I need to remind you that you're the lawyer here? You're meant to get *me* out of sticky situations."

"Are you saying that being your girlfriend doesn't come with any legal privileges?"

"Unfortunately, it does not."

"Why am I even here then?"

He taps the side of his nose. "As I said before, I haven't figured that out yet."

"Hm," I say, drumming my fingers on the coffee table. "I'm sure you must bring something to the table."

Eddie wraps his arm around my waist and starts kissing my neck.

"Mm," I murmur. "Yup, this might have something to do with it. Should we skip dinner and head upstairs?"

"I wish we could," Eddie says, breaking away from me. "I'm due back in another briefing session in the office in twenty minutes. Henry only let me leave because I told him Mum's office had asked me to come by at the last minute. He must be even more worn out than I am if he didn't even question why the request didn't come through him."

"Should I stay here? I can wait up for you."

"I wouldn't bother," he says, looking rather downtrodden. "I've no idea how long I'll be there. You should go back to your flat, and I'll ring you in the morning. I'll call a car around."

"All right, I'll see you tomorrow then."

Half an hour later, a Range Rover drops me off in front of my flat where, mercifully, there's still no sign of any photographers. If—or when, rather—they turn up again, I'll cope. After what I've been through over the last few months, I've learned to tune out the noise, keep my eyes trained on the ground in front of me, and focus on taking one step at a time—but being surrounded by a pack of men clicking away and shouting awful things designed to get a reaction out of me still isn't my idea of a good time.

When I walk inside, Penny is sitting on the sofa, eating takeout pasta and watching the news. "Mils! I didn't expect to see you back tonight."

"You don't want to see me?"

"Of course I do. I want to make the most of my time living with you before you go and move into Kensington Palace." Her eyes grow wild. "Or Buckingham Palace! Is Edmund moving?"

I wrinkle my nose. "Good question. I suppose he probably will—it *is* tradition for the monarch to live at Buckingham Palace."

Penny squeals. "Buckingham Palace! You're going to live at Buckingham Palace! You, Amelia Marie Glendale, who hasn't washed her sheets in at least a month and uses my toothpaste when I'm not looking because she's not organised enough to buy her own, living in a palace."

"Hey, slow down there," I say, shaking my head. "No one has said anything about me living in a palace."

"You will though, right? Two days ago, you two were planning to move to Australia together. That's obviously not an option for him anymore, so I assume he'll expect you to move in with him here."

Huh, she's probably right. Another thing I hadn't thought about. We were going to move to Australia together, but moving into a palace is an entirely different proposition. Dating Eddie isn't like dating just anyone off the street; he has traditions to uphold and a public image to worry about. Moving in together wouldn't only be a convenient way to see each other every day; it would be taken by the palace and the public as a signal we are going to get married and an opportunity for me to prepare for life as a royal. But I'm not at all sure I'm ready for that.

"Can we talk about something else?"

"Sure. Can you believe Aung San Suu Kyi was arrested again? The way female politicians are treated in some countries is unbelievable."

"Uh, no offence, but what's even more unbelievable is that you even know who Aung San Suu Kyi is. She's not exactly a regular feature in the tabloids."

"Excuse me," Penny says, glaring at me. "I keep up to date with world events."

"Do you now?" That's news to me. Penny's idea of keeping on top of current affairs is normally knowing who Leonardo DiCaprio is dating.

"Yes, I do. I read all about the arrest on Beyoncé's Insta."

I roll my eyes. Well, that explains it.

CHAPTER 4

THE NEXT MORNING I send an email to work and let them know I'll be staying home for the week and only be taking urgent calls. The foundation's CEO spoke to Henry last night, and they agreed the foundation will carry on serving as Leo's charity and nothing will change for the next month at least—other than the name changing to the Prince's Trust as Eddie gets involved in the King's Trust instead—so I don't feel too guilty about letting the junior lawyers in my team handle things for now. My priority is being there for Eddie.

I'm dressed, up to date on emails, and sipping my coffee by the time Penny emerges from her room, yawning. "Morning. I was thinking about it last night—if you move in with Edmund, how am I going to keep the flat?"

"Don't worry, Pen, it's not going to happen any time soon. Even if it does, I'll keep paying my rent until you find someone else to take my room."

Penny relaxes. "Phew, that's a relief. If you do leave, can I also keep all the clothes in your wardrobe? The nice ones I chose for you anyway. Oh, and your bedside lamps. But not the bedside tables—they're not exactly my style. You know what? I think it would be easiest if I go around and put some stickers on all the things I want. I'll do a full assessment while you're at KP today." She grabs the coffee I'd left for her on the table. "When are you leaving, by the way?"

"Er, I'm not sure, actually. Eddie said he'd call in the morning, but I haven't heard from him yet. I sent him a text earlier but didn't get a reply."

"I'm sure he'll call soon," she says, smiling sympathetically.

"Yeah, he's probably still asleep."

"Anyway," Penny says, taking a gulp of her coffee. "I need to head out soon. What's the paparazzi situation outside today?"

"There was no one there earlier." I walk across the room and peer out the window. "Nope, still no one. I should thank Sibella for the distraction one day."

Penny frowns. "When is he calling that off publicly? I know the timing is bad, but he's got to announce it eventually."

"Aren't you full of questions this morning? Auditioning for a role on a TV talk show, are you?"

"Mils, none of these are unreasonable questions."

"True, but they're things we haven't had time to think about. I'm sure he'll announce it soon and try to use the funeral to deflect a bit of attention. On the plus side, we won't have to deal with Albert's rage now." I shudder as I think back to a particularly awful conversation I had with Eddie's dad in which he demanded I leave Eddie. "Am I a horrible person to be kind of glad he died before we had to tell him?"

"Yes, definitely. But I love you anyway."

I throw a handful of dry cereal across the table at Penny, and she dodges out of the way, letting it all fall to the ground.

"I hope you're going to clean that up, Your Majesty. We don't have maids here."

~

At lunchtime, I'm sitting on the sofa eating peanut butter out of the jar with a spoon—I maintain that when you haven't done any shopping, it counts as a meal, and I won't hear any different—when my phone buzzes with a text from Penny.

Penny: *Hey, how's Edmund doing?*

Me: *Doing okay, thanks.*

At least I think he's probably doing okay. To be honest, I have no idea. He still hasn't called or replied to any of my messages. My phone buzzes again.

Penny: *What's the deal with this?*

There's a link in Penny's message to an article in *The Sun*—one of the most inflammatory and least factually accurate newspapers in the country. Penny knows that, for my own sanity, I've sworn off reading tabloids, so if she's sending it to me anyway, it must be something important.

Sibella comforts new King

The world was left reeling yesterday after Buckingham Palace announced the shocking death of King Albert at age sixty-three. The late king spent only three months on the throne before an ill-fated helicopter flight cut his reign tragically short. Sources say the king was piloting the helicopter himself when the engine failed en route from Buckingham Palace to the royal family's country estate at Sandringham. Two elite Scotland Yard protection officers were also killed in the crash.

The accident means that for the second time in less than a year, the nation has a new monarch. All eyes are now on royal heartthrob Prince Edmund, who has skipped the queue and become king decades earlier than expected. The former prince is no stranger to public attention. After years of impeccable behaviour, he was recently embroiled in scandal after he was left at the altar by Lady Sibella Cavendish and then moved on immediately with gold digger and alleged mistress Amelia Glendale.

These days, Edmund and Sibella, who became re-engaged last month, seem to have put their issues behind them. Lady Cavendish (pic-

tured) was seen entering Kensington Palace late yesterday wearing a four-hundred-pound dress by Stella McCartney and carrying a large Hermès overnight bag valued at over thirteen thousand pounds. Lady Cavendish, who is the eldest daughter of the Duke and Duchess of Chester and an amateur equestrian, hasn't left the palace since. Insiders say the future queen is currently holed up at King Edmund's Wren House digs, doing her best to comfort the bereft monarch.

. . .

Eddie sent me home and then had Sibella come and stay? I know I shouldn't trust anything the papers say—after all, they did call me a gold digger—but you can't argue with the photo of Sibella driving through the KP gates and walking down the drive with her fancy dress and unnaturally shiny hair. She must have extensions, right? No normal person's hair has that much volume and that little frizz. I run my fingers through my own not-at-all-shiny hair. Maybe I should find out where she has hers done.

Wait, what am I thinking? Hair is the least of my problems right now. She's an old family friend, so I'm sure she's just there to support the family and there's nothing to worry about—but Eddie has been so non-communicative lately, and it's starting to make me paranoid. I should call him and check or send him a message and casually ask if he kicked me out last night so his ex-girlfriend/current fake fiancée could come to stay.

I scroll through our message history. Hm, I've sent him five messages in a row with no reply. A sixth might start looking desperate. I'll wait until he calls and let him explain. That would be the mature option.

I spend the rest of the day resisting the urge to call Eddie and demand to know why Sibella is staying at KP. At some stage, I fall asleep on the sofa and wake up with my phone smooshed under my face. I check and see I've got two missed calls and thirteen messages. None from the only person I want to hear from, though. A key rattles in the lock, and Penny appears in the doorway.

"Mils! What are you doing here?"

I don't want to admit to her that I've been here all day and haven't had so much as a text from Eddie. "Eddie had meetings again tonight, so I decided to come home for dinner."

Penny's cheeks flush. "I wasn't expecting you to be here."

"That's okay. Should we order something in for dinner and find a cheesy movie to watch?"

"Er," Penny says, fidgeting.

"What is it?"

Penny swings the door open to reveal a man I've never seen before standing next to her. "This is Josh."

"Oh, right. Hi, Josh, come in. Nice to meet you."

Josh strides into the living room and closes the door behind him. "Nice to meet you," he says, extending his hand.

I shake his hand. "Were you two planning to have dinner here?"

"We were," Josh says, smiling. "Would you like to join us?"

I glance across at Penny, who is standing out of Josh's view, shaking her head violently.

"No, that's okay—thanks for asking, though. I'm pretty tired, so I might go and read in bed."

"Good night," Penny says way too quickly.

I trudge off to my room and close the door. Maybe living at the palace wouldn't be so bad after all—at least there's someone at the gate making sure no random men walk into your house unannounced.

CHAPTER 5

By mid-afternoon two days later, I still haven't seen Eddie. He sent me a couple of brief messages yesterday, so I know he's alive, but beyond that, I have no clue what he's been doing or how he is.

I jump as my phone rings. I grab it, hoping it's Eddie calling, but instead see Princess Lucy's name on my screen.

"Hey, Lucy, how are you?"

"Hello, darling, I'm doing okay, all things considered. How are you and Eddie faring?"

"I'm fine, thanks. Eddie is . . . also fine, I think? To be honest, I don't know how he is. I haven't seen him in days. He hasn't even called."

"If it makes you feel any better, we haven't seen him either. Give him time—he's got a lot going on right now."

I nibble on my bottom lip. "Can I ask you something?"

"Anything, darling."

Here goes nothing. "I saw some weird reports the other day. Do you know if Sibella is staying with him?"

The line goes silent.

"Lucy, are you still there?"

"I'm here," she says in an even tone.

"So, have you seen Sibella? The papers say she's staying at Eddie's."

"Yes, I've seen her. I didn't speak to her, just saw her across the lawn when I was taking a walk around the grounds yesterday."

"So it's true? Eddie asked her to come and stay with him?"

"I don't know for sure. I wouldn't be too concerned, though. She's probably staying with Caroline. You should ask him."

"Well, that would be a convenient excuse, wouldn't it? I'll be demanding answers next time I talk to him! Or I will if he ever calls me again."

"Amelia, were you exaggerating before when you said you were fine?"

I sniff. "Maybe."

"Okay, you're coming over here tonight for dinner."

"Are you sure? I don't want to impose."

"You would absolutely not be imposing. It's been so gloomy around here this week, and we're desperate for entertainment."

"All right then, if you're sure."

"I am. Be here by six."

Two hours later, I'm waved through the gates at KP—Lucy made sure I was on the list this time.

When Lucy greets me, she's wearing a vivid green, floor-length silk robe with fur trim and six-inch stilettos. It's quite a look.

"So good to see you, darling. Em and I have spent the last few days with Mummy and Aunt Louisa, and it's been hideously depressing. Come in so I can tell you all about it and make you share my pain." Lucy steps aside, and I move through the small foyer and into the princesses' cosy, Hamptons-style living room decorated with linen sofas and breezy white furniture.

"Whoa!"

"I know," she says. "It's quite a lot, isn't it?"

The room, which normally features a tasteful amount of greenery, looks like it has been transformed into a pop-up floristry studio. There are enormous bouquets lining every surface and even more on the floor. I try to count them but give up once I hit sixty.

"You should see the collection in Aunt Louisa's apartments. She's got trucks coming in twice a day to take flowers away and donate them to hospitals and anywhere else that will take them."

I gaze around the room, wide-eyed. "I suppose I shouldn't be surprised. I just didn't think King Albert was that popular."

"Oh, he wasn't," Lucy says with a sparkle in her eye. "Don't be fooled—these are not flowers of adoration. At best, they're flowers of grudging respect."

"I can't even imagine how many there would be if people actually liked him."

"I don't need to imagine. The deluge after Gran died was incredible. Emma and I obviously weren't sent as many as Mummy or Albert and Louisa, but we had days where we had hundreds of deliveries. Not to mention the thousands of bouquets left at the gates. Once I got trapped in my bedroom after security filled the hallway with vases not realising I was in there."

I laugh. "Trapped by too many flower deliveries. What a first-world problem. Actually, is there something more elite than a first-world problem—an aristocratic problem, maybe?"

"Don't you laugh at me, Amelia, it was a genuine issue! I had to have a protection officer lift me out my bedroom window. Well, technically, I could have waited for them to clear the hall instead, but I'd take any excuse for more hands-on time with that particular PPO."

"Ooh, which one?"

"His name is Haines, but you wouldn't know him. Mummy and Uncle Albert had him reassigned a few months ago when they found out we were involved."

My eyes boggle. "You were dating one of your security guards? How did I not know that?"

Lucy raises an eyebrow. "I don't know that I'd call what we were doing 'dating' as such . . ."

"How has that not been all over the papers?"

"Because, my dear, believe it or not, I can be incredibly discreet when I want to be."

"No offence, but I'm not sure I do believe that. As far as I know, you're the only member of your family who goes out of their way to pose for paps."

"Can you blame me?" she asks, before twirling on the spot and striking a pose. "I spend a bloody fortune on my wardrobe. What's the point if no one sees it?"

I chuckle. "Fair enough. Anyway, tell me more about the mysterious Haines."

Lucy's eyes glaze over as she stares into the distance. "Maybe another time."

Hm, I get the feeling there's more to the story there than a couple of casual hook-ups. Time for a change of subject. "Is Emma here?"

Lucy spins around to face me. A mischievous gleam has replaced the glazed look in her eyes. "She's in the kitchen. Making dinner."

"Oh, I didn't realise she could cook."

Lucy cackles. "She absolutely can't. Shall we go and watch?"

"Definitely!"

We walk through the living room to the kitchen. It's all marble and white subway tile with an enormous farmhouse sink and shiny brass tapware. Everything gleams in the way only a barely used kitchen can, even when you have daily maids.

Emma is standing in the middle of the kitchen, flushed, her dark hair flying everywhere. The oven is on, and there are three pots on the stove. The marble island is almost entirely covered with bowls and chopping boards. We stand and watch for a minute as she flits between stirring pots and checking her phone.

"Hi, Emma," I say, waving at her.

"Oh, Amelia! Sorry, I didn't see you there." She wipes the sweat from her forehead with the back of her hand and leaves behind a smear of something red.

"No worries. How are you? And more importantly, what are you cooking?"

"I'm about as well as is to be expected. Dinner, on the other hand, is in rather dire straits, I'm afraid."

I glance around the chaotic scene. "It looks quite . . . involved."

"It's meant to be a mushroom risotto and roast beetroot salad, but I'm not sure it's quite working out."

"I'm sure it'll be delicious." I'm not at all sure of that, but what I do know is that if I say anything even remotely judgemental, I'll probably end up with the most thoroughly burnt part of the dish.

"Hm," says Emma, pursing her lips. "We'll see."

Just then, the doorbell rings.

"That'll be Leo and Kayla, I expect," Lucy says. "I'll fetch them."

A couple of minutes later, Eddie's younger brother Prince Leo and his secret girlfriend, Kayla Monroe—influencer and frequent reality TV contestant—appear in the kitchen.

"Hi, Leo. I'm so sorry about your father. How are you holding up?" I say. "Good to see you, Kayla."

"Amelia," Leo says curtly before striding across the kitchen to help himself to a drink.

Kayla glances at me but makes no move to greet me. She's never been my biggest fan. King Albert didn't approve of Kayla and refused to let her and Leo go public with their relationship. Albert didn't like me either, but he wasn't so mortally offended by me that he made sure I was kept hidden. I think Kayla resented people thinking of me as a slightly more suitable partner, so she set about leaking awful stories about me to the press. Thanks to Kayla, half the country thinks I'm some kind of crazed Leo-stalker who targeted Eddie after Sibella left him at the altar. The other half thinks Eddie and I were having an affair and I'm the reason Sibella left him at the altar. Needless to say, I'm not exactly disappointed she doesn't want to talk to me.

"The table is covered in flowers," Lucy announces as she walks back into the room. "So I think we'd better eat in here."

I gaze down at the pile of bowls and mess on the island. "Let me help clear these dishes."

"Thanks, darling," Emma replies.

I get to work stacking mixing bowls and clearing up food scraps and wrappers. Instead of coming to help, Lucy pours herself a large glass of champagne. Typical. When the bench is clean and Emma has dished up dinner, the five of us sit down to eat.

"Thanks for cooking for us, Emma," I say.

"It was my pleasure. Enjoy, everyone." She looks at me expectantly.

I glance down at my plate. To be honest, her risotto doesn't look particularly appealing. I'm sure it's fine though—risotto is basically rice, butter, and wine. I'd happily eat any of those things by themselves, so how bad can it be? I bring my spoon to my mouth and smile at her. I take a bite.

Jesus. This is so bad. I don't even know how she's managed to do this. Other than by adding what tastes like approximately five cups of salt, that definitely hasn't helped. Even Eddie's dog wouldn't eat this. "Mm," I say, choking down the spoonful.

Suddenly there's a scream across the table. I look up and see Lucy spitting a mouthful of food onto the table.

"Em, what on earth did you put in this?" Leo asks.

"We didn't have all the ingredients, so I had to improvise a bit."

"Please never do that again," Lucy says.

Leo puffs up his chest. "As the most senior member of the family here, I'm making an executive decision. We're ordering pizza."

Half an hour later, a stack of pizzas arrives at the door—carried by the guard who intercepts deliveries at the front gate. As Leo walks into the kitchen carrying the boxes, the doorbell rings again.

"Did they deliver the wrong pizzas?" I ask.

"They all look okay to me," Leo replies.

Lucy stands up. "I'll check what he wants."

I grab a couple of slices of four-cheese pizza from the nearest box and start eating.

"Amelia, what are you doing here?"

I jerk my head up. "Eddie!"

Oh god. It's not just Eddie, he's standing there flanked by Princess Caroline and none other than Lady Sibella Cavendish. Caroline and Sibella both look at me and wrinkle their noses. Are they cringing at my presence in general or at my face in particular? Is there something wrong with my face? I sneak a look at my reflection in my spoon. Yup, it's my face—my chin is covered in tomato sauce. Excellent.

I swipe at my chin with a napkin. "I didn't know you were coming tonight."

"I wasn't planning to, but Caro and Sib insisted I needed to eat."

"That's right," Caroline says, patting Eddie's arm. "Someone has to look after you."

Should I be taking responsibility for making sure he performs basic human functions? No, he's a grown man, he doesn't need someone to micromanage when he eats. Well, he doesn't normally anyway, but—based on how dishevelled he looks tonight—maybe he does right now. I'm pretty sure that's literally part of someone else's job description, though. Like his housekeeper, or his assistant.

"I can look after myself, thank you very much. Unlike the rest of you lot," he says, gesturing to the pizza boxes. "Is this what happens when I stop cooking for you for a couple of days?"

"Excuse me," Emma says, lips pursed. "I'll have you know I spent hours cooking dinner for everyone."

"Did you buy a pizza oven I don't know about?"

"All right, so we're not actually eating the food I made. But that doesn't change the fact that I cooked."

He tilts his head and looks at Emma softly. "You've missed me, haven't you?"

"So much," she gushes. "You have no idea. I almost wish you'd tried my risotto and seen how useless we are without you. I'm glad you didn't, though—I don't want to be thrown in a dungeon for poisoning the king."

"I'd never have you thrown in a dungeon, cousin. I'd have you locked in a tower somewhere with a marvellous view. I'm not a monster." He smiles, but there's no sign of his usual mischievous gleam in his eyes.

"Thanks, Eddie," she says, sweeping into a dramatic bow. "Your magnanimity is appreciated as always."

Eddie turns to me. "Mils, you haven't met Sib before, have you?"

No, I haven't, and I didn't particularly want to, but it doesn't look like that's an option anymore. I'm going to have to take the high road here though, aren't I? It's probably for the best that I'm not holding a drink I could "accidentally" throw at her. I extend my hand to Sibella. "No, I haven't. Nice to meet you."

"It's a pleasure," Sibella says, ignoring my hand and pulling me into a hug.

CHAPTER 6

After an hour of watching Sibella talk to Eddie and the others, I can't take it any longer. I need to find out what she's doing here. I lean over to Eddie and whisper to him, "We need to talk."

"Shall we go back to mine?"

My jaw tightens, and I nod.

He stretches his arms over his head and lets out an exaggerated yawn. "Time for me to be getting to bed. I would say thank you for dinner, but the real thanks should go to Domino's."

Emma gives a round of applause in the direction of the pizza boxes. "That's why you're cooking next time, cousin dear."

"That would probably be advisable. Honestly, though, thank you—I needed this."

Lucy, who is sitting next to Eddie, puts her arm around his shoulder. "It's been a tough week. You get some sleep. We can't have you falling asleep during an audience with the prime minister—even if he is incredibly dull."

Eddie stands and takes my hand, urging me up with him. "Have a good night, everyone."

We walk silently, hand in hand, down the cobblestone path to

Eddie's house next door. When the door closes behind us, I crack. "What is she doing here?"

"Excuse me?"

"Sibella. Why is she staying with you?"

He squints at me. "What are you talking about?"

"You know exactly what I'm talking about. You sent me home earlier in the week, and next minute, your ex-fiancée comes to stay and you stop answering my calls. That can't be a coincidence!"

"Amelia," he says, rubbing his jaw. "Calm down, you're not making any sense."

"Don't tell me to calm down! I am an appropriate level of worked up for someone in my position."

"I haven't a clue what you think is going on here, but I promise you that whatever it is, you're mistaken."

"Okay, let me spell it out for you, then. Three days ago, you told me I should go home and you'd call me in the morning. Correct?"

Eddie looks me straight in the eye. "I'm with you so far."

"Okay. Except you didn't call me in the morning. Instead, I woke up to paparazzi photos of your former fiancée waltzing into your house carrying an overnight bag. Care to explain?"

Eddie rakes his fingers through his hair and gives a hollow laugh. "Amelia, after all the stories people have printed about you, don't you know by now not to believe everything you see in the papers?"

"It's not only the papers. You were supposedly too busy to see me today, but then you turned up to dinner with her."

"Haven't we had this conversation before? Sibella and I were not in love. It was a relationship of convenience and purely platonic. You have nothing to be worried about."

"Then why is she staying with you while I sit at home by myself, feeling completely useless?"

Eddie shakes his head. "She's not staying here."

"But I saw the photos. And I saw her here tonight!"

"I haven't read the news, but I assume what you saw was Sibella walking down the drive to Apartment 1A. Where she is staying. With Caroline."

I scrunch up my face. "She's staying with Caroline?"

"Yes, Sib is Caro's best friend—she just wanted to be here for her."

I blink. "So she's not here to try to win you back?"

"No."

"And you're not trying to win her back?"

Eddie shakes his head. "I absolutely am not. Why would I do that when I have a beautiful woman standing right in front of me who I am madly in love with?"

Hm, he doesn't sound like someone trying to dump me for his ex-fiancée. I might have gotten the wrong end of the stick on this one. "Well," I say, laughing nervously. "When you put it that way, it doesn't make much sense, does it?"

"It really doesn't."

"I'm sorry, I shouldn't come in here accusing you of anything. On some level I knew nothing was going on, but it's been such a stressful few days, and you've barely spoken to me. I started panicking that you'd gone radio-silent because you were hiding something."

He leans down and kisses me softly. "It's quite all right. We're all dealing with things as best we can. And I promise I wasn't hiding anything from you, I've been sucked into a vortex of palace business and grief. I'm sorry I haven't called more. In the little time I've had to myself, I've been so drained, and I haven't felt much like speaking to anyone, even you."

The tension in my shoulders releases, and I feel my jaw relax. Everything is fine. Of course everything is fine—we love each other, and it was ridiculous of me to be worried over some silly paparazzi photos. I should know better by now. I wish Eddie had spoken to me about it sooner, or had spoken to me at all.

"Do you think Caroline hates me for taking you away from Sibella? Your dad didn't like me, and I obviously have issues with Leo. Meanwhile, your mother has never even acknowledged my presence. I want your family to like me. I don't think I could handle it if Caroline decided she was anti-Amelia too."

"Don't worry, I'm sure Caro doesn't hate you. She's a tad reserved and has some trust issues, so she may take some time to warm up, but she'll love you once she gets to know you. Lucy and Emma do, and they're much better judges of character than Leo. I'm sure Leo will come round too, eventually. He doesn't have an issue with you as such—he doesn't like that we were briefly able to have a relationship in public while he and Kayla are still sneaking around."

"Hm, I'm not so sure, but we'll see."

Eddie bites his lip. "Are we okay?"

"We are," I say, smiling.

He leans in and kisses me slowly. "Will you stay with me tonight?"

"I thought you'd never ask."

I WAKE up early the next morning and stretch out in Eddie's amazing bed. I don't think I'll ever get used to how comfortable this thing is. I'm convinced there's a secret underground lab somewhere where scientists funded by shadowy philanthropists have invented a special kind of ultra-comfortable foam reserved only for heads of state. Better sleep means leaders in better moods and fewer wars. Either that or it's just a really expensive mattress.

My eyes are still closed as I luxuriate in bed, but I can sense something is wrong. It takes me a moment to realise that when I flung my arms out across the bed earlier, I didn't hit anyone. I roll over and open my eyes. Nope, no Eddie.

My stomach rumbles. I hope he's downstairs making breakfast. I like to think I'm not a violent person, but I may actually strangle someone with my bare hands for one of his ricotta pancakes or fruit Danishes right now.

I wrap myself in a fluffy robe from Eddie's bathroom and pad down the stairs. Side note: his robes are also incredible. After I first stayed here, I looked them up online so I could buy one for home and found that they cost five hundred pounds. Five hundred pounds! Meanwhile, Eddie has a whole stack of them neatly folded in his bathroom cupboard. On a scale of one to everyone insisting on dating Pete Davidson, how weird would it be to steal a robe from my boyfriend's house like it's a hotel?

"What's for breakfast?" I call out from the bottom of the stairs. Of all the things I love about Eddie, his penchant for making breakfast pastries is up there.

My question is met by silence. I make my way down the hall to the kitchen but find it dark and empty. After exploring the rest of the house, I realise Eddie isn't home. I check my phone to see if he sent me a message saying he was going out somewhere. He didn't.

Me: *Hey, will you be back for breakfast?*

I make myself a coffee while I wait for Eddie to reply. Fifteen minutes later, I've finished my coffee and haven't had a response. I guess I'm organising my own breakfast.

Two hours later, I've eaten some toast—the limit of my breakfast-cooking abilities, as demonstrated by the pancake fiasco—had a shower, watched a morning talk show, and am now scrolling through my emails. Still no reply from Eddie. I'm curled up on the sofa in the den with Poppy at my feet, replying to an email from a donor about a liability clause in a funding agreement, when the doorbell rings. Should I answer it? I suppose anyone who made it past the gates is authorised to be here, so it's probably not a serial killer—or worse, a photographer. The doorbell rings again.

I jump up and rush to the door. When I open it, I see Leo standing outside.

"Hi," he says, pushing past me into the foyer. "Where's Eddie? I need to talk to him."

"He's not here, sorry."

"When will he be back?"

"I'm not sure."

He taps his foot on the floor impatiently. "Right. Where did he go? I need to talk to him as soon as possible."

"He didn't tell me where he was going. Probably a meeting in the main building," I say, shrugging. Trust me, Leo, I'd like to know the answers to all these questions as much as you would. Probably more.

Leo rolls his eyes. "Well, you've been no use. Tell him to call me when he gets back."

Ugh. Why is he always so rude? I plaster on a wide smile. "Of course, I'll pass on the message."

Leo turns around and walks out without another word.

At eleven, I send Eddie another message.

Me: *Are you coming home for lunch?*

A few minutes later, my phone buzzes.

Eddie: *Sorry—got tied up. I should be back for an hour at four.*

I'm tempted to "forget" to tell Leo when Eddie is due back, but he *is* my boyfriend's brother and—now that Eddie has moved on to the King's Trust, leaving Leo as the sole patron of the Prince's Charitable Foundation—my boss, so I should probably keep him on side. The last thing I want to be doing is working for a man who hates me.

Me: *Eddie's due back at four.*

Leo: *OK*

Leo, eloquent as always.

~

It's half past four when the front door creaks open again. "Amelia, are you here?"

"In the den," I call out. Seconds later, Eddie appears in the room, looking exhausted.

"Hey."

"Hey to you too," he says, the corners of his eyes crinkling.

He walks over and flops onto the sofa next to me. Straight away, he takes his phone out of his pocket and starts checking messages. He doesn't even say hello to Poppy, who bounded into the room when he arrived and has been running around in circles trying to get his attention.

"How was your day?"

"Long."

I wait for him to elaborate, but it looks like that's all I'm getting. "Are you getting a break tonight?"

He winces. "No, I've got a meeting with the coronation planning team in half an hour."

Although Eddie automatically became king when his father died, there will be a formal ceremony with crowns and sceptres in about six months. The palace team have insisted they need at least that long to plan for it. I'm not exactly sure how much planning Eddie needs to do given he effectively just needs to sit there and wear a crown, but I suppose I'd want to be well prepared too if over a billion people were going to watch me do something. "Will you be home for dinner? I could stay here and order us something to eat."

"I'm not sure how long the meeting will run for. Perhaps you should go back to your flat, and I'll call you in the morning."

Well, that sounds familiar. "To be honest, I'm not wild about that plan. Last time you suggested I do that, I didn't hear from you for three days."

"I know, I'm sorry. Things are all a bit out of my control right now."

"It's okay, I understand. But that's why I want to be here for you, and it's hard to do that when I never see you." I take Eddie's hand and lean my head against his shoulder. "I miss you."

"I miss you too, Amelia. I want to be able to spend time with you and for you to be here whenever I get home, but I'm never quite sure when that's going to be." He jolts and sits bolt upright. "That's it! I don't know why I didn't think of it earlier."

"Think of what?"

"You should move in."

My eyes widen. "Move in here?"

Eddie looks deep into my eyes. "Yes, move in with me. Before Dad . . ." He clears his throat. "Before . . . everything happened, we were going to move to Australia together. We obviously can't do that now, but we can still live together. Move in with me. I want you to be here when I get home, whenever that might be."

"The palace wouldn't mind? None of your relatives have lived with a partner before they got married. Especially not a reigning king or queen." At least him asking me to move in answers my question about whether he was planning to propose—in this family, moving in with someone is as good as a proposal.

"I wouldn't be too sure about that. I'd hazard a guess that plenty of my ancestors had mistresses living with them."

Right, maybe I shouldn't be planning a wedding anytime soon. "Excuse me! Are you suggesting you're going to keep me here as a secret mistress like we're living in the seventeenth century?"

Eddie chortles. "I wouldn't dream of it. I'm merely suggesting that, as king, I get to decide what the palace approves of and what it doesn't. And I approve of you."

"I'm glad to hear it."

"So what do you say?"

"Yes. I'd love to. I know it's only been a few days since we got back from Kenya, but I've found it so hard not seeing you every day. I'm in favour of anything that means I get to see you more often."

Eddie jumps off the sofa and sweeps me up into his arms, spinning me around the room. "I can't tell you how happy you've made me. Everything feels so much more manageable already knowing you'll be here."

I kiss him, then jerk back. "Wait. When you say 'here,' will we be staying here, or do you need to move to Buckingham?"

He drops his arms from around me and tugs at his earlobe. "You know, I hadn't really thought about it. I suppose it is tradition for the monarch to move into Buckingham when they take the throne—that's what Gran and Dad did—but I don't think I want to. I wouldn't feel right moving into Gran's apartments. This is my home. Besides, I only just bloody finished redecorating." He looks at me appraisingly. "Unless *you* wanted to move to Buckingham?"

"God, no! I love it here—it's comfortable and homey. Buckingham Palace is too intimidating and *royal* to live in."

"Amelia, do I need to remind you that I am the king of England? If you feel that way about Buckingham, shouldn't you be intimidated by me too?"

"Eddie," I say, patting his arm, "I've seen you tear up watching an old episode of *Say Yes to the Dress* at three in the morning. You couldn't intimidate me if you tried."

"The woman had been in a horrible accident and was told she'd never walk again but spent years in physical therapy so she could walk down the aisle. Only a heartless monster wouldn't cry at that story! Also, don't let anyone else hear you speaking ill of your king like that. They could have you locked up for it."

I tug at my collar. "And you'd let them?" Note to self—whatever you do, do not steal a robe.

"Never. It'd be more of a punishment for me than anything else. I'd break you out with a file hidden in a cake if I had to. Or pardon you. Sounds much less romantic that way, though."

"It really does."

"So," he says, grinning at me. "You're going to come and live with me?"

"I think I am."

"Is tomorrow too soon? Now that you've said yes, I don't want to wake up without you here for a single day longer than I have to."

I blink. Tomorrow. This is all happening so fast, but I'm sure everything will be much easier once we're living together. We never would have had that fight last night about Sibella if I'd been here and known what was happening, so I draw a deep breath and smile. "Tomorrow."

CHAPTER 7

I WALK into my flat and look around. "Pen, are you here?" I make my way over to the kitchen and start making coffee.

Penny pokes her head out of her bedroom. "Hey, I didn't think you'd be home for dinner."

I cast my eyes around the room, looking for a sign I've interrupted something. "You don't have another Tinder date in your room, do you?"

"I'll have you know that I'm off the Tinder market. I'm still seeing Josh, and we met through a friend. An actual, old-school meeting that didn't involve any swiping."

"I don't believe it!"

"It's pretty crazy. He's a friend of a friend, recently moved here from Singapore. We met a couple of weeks ago at some birthday drinks. He's sweet and funny, and generally a normal human. Enormous improvement on most of my app finds."

"That's so great, Pen. I'm happy for you."

"Don't get too excited, it's only been a couple of weeks. And we all know what happened last time I thought I'd met someone nice."

I cringe. I don't think I'll ever forget the moment I walked in on Penny's boyfriend, who turned out to be an undercover reporter, taking photos of my bedroom to sell to the tabloids. "I won't get ahead of myself, I promise. I'll just be quietly optimistic."

"I'll allow it."

"Good," I say, raising an eyebrow. "Because you can't stop me."

Penny laughs. "God, you're so stubborn. Why are we friends again?"

"Because I'm hilarious, have excellent taste in TV, let you borrow my shoes, and am generally fantastic company?"

"Oh, yeah," she says, shrugging. "That's probably it."

"Can we have a date night tonight, or are you seeing Josh?"

"I was actually planning to meet up with him for dinner. Can we hang out tomorrow?"

I take a deep breath. I'm not sure how Penny is going to feel about me moving out. I'm not even sure how *I* feel about me moving out. Eddie is fantastic, obviously, and living with him is the next logical step, but I love Penny too. My eyes are getting a bit misty thinking about not having our morning chats or movie binges anymore. "Actually . . . I won't be here tomorrow night."

"That's fine, we can do it the day after."

"I won't be here then either."

Penny looks at me, and I avoid catching her eye. "Well, aren't you popular this week? Do I need to start making bookings in advance if I want to see you?"

"You probably will."

She rolls her eyes. "Honestly, you date *one* king, and suddenly you're too busy and important to hang out with your best friend."

"Pen," I say, my eyes crinkling, "this isn't about my ego, it's about practicalities. I'm not going to be here because I'm moving in with Eddie. At KP."

The room is filled with an ear-splitting shriek. "Oh my god!"

Okay, now she's jumping up and down.

"You're going to live in a palace," Penny says, wide-eyed. "You're going to live in a palace!"

I chuckle. "It looks like it."

"Can I visit you? Can I come and have dinner with him? No! I want to visit when he's not there so I can snoop around his house."

"You can visit anytime you like. Maybe you can come for dinner on the weekend?"

Penny wraps her arm around my shoulders and squeals. "You won't be able to keep me away. Wait, this weekend? When are you moving?"

I look down at the floor and fidget with my watch. "Tomorrow."

"You're moving tomorrow? But that's so soon."

I force myself to look up at Penny. The look on her face breaks my heart. "Oh, Pen, I'm sorry. I don't want to leave you, but Eddie and I aren't getting to spend any time together. If we're going to get through this crazy time, we need to be in the same place."

Penny sniffs. "I get it, I do, but I wish your being with him didn't mean you had to abandon me."

"Pen, I'm not abandoning you! I'm moving twenty minutes away."

"But you won't be *here*," she says, wiping her eyes.

"Are you crying?"

"No! Okay, maybe a little bit." Her eyes soften as she gazes at me. "I'm going to miss you so much."

I gulp. "I'm going to miss you too. Will you cancel on Josh and stay in with me tonight instead?"

"Consider him cancelled. Lady, there's no way I'm missing your last night living here."

We spend the rest of the night curled up on the sofa watching movies, eating popcorn, and reminiscing. I know that I'm the one who said that it won't change things and I'm only going to be twenty minutes away, but leaving Penny and this flat—it feels like a big deal. It feels like the end of something, and it's already left a little hole in my heart.

THE NEXT MORNING there's a knock on the front door at seven in the morning. I blearily check through the window to see who it is and find Michael, my old security guard, standing on my front step.

He knocks again, and I crack the door open. "Michael! What are you doing here?"

"May I come in, Ms Glendale?"

"Of course, sorry. Come in." I step aside and wave him through to the living room.

He closes the door and scans the minuscule room. It's only big enough to hold an old sofa, coffee table, a TV, and a two-seat dining table, so I'm not sure what he's looking for—hidden cameras? A bomb? Whatever it is, he's got no hope of finding it under the mountains of stuff piled around the room.

"I've been packing," I say.

Michael simply raises his eyebrow and curls his lip. "His Majesty arranged for me to load the car and escort you to the palace. Do you need any assistance with your packing?"

"No, I'll be okay, thanks. I wasn't planning to leave until this afternoon, though, so can you come back later?"

"My instructions are to collect you and your clothes this morning."

"Right, I'll keep packing then. Is there a truck coming later for the rest of my things?"

Michael looks at me, brow furrowed. "The rest, ma'am?"

"You know—furniture, kitchenware, my outdoor table . . ."

Michael looks at me as if I've suddenly sprouted enormous peacock feathers out of my shoulder. "I've not been told about any truck, Ms Glendale." He clears his throat. "I, uh, don't believe you'll need your furniture."

I slap my forehead. Of course, why would I need my furniture? I'm moving into a palace residence that Eddie spent a year and millions of pounds renovating. There's not going to be anywhere to put my mismatched dining chairs or the coffee table I salvaged from a rubbish pile on the street. What do I need to take? My clothes, obviously. My make-up and jewellery, and my books. And . . . what else? There's no point taking any of my linen, towels, or any of the other things Eddie already has a much better version of.

"Hm, you're right. I won't need my furniture. I guess it won't take long to pack what I need, probably a couple of hours. Are you sure you want to wait?"

"Those are my instructions, ma'am."

"Great, well, make yourself at home. and I'll get to it." I jerk my head towards the sofa, but Michael remains standing ramrod straight in the corner of the room.

Two hours later, I've assembled my laptop, iPad, Kindle, clothes, shoes, accessories, toiletries, books, and photos into a suitcase, some tote bags, and a couple of big, blue IKEA bags.

"Is this all, ma'am?" Michael asks, not having moved an inch from his post in the living room.

"Yup, that's it." It's a bit sad, looking at the measly pile of luggage by the door. Everything in my life worth keeping will fit in the back of a sedan. I don't even need a minivan, let alone a truck.

It's almost ten by the time we're loaded in the car and ready to go. I text Eddie from the back seat, a bag of make-up and handbags crammed next to me.

Me: *On my way! Will I be able to get in? I assume you're out already.*

Eddie: *That's great news. I'll make sure someone is there to let you in.*

When we arrive at KP, the guard at the gate spots me in the car and raises the boom gates—I suppose there's no need to sign in when you live here. When the car stops, Michael jumps out and walks to the boot to unload my things. I step out onto the path and go to pick up the suitcase.

"Don't worry about these, ma'am. I'll bring them inside for you."

"Thanks, Michael."

He lifts an IKEA bag in each hand and gestures for me to walk in front of him. I walk up to the door and ring the brass doorbell. A moment later, Eddie himself opens the door, shouting "Surprise!" He grins, scoops me up, and carries me into the foyer. "Welcome home."

I tilt my head up, and our mouths meet.

"What a welcome!"

"Don't worry," he says. "There's more where that came from." He traipses through the foyer and sitting room into the kitchen, carrying me all the way. As we approach the kitchen, the aroma of warm pastry hits me. We follow the scent to Eddie's large marble-topped island bench, where he deposits me on a stool. In front of me is an enormous spread of deliciousness—croissants, Danishes filled with blueberries and raspberries, chocolate chip muffins, scones, and cinnamon buns.

"Did you make these all for me?" I ask, wide-eyed.

Eddie puffs out his chest and nods. "I did. Special new-resident breakfast offer, one day only."

I snatch a Danish from the plate in front of me and bite into the flaky, buttery pastry. As I do, my eyes roll back. "Mm, this is so good. I should move in more often."

"You should probably also eat something healthier for breakfast, but we can work on that now that you're here."

I clutch my chest. "Don't you dare judge me for eating breakfast pastries when you're the one who makes them for me!"

Eddie chuckles. "What can I say? I don't find scrambling eggs as relaxing as folding layers of pastry."

"You enjoy making them, I enjoy eating them—it's perfect. Don't take that away from me."

"Very well," he says, raising his hands in surrender. "The pastries stay."

"Phew! In that case, so do I. If you started serving me green juices, I might have to move right back out again."

"Noted." Eddie winks at me as I reach across and take a muffin. "I have to head off shortly to a meeting, but I wanted to see you before I went. I also have something for you."

He sticks his hand in his pocket and pulls out a small black box. I inhale sharply. Is that a ring box? Is he finally going to finish proposing? I can't tell if it's the same box he had with him in Africa; with everything going on, I never got a good look at it. Eddie places the box on his upturned palm and offers it to me. Trembling, I reach out and open the lid.

Oh. It's a key.

"Now you can really make yourself at home."

This is not quite what I was expecting. Maybe I totally misread the situation in Africa and he was never planning to propose in the first place. Where does he think this is going? Maybe I actually am his seventeenth-century mistress? I want to ask, but he finally seems genuinely happy right now for the first time since Kenya. I don't want to ruin that.

"Amelia?"

My head snaps up. "Uh, thank you."

Eddie squeezes my hand. "I'm so glad you're here. I have to run, but I'll see you later."

Lost in thought, I munch on my Danish and then notice

Michael is standing in the doorway and probably saw the whole key exchange. "Would you like something to eat, Michael? There's plenty."

"No, thank you, ma'am."

"Are you sure? There's no way Eddie and I will get through all of this."

He eyes the platters and then looks down at his washboard stomach. "I shouldn't, ma'am. Recovering croissant addict, you understand."

"Don't worry, it's an addiction I know well."

CHAPTER 8

After Eddie leaves, I take a croissant for the road and trek upstairs to the bedroom where Michael has left my luggage neatly piled by the door. I lug the bags into Eddie's closet and find he's cleared a section out for me. It takes even less time to unpack my things than it took to pack them. What now? Maybe I should go to the office. I'm not meant to be going back until Monday, but with Eddie out all day, I don't have much to do here.

I'm in the living room packing my phone and some papers into my handbag when there's a rap on the door. I check the time —Eddie's only been gone for forty-five minutes. Perhaps he forgot something. Why would he knock on his own living room door, though? Weird. "Hello? Eddie?"

The door opens, and a man strides in. He stops in front of where I'm sitting on an ottoman in front of the fireplace. It's not Eddie, though—it's Henry.

"Oh, hi, Henry. How did you get in here?"

"Ms Glendale, I'm His Majesty's most senior adviser—I have a key."

I know Henry works incredibly closely with Eddie, but

turning up unannounced in his house seems like an overstep to me. But who knows? It might be normal. There are plenty of things about how this family works that I don't understand yet.

"I've become aware that you are staying here presently."

"Yes, Edmund asked me to move in."

Henry's lip curls. "He didn't have permission to do that."

Permission? This is *his* house. I'm pretty sure he doesn't need permission to decide who lives here. I don't want to cause any unnecessary issues with Henry by pointing that out, though.

Before I say anything, Henry speaks again. "Don't get your heart set on the idea of living here. I'll be speaking to His Majesty about the situation shortly, and I expect your stay here will be rather short-lived."

"Excuse me? Why would it be short-lived?"

He laughs. "You are not from this world, Ms Glendale, and you do not fit into it. King Albert did not approve of your association with his son, and neither do I. You may have some brains and decorum, but you are wholly inappropriate to fulfil the role of a royal consort. You cannot even begin to appreciate the intricacies of the monarchy. You simply haven't been bred for it like Lady Cavendish. I cannot envisage any circumstance in which your relationship survives."

Right. Looks like I'm not the one creating issues here today. I can't believe he actually said I wasn't bred for this. I joked about being a seventeenth-century mistress, but I think Henry and his values may have actually travelled here from three hundred years ago. "Henry, I don't know that it's your place to be commenting on Edmund's personal relationships."

"With all due respect, Ms Glendale, you wouldn't have the first idea of what is or isn't my place to comment on. That is part of my concern."

I pull my phone out of my bag. "I'm also not comfortable having this conversation without Edmund here. I'm going to call him."

Henry reaches out, grabs my phone from my hand, and throws it onto the sofa. "There's no need to disturb the king. We can discuss this like adults, just you and me."

Whether Henry is acting like an adult right now is extremely questionable. "I'm not sure there's anything to discuss."

"To the contrary, there are extremely pressing matters to discuss. Given the current stressors the king is facing, I'm reluctant to ask him to end this relationship. However, if there is something that could persuade you to end it yourself, I could facilitate that."

"Something that could persuade me to break up with Eddie?"

"Yes, a payment perhaps? I believe we could arrange quite a generous bonus to be paid through the foundation."

"Sorry, are you trying to *bribe* me?"

Henry rolls his eyes. "I'm simply attempting to ensure we both achieve our goals."

All right, I was mad after the poor breeding comment, but now I'm furious. "I can't believe I have to say this, but I'm not dating Eddie for the money. And I'm not going to break up with him because you don't approve of me."

"Very well." He fixes me with a steely glare. "If you insist on staying with him, be aware that as long as I am part of this institution, you will never have a role in it. You will not be seen with the king in public. You will have no influence. You will have no voice."

Wow. I've barely even spoken to Henry before. I never knew he hated me so much. And for what—because I didn't grow up in a mansion in the country going on fox shoots and hosting tea parties? This is ridiculous. Eddie's going to be incensed when he hears about this. "Henry, you need to leave."

He sneers at me before leaving the room. I definitely need to get out of this place for a while.

~

On my way to the office, I try to call Eddie but can't get him. So when I arrive, I push Henry out of my mind and go upstairs only to find Daisy Mellington, one of my junior lawyers, sitting at my desk. When I walk into the room, I cough, and she jumps sky-high and throws the cup of coffee she was holding into the air. It lands on the desk and spills everywhere, drenching all the stacks of paper I'd strategically scattered around so I wouldn't lose them.

"Amelia! I didn't think you were coming in until next week!"

"Sorry to startle you. I had a free day, so I decided to come in. Let me grab some paper towels to clean this up."

I run off to the kitchen and pick up a wad of paper towels. When I walk into my office again, Daisy is standing next to the desk trying to wipe coffee off her pencil skirt with a piece of paper. "Here," I say, handing her some of the towels. "This might work better."

She takes them gratefully and starts scrubbing at her skirt. "Thanks, Amelia. And sorry for getting coffee everywhere. I was surprised to see you and a tad embarrassed to be caught using your desk. I came in here because I'm having a completely frantic day and needed to concentrate."

"Don't worry about it, Daisy. You're welcome to use my desk whenever I'm not here. But now that I am here, can I take anything off your plate to make your day a bit more manageable?"

"We need to get back to Doctors Without Borders with any comments on the project report for the vaccination clinics by the end of today. Could you look at that?"

"I'd be happy to. That project is my baby." I cough. "But I'll probably need my desk back, though."

Daisy's cheeks flush. "Of course, sorry again." She scuttles out of the room, and I sit down at the desk and exhale. Being back here makes me feel useful again. I've been trying to do what I can to help Eddie at home, but frankly, there's practically nothing I can do. At least here I've got a to-do list I can work through. What a relief.

I bunker down and spend the day reviewing reports on the progress of the vaccination clinics we recently opened at some of the schools we run in Kenya. It's great to see the pilot program has been going so well—the school infrastructure and connections to local communities are already there, so the incremental investment to provide health services is minimal, and the reach is extensive. Based on the progress to date, I think the program should definitely be expanded. Program development isn't strictly my job, but I'm going to find some time to research where we should roll the clinics out next. I enjoy the legal work I do, but there's a satisfaction in coming up with an idea for a project and seeing it come together that I haven't experienced before. Knowing something I created has directly improved people's lives is the most rewarding thing. I also love that taking the clinics from idea to reality is something Eddie and I achieved together. I wish we could do more of that work together, but based on my conversation with Henry earlier, there's no way that's ever going to happen.

CHAPTER 9

Back at home—I don't think I'll ever get over how weird it sounds to hear myself describe a palace that way—Eddie and I are eating dinner on the sofa when Leo walks into the dining room. Exactly how many people have keys to our house? This is starting to feel like a security issue.

"Hello, Leo, good to see you," Eddie says.

"You've been hard to track down lately, Eddie."

"I have, I'm sorry. Things have been a tad hectic."

Leo huffs. "We need to talk about the arrangements for the funeral."

"Is it something my office can deal with? My protocol secretary, James, is the best person to speak to about the logistics."

Leo lets out a short bark of laughter. "Don't fob me off."

Eddie blinks. "Pardon? I'm not trying to fob you off. I'm simply not the best person to speak to about details. I'm not across everything."

"I've spoken to your office. They told me to speak to you."

"All right then, what exactly about the funeral was it you wanted to discuss?"

"Your office told me Kayla has to sit at the back of the abbey, and she can't arrive or leave with me."

"Leo," Eddie says, rubbing his temples. "You know it's protocol that only engaged and married couples attend official events together. I was happy to approve Kayla to attend, but she can't sit with the family. It's not how things are done."

Leo scoffs. "It's now how things are done? Wake up, Ed—you're in charge now. You're the one who makes the decisions. You can't hide behind protocol. You've got your girlfriend secretly living here. How does that fit with protocol?"

Eddie takes a deep breath and exhales slowly. "Leo, I'm sorry, but I'm not going to break with tradition for this. The funeral is about Dad. I can't let you distract from that by using it to announce your relationship."

"Are you kidding me?" Leo yells.

"I mean it."

Leo shakes his head and paces around the room. "Is this because you don't think she's good enough for our family? Because she's been on TV? You're as bad as he was."

"Leo, it's got nothing to do with that. I promise you, it's purely a matter of timing and ensuring we don't distract from the funeral."

Leo scowls at Eddie. "Whatever. You're just jealous."

"I'm jealous?" Eddie splutters. "I am *not* jealous. Let's calm down here."

"Don't tell me to calm down!" He spins around, grabs a pile of briefing papers from the coffee table, and throws them in the air, letting them fall to the floor like confetti.

"Look," Eddie says in an even tone, "how about this? Kayla comes to the funeral by herself, and then, a week after the funeral, once we're out of the official mourning period, you can go public."

Leo cocks his head to one side and rubs his chin. "We can do interviews?"

"You can do as many interviews as you like, as long as you wait a week."

He paces back and forth in silence for what seems like minutes before fixing Eddie with a stare. "All right, you've got a deal. I'm only agreeing as a favour to you, though. You owe me."

Eddie opens his mouth and then closes it again and purses his lips, clearly thinking better of engaging any further.

"I'll see you at the funeral," Leo says. He turns on his heel and walks out of the room.

"What was that?" I ask, shell-shocked.

"I take it you haven't been properly introduced to Leo's temper?"

"Apparently not. I've seen him snap before, but nothing like that."

"He gets rather worked up sometimes. He's harmless, but he can take a while to cool off."

"Do you think he'll keep his word on not going public with Kayla until after the funeral?"

"Mm, I expect so. He's got a lot of bravado, but he won't want to incur our mother's wrath by taking attention away from Dad."

"Fair enough. By the way, what are we doing about the funeral? Henry came to see me today, and he said he doesn't want me to be seen with you in public. I assume that means we can't officially attend together?"

Eddie turns to gaze out the window and starts fidgeting with his watch. Almost a minute later, he still hasn't spoken. "Eddie?"

"Mm?"

"The funeral? Should I talk to James about the details?"

"No, no need to speak to James."

"Okay, what time should I get there? And am I meant to sit anywhere in particular?"

"About that . . ." Eddie turns to look at me, his face drawn. "You can't come to the funeral."

"What, not at all?" I ask, my nose wrinkling.

"No. It's been discussed, and the team considers that, given how much public attention you've attracted over the last few months, it's best for you not to attend."

"Is this because of Henry? I know he doesn't want me to be seen with you, but I thought I'd still be able to come to the funeral and hide in the crowd so I was still there for you."

He winces. "Yes, it was Henry who decided you shouldn't be there. And there's something else you should be aware of."

What now? I'm not sure how much I can take. It's been a long day.

Eddie's shoulders are hunched, and he's frowning. "Sib is coming to the funeral."

"Oh, okay, that makes sense. She's been close to the family for a long time. I'm sure Caroline will be glad to have her there."

"She's coming to the funeral with me. As my fiancée."

The words crash over me, and time seems to screech to a halt. What on earth is going on? I thought we had this conversation already. He said they weren't together. He asked me to move in. This makes no sense. "Sorry, can you say that again? I thought I heard you say Sibella is going to your father's funeral with you as your fiancée."

Eddie gulps hard. "That is indeed what I said."

"I . . . I don't understand. You're not together, so why would you do something to perpetuate the idea that you are?"

He sighs. "You know Sib and I never made our split public."

"Of course I do. But I didn't expect you to go out of your way to pretend you're still with her. I thought you'd be making some kind of announcement before the funeral. Especially now that I've moved in here."

"I know it's not ideal, but as I said to Leo, the last thing we want to do is detract attention from the funeral and national mourning. Henry and the other senior staff have been quite insistent that I not upset the cart by announcing the broken engagement yet."

"I can kind of understand that, but there's a big difference between not announcing you've ended the engagement and parading her around in front of the world at official events."

"I'm not sure I've got a choice. If Sib doesn't come with me, the press will have a field day, and there will be an avalanche of speculation about the state of our relationship."

I give a hollow laugh. "As there should be. You broke up!"

Eddie grimaces. "I understand it's hard to accept, but my advisers are quite set on it. It's only going to be for the funeral. After that, I can stop being seen with her in public before quietly announcing we're no longer together."

"Eddie, I don't like this. It feels like you want me to skulk around and pretend not to exist."

"Mils, I'd never want you to pretend not to exist. I want you here. Believe me, if there were any other option, I'd take it, but my advisers won't budge on this one."

After the discussion I had with Henry earlier today, this feels much more like a personal vendetta than a legitimate concern on his part. He'd love for Sibella to keep playing the role of queen-in-waiting if it means keeping me in the shadows. Maybe Eddie can talk to someone else on the team about it who might be slightly more reasonable. "I hate agreeing with Leo on anything, but like he said earlier, you're the one who gets to make the decisions now. Are you sure you can't do something?"

"There's nothing to be done," he says, dropping his head. "I may be in charge, but my ultimate duty is to the country and my family. I can't go against protocol or do anything to distract people from Dad's funeral any more than Leo can. In fact, I have less scope than anyone to step out of line. I'm the one who gets the most attention, the one who needs to be seen as infallible. Henry has made it clear to me it would be problematic for us to be seen together."

I scoff. "I'm sure he has. That's why I tried to call you earlier today, Henry came over here and accosted me. He tried to bribe me to break up with you."

"What?" Eddie asks, looking startled. "Are you sure? Maybe it was a misunderstanding."

I wish it was a misunderstanding. There are only so many ways you can interpret being told that you weren't bred for something, though. "I'm sure. He was incredibly rude to me."

"Well, I'll certainly take care of that. I won't allow anyone to speak to you in that way. If Henry has an issue with you, he can raise it with me."

I sigh. "Thank you. But that doesn't solve the issue of my place here. Where does all of this leave us?"

"I don't want it to change anything. I love you and want us to spend our lives together."

He wants us to spend our lives together, but suddenly it's going to be in secret? I do not feel great about that. At all. I rake my hand through my hair and sigh. "How does that work? Am I meant to pretend we're not together? I don't want to do that."

"I can absolutely understand that. I promise you that very soon we'll be able to be together in public. In the meantime, my family and the staff are aware we're together and you're living here, so at home, there's no reason to hide."

I exhale slowly. "I don't know how that's going to work. I don't want to feel like we're sneaking around."

Eddie takes my hands in his. "We're going to make it work. I need you. And we definitely don't have to sneak around." He wrings his hands. "Other than at the funeral."

I pull my hands away and stare out the window.

"Why don't you come to the reading of Dad's will with me next week? The family will all be there and some senior advisers. It will show everyone here that I'm serious about making you part of my family. Because I am."

"I'm not sure. That seems like exactly the kind of thing Henry is trying to keep me out of."

"Let me worry about Henry. I'd really appreciate it if you came. Going through these processes makes everything feel real. Each step takes me closer to having to accept that he's gone and this is my life now. I could do with your support."

I soften at that. "Oh, Eddie." I stroke his arm. "If it'll help you, I'll be there."

CHAPTER 10

ON THE DAY of the will reading, I wake to the sound of Eddie pacing around our en suite. "Hey, honey, is everything all right in there?" No response. I pull on one of those amazing robes and go over to see what's happening. In the bathroom, I see Eddie walking back and forth with his eyes closed and headphones in. I go over and tap on his shoulder. His eyes snap open, and he pulls an earbud out.

"Sorry, did I wake you?"

"Don't worry about that, are you doing okay? Big day today."

He closes his eyes again and rolls his shoulders. "I'm rather stressed at the moment, so I thought listening to some meditations might help me relax."

"That's a good idea. Has it helped?"

"Mm, yes and no. I'm not hyperventilating anymore, which is positive, but I still feel like my chest is in a vice."

I pat him on the arm. "Baby steps. Anything else I can do?"

"Would you mind terribly tying my tie for me? My hands are shaking."

I survey the room and see a navy silk tie waiting on the bathroom counter. "That I can do." I take the tie, slide it under his collar, and tie a perfect Eldredge knot. Finally, my weird habit of watching tie-tying videos on YouTube has paid off.

"That's a rather splendid knot. I should have asked you to become my official tie tier months ago."

I take a bow. "We all have our skills."

"Colour me impressed." He checks his watch and groans. "Half an hour until go time."

"Are you ready?"

He grits his teeth. "Not at all, but we'll do it together."

The atmosphere in Eddie's office is stifling—and not just because Henry is shooting daggers at me from behind the desk. I'm hovering at the back of the room with a group of palace staff, fanning myself with a piece of paper and trying to fade into the wallpaper. Meanwhile, Eddie sits behind his desk, surrounded by Queen Louisa, Caroline, Leo, Princess Helena, Emma, and Lucy perched on an assortment of antique chairs someone has dragged into the room. The room is silent but for the sound of Eddie drumming his fingers on his desk and occasional sniffling from Louisa. After twenty painful minutes, a tiny and impossibly old man walks into the room, followed by three other men in black suits.

The ancient man bows as he enters. "Good morning, Your Majesty, Your Highnesses. Apologies for keeping you waiting."

"That's quite all right, Alfred," Eddie says. "We do have a limited amount of time available this morning, though."

"Of course, sir." Alfred looks around the room for a spare seat. I can only assume he's no longer physically capable of standing for more than three minutes at a time. Clearly, I'm not the only one who is concerned because one of his colleagues disappears from the room and quickly reappears with a chair. Alfred creaks into place and fishes a pair of reading glasses out of his briefcase. "Shall we get started?"

"Yes, please," Eddie says.

"Very well, sir." Alfred extends his hand, and one of his colleagues hands him a sheaf of paper. He pushes the glasses up the bridge of his nose and clears his throat.

"This is the last will and testament of His Majesty King Albert the Second, made on fifteen July, twenty-twenty. His Majesty signed this will in my presence, and I have stored it in a safe in my office ever since."

Alfred spends what feels like hours droning through the standard provisions of the will, and I swear I see Helena fall asleep at one point.

"I will now read the list of specific bequests from His Majesty's will. First, to my son Edmund, I leave my art collection. To my daughter Caroline, I leave my estate in Aberdeen. To my son Leopold, I leave my estate in Norfolk. To my sister Helena, I leave my collection of antiquities." Alfred adjusts his tie and coughs. "To Lady Sophia Sumner-Jones, I leave the contents of vault 385 at the Bank of England's Oxford Street branch. To Lady Isla Barrington, I leave twenty-five million pounds and my estate in Derbyshire. Finally, to my wife Louisa, I leave the remainder of my estate and personal effects."

A heavy silence falls over the room. The rustling of pages as Alfred places the will back in his briefcase is deafening.

Oh my god. I've suddenly realised that in all the drama, I never told Eddie that I found out his dad was having an affair with my old boss, Soph. And now he's left her a mysterious package in his will. And he's left a house and money to Soph's daughter . . . Does that mean she was their love child? He wouldn't be that careless, would he? Then again, he wouldn't be leaving her all that money for nothing. Ugh. This is not going to end well.

Eddie and his family are all looking around the room in

disbelief, while Alfred, his colleagues, and the palace aides try to be invisible.

Alfred mops his brow. "Your Highness," he says, addressing Queen Louisa, "His Majesty also left this letter to be given to you when the will was read."

Louisa stares at Alfred, looking like a deer in the headlights. He holds the letter out towards her, and she recoils. "Shall I read it?" he asks.

Louisa startles. "No. I'm going to read it in private," she says, reaching out to take the paper.

But before Alfred can hand it to Louisa, Leo strides across the room and snatches it from his hand. "I don't think so, Mother," he says. "I'd like to hear why on earth Dad left money and our best country home to a random family friend. I'm sure everyone else would like answers too."

Louisa furrows her brow and glares at Leo. Everyone else is silent.

Leo holds the letter above his head. "Ed, you're in charge. You make the call."

Eddie looks at the floor and rubs his temples. "Mother," he says, turning to Louisa, "I think we should all read it. We all need to understand what is going on here."

After a long silence, Louisa groans. "As you wish, Edmund," she says, wringing her hands.

Leo rips the envelope open. He clears his throat dramatically and begins to read.

"Dearest Louisa, you will not see this letter until the time has come that I have passed and you have been provided with a copy of my will. I imagine that having read my will, you will be full of questions. Before I explain the reason for the bequests I have made, I want you to know I valued our life together greatly."

Oh dear, I get the feeling that this letter is about to drop some major truth bombs. My eyes dart around the room madly. I'm searching everyone's faces, trying to glean if they've figured out where this is going. So far, everyone just looks confused.

Leo continues. "However, as I suspect you have known for some time now, ours was not the only significant relationship in my life. I have loved Sophia for as long as I have known her."

Suddenly, the room explodes. Emma squeals and slaps Lucy's arm. Louisa crumples onto the floor.

Eddie swings around to face Helena. "Did you know about this?"

Helena mutters something incomprehensible before Leo shouts out to silence everyone. "Quiet! There's more."

When everyone has stopped talking, and two aides have lifted Louisa into a chair, he continues reading.

"What you may not know, or may not have wished to know, is Sophia and I shared more than love. We also shared a daughter. It is my most ardent desire that when I am gone, you will accept my dear Isla as part of our family. I left instructions with my attorneys that after my passing, Isla should be afforded her rightful rank and titles and be known as a princess of the United Kingdom. I trust you will honour my wishes and embrace Isla as one of your own."

Leo slaps the letter down against his leg, and Louisa sobs. The sound of her gasping breaths reverberates around the room, and the assembled group stare at each other in silence.

My mind is spinning. Soph told me about her affair with King Albert, but it had never even occurred to me that he may have been the father of her daughter Isla.

"Shit," Lucy says.

Well, that's an understatement.

She bites her lip before speaking again. "Edmund, isn't Isla around the same age as you?"

I turn to face Eddie. His jaw is slack, and his face is pale. Henry, meanwhile, is twitching around in the corner, looking like he's having both a seizure and a heart attack simultaneously.

Eddie coughs, and instantly all eyes in the room are on him. Wait, *is* Isla older than Eddie? How would that even work if she was? Would he be stripped of the throne and be forced to let Isla take over? Or would her being illegitimate mean she didn't have a claim? This could get messy. Really messy.

"Alfred," he says. Every eye in the room is on him. "Do you have Lady Barrington's details?"

Alfred gulps hard. "Details, Your Majesty?"

"Yes," Eddie says, gritting his teeth. "Her details. Her date of birth."

The lawyer reddens and madly shuffles papers around in his briefcase. He grabs a sheet and thrusts it into the air. "Got it!"

Louisa lets out a yelp.

Eddie stares at Alfred. "Well?"

"Lady Barrington was born on the seventeenth of July 1990. Three weeks after you, Your Majesty."

Everyone assembled in the room lets out a collective breath. A moment later, Leo is the one to break the heavy silence that has descended. "Thank Christ for that!"

Eddie clutches his forehead. Emma laughs deliriously. Louisa is back to sobbing. Helena sits in the corner, quiet and withdrawn, looking suspiciously like someone who isn't as shocked by this news as she should be.

"Well," Alfred says, clearing his throat. "Uh, I think that's all I needed to communicate, so I might be going."

He awkwardly packs his papers back into his briefcase while the crowd watches in silence. As soon as his case snaps shut, he scuttles towards the door and walks out before quickly reappearing in the room looking flustered. "Your Majesty, Your Highnesses," he says with a bow before disappearing again.

Appearing from the corner of the room, Henry claps. "Right. It looks like there are some issues to discuss."

Eddie raises his head and glares at Henry. "Out," he roars.

"Pardon, Your Majesty? We need to discuss where to go from here."

"Out. All of you."

Aides glance around at each other and start making for the door. Helena also stands to leave.

"Not you, Helena. Everyone who isn't family, leave this room immediately."

Both Henry's and Leo's eyes flick to me. "After you, Ms Glendale," Henry says.

"Yeah," Leo chimes in. "Last time I checked, she wasn't family."

"Amelia stays," Eddie says firmly.

"But, Your Majesty . . ." Henry says.

"No buts."

Henry purses his lips, and Leo huffs.

As the last of the staff scamper out into the corridor, the door slams shut, and the room is quiet again other than for Louisa's overwrought sobs. Eddie slams his head down on his desk with a thunk, and his gravelly groan melds with his mother's crying. After an eternity, he looks up and surveys the room. "What on earth are we going to do?"

Leo crosses his arms. "*We* aren't going to do anything. This is way above my pay grade. This one is all yours, brother. Enjoy."

Eddie turns to Louisa. "Mummy, what do you think we should do?"

She tries to speak but instead dissolves into increasingly dramatic tears and starts rocking back and forth while Helena tries to comfort her. Eddie slumps in his chair. "We're clearly not going to figure anything out right now. I'm going home to have an exceptionally large drink."

CHAPTER 11

Eddie and I make our way back to Wren House in a blur and plant ourselves on the sofa. Eddie sits silently, clearly struggling to process what he's learnt. I'm going to have to admit that I already knew, aren't I? I can't imagine he's going to be thrilled about me not having told him sooner, but we're a team—I can't keep this from him. I clear my throat. "Eddie, there's something I need to tell you."

"What is it? Is something wrong? Fair warning, I'm not in much of a mood for bad news."

This isn't going to go down well. At all. But it's bad enough that I kept the affair secret from him for this long; no good can come from me pretending I'm only learning about it now. "It's about your father and Soph."

"Don't say her name!" Eddie spits. "I don't want to talk about them."

"I can understand why you don't want to, but I need to get this out." Deep breaths, Amelia. "I knew. About the affair, that is."

Eddie's jaw goes slack. I rush to speak again before he can say anything. "Not for long! Soph told me when she came to see me the morning we got back together. I'd had no idea before that! I was going to tell you, but then we were on our romantic trip, and I didn't want to kill the happiness. And then your dad died, and it didn't feel like quite the right time to bring up that he'd been cheating on your mum for decades." I peer nervously up at Eddie. He's silent, but his face is thunder. I grimace. "Are you mad at me? I'm so sorry. I should have told you straight away."

"Mad!" Eddie barks. "Too bloody right I'm mad! I'm mad at you for not telling me. I'm mad at Dad and Soph for having the stupid affair in the first place. I'm mad at Henry for trying to control how I react. I'm mad at everyone!" Suddenly, he drops his head into his hands and sobs. When he speaks again, it's barely a whisper. "I'm mad at Dad for dying and leaving me to handle all of this alone. I'm not ready."

And just like that, my heart breaks for him. The Eddie I know is strong, funny, and passionate, but when I study him now, all I see is a scared little boy who needs a father—preferably one who isn't as emotionally distant and judgemental as King Albert was. I lean over and rub his back. "It's okay, everything's going to be okay."

"How can it be?" he asks between ragged breaths. "I wasn't meant to do this—to be king—for decades yet. I didn't have enough time to prepare. It's too much."

I slip my arm around his waist and rest my head on his shoulder. "Oh, honey, it's so hard, I know. Well, I don't really know, and that's the problem. There are so few people in the world who can truly understand what you're going through. I can't even begin to comprehend how isolating it must feel. But whatever happens, I'm here for you, and we'll deal with it together. There can only be one king, but that doesn't mean you have to do any of this alone."

"I'm not so sure. Lately, I feel rather alone."

"I can see that, but you've got a whole team of people to support you as king and so many people who love you as a person. Me, your mum, Lucy, Emma, Caroline, Leo. Like it or not, none of us are going anywhere. Other than Leo, I mean. He may well make a break for Majorca at any minute. The rest of us, though, you're stuck with for life. And not only because you've got the biggest TV and always remember to stock up on snacks."

He looks over and gives me a watery smile.

"I love you, and I'll do anything to make you feel better. If you need someone to throw something at Soph or spray-paint inappropriate words on her car, I'm your girl."

"Oh, Mils, I love you so much. Please never leave."

"Never. Stuck with me for life, remember?"

WHEN I WAKE up in the morning, I yawn and stretch out in bed. Even if Eddie weren't funny and attractive as hell, I probably would have moved in with him just for the bed. I've said it before, and I'll say it again—this mattress is out of control.

I'm so relaxed that it takes me a minute to realise that, yet again, I've sprawled out on the bed without hitting the perfectly toned arms, chest, or any other body parts of Eddie. I spring up and peer around the room, but there's no trace of him. "Eddie? Are you up here?"

No response.

I grab some sweatpants from the pile of clothes I've left on the floor and pull them on as I make my way downstairs.

"Wow."

I have no idea what I've walked into here. Eddie is buzzing around the kitchen with AirPods in, and if there weren't armed guards outside the front door twenty-four seven, I'd swear we'd been robbed. What looks like every pot, pan, dish, and utensil in the house is strewn around the kitchen. There are trays on the table, whisks on the floor, and flour everywhere. Everywhere.

"Eddie? Eddie!"

He startles and swings around to face me. "Sorry," he says, pulling out his earbuds. "I didn't hear you come downstairs."

I survey the kitchen massacre. "So, uh, what are you doing?"

"Just baking."

I plant a hand on my hip. "Just baking?"

"It may be more aptly described as stress baking."

"And how long have you been up stress baking for?"

He glances at his watch. "About five hours now."

"So you've been up cooking since three in the morning. You've been doing this quite a lot recently."

"Are you saying you don't want my red velvet cake, coconut blueberry layer cake, raisin croissants, and chocolate-raspberry brownies?"

How is he so much more productive when stressed than I am? When I'm finding things too much, I'm more likely to hit a bar and make terrible life choices than hit the kitchen.

"Eddie," I say, walking around the island and taking his hand in mine. "I love that your pain manifests in dessert, but I'm worried about you. You're dealing with so much right now, and as much as I provide excellent moral support, if I do say so myself, I think perhaps you should talk to someone. A professional, that is."

He gives me a wry smile. "I'm flattered you think I'm so well adjusted that I've made it this far in life without a therapist. Don't worry, the official palace psychologist is due to visit in a couple of hours to ensure I haven't completely fallen apart."

"Oh! I didn't realise. Well, that's great. I'm glad you've got someone to talk to."

"I'm sure I'll be quite all right once I have a chance to process. It's all been quite a shock."

I rub his back. "I can't imagine. Early morning baking aside, you're handling it so well. I'm really proud of you."

Eddie's shoulders relax, and he kisses me on the forehead.

"Thanks, Mils, that means a lot to me. Can I reward you with some breakfast cake?"

"Early morning sugar sounds great, if somewhat unhealthy. Has anyone ever told you that you're not a very good influence?"

"I resent that implication, Amelia. I'm an excellent influence, and I have the public opinion polls to prove it. Are you aware that eighty-five percent of women aged thirty to fifty-five would trust me to take care of their children? Curiously, though, less than fifty percent would trust me to look after their dog. I'm not entirely sure if that reflects poorly on me or on the public's judgement."

I cackle with laughter. "If only they knew you've managed to keep a dog alive for years but have a pathological fear of children's sticky hands."

"How are they always so sticky? I find it both confusing and incredibly off-putting. I'm sure I was never like that as a child."

"To be fair, I assume you also had at least one nanny dressed as Mary Poppins following you around at all times. You could have had a nanny whose entire job was to keep you clean."

His mouth twitches. "I'll have you know I only ever had two nannies at a time—hardly enough to dedicate one solely to hand wiping."

"You royals," I say, smiling, "you're just like the rest of us."

Eddie chuckles and relaxes a fraction, which is why I'm not certain that what I'm going to say next is a great idea, but I feel like I have to do it anyway.

"Eddie, all jokes aside, have you thought about speaking to your sister to see how she's holding up?"

He knits his brow. "Caro? I spoke to her last night. She's livid with Dad, but she'll survive. She's looking forward to getting back to Scotland and having some space from all the family drama."

I look into Eddie's warm hazel eyes. "I meant your other sister."

Confusion fills his face before swiftly being replaced by anger. "Don't call her that!" he snaps.

"Eddie," I whisper. "Like it or not, she is your sister, and I'm worried about her."

"She may share my DNA, but that doesn't mean that she's part of my family. Quite to the contrary, she represents everything that's wrong with my family. If I ever see her again, it will be too soon."

All right, time to drop that topic.

As we're sitting at the table eating breakfast, the doorbell rings. Eddie jumps up to answer it and soon returns carrying a large red leather briefcase.

He places the case on the table and flips it open. Inside is an intimidatingly large stack of papers—the daily dispatches from Eddie's office, which normally include a combination of briefing papers, political and financial updates, and new legislation to be officially approved.

"Some light morning reading?"

He picks up the top piece of paper, briefly studies it, and then rubs his eyes and puts it back down. "That's one way to describe it. I'm not sure I can muster the motivation to deal with all of it today. Or any of it for that matter."

"Maybe I can help. What's first on the list?" I walk over and take the paper he's discarded. "Eddie!" I squeal. "It's a new law! I know you're stressed, but the law nerd in me is freaking out that you get to literally approve or veto laws over morning coffee. Can you please let me take a photo of you signing it? Being this close to the legislative process is pretty darn exciting."

Eddie grimaces. "I'm not sure that 'exciting' is the first word that springs to mind, but I appreciate your enthusiasm."

"Come on, it's definitely exciting. You're changing the world here, buddy."

"Did you read the details?" he asked with an arched brow.

I glance down and read the first couple of pages of the document. "Okay, so rules about the size and colour of parking signs aren't the most fascinating things in the world, but they're still an important part of our society."

He rolls his eyes. "Indeed. I can't even begin to comprehend the anarchy we would be plunged into if some parking signs featured black text while others used charcoal." There's a bitter edge to his voice that I'm not used to.

"Hey," I say, squeezing his arm. "Sure, there's a lot of admin and paperwork, but don't forget the difference you can make to people's lives with your work."

He exhales. "I don't know, Mils. Since Dad died, I haven't been able to spend any time working on my charity projects. I'm constantly being shuffled from one meeting to another, reading mundane briefings, or dealing with palace issues. I always thought when I eventually took the top job, it would mean having more control over my life, but it seems like I have less influence now than ever."

"It's always hard adjusting to new jobs. Especially when it's thrust on you so suddenly."

He shakes his head. "I'm not convinced it's an adjustment issue. The palace machine seems to steam along with minimal input from me. I'm a hollow figurehead. My job description is to appear at the times and places listed on my daily schedule, smile, and say nothing offensive. I'm not trusted to do anything else."

"Have you spoken to anyone about it? The advisers are probably just trying to help by taking care of things for you."

"I've attempted to speak to Henry about me exercising more control over what makes it onto my schedule several times now, and I've made no headway at all. I haven't even been able to convince him to let me hold a meeting with the King's Trust team, and it's bloody well named after me." He drops the papers onto the table and rubs his eyes. "Sorry, I'm a tad stressed. A change of scenery may help. I might take the case and head over to the office to work through the documents there."

"Can't focus here?" I ask.

He looks me up and down and smirks. "There are certainly some distractions here that I would be best to avoid until I've managed to tick at least one task off my unending to-do list."

"All right, I'll allow you to leave. Will you come back for lunch so I can distract you some more?"

"You couldn't keep me away if you tried."

AFTER A VERY *DISTRACTING* AFTERNOON, Eddie and I stroll over to Ivy Cottage to have dinner and debrief with Lucy and Emma.

As we approach, the front door flies open. Emma stands in the doorway wearing pyjamas and holding a bottle of Dom Pérignon. She beckons for us to come in.

"Celebrating something, are we?" Eddie asks as we move into the foyer.

Lucy stares blankly at him. "Pardon?"

He gestures towards the bottle.

"Oh, that. No, no celebration—I'm just a girl, stress drinking champers."

"Stress drinking?" he echoes. "What are *you* stressed about?"

Emma laughs hysterically as she gestures madly around the room. "Everything! First, your dad goes and drops dead—which changes everything—and next thing you know, he's got a secret family. Aunt Louisa isn't talking to Mummy. Leo is being weird. You never have time for us anymore. Everything is wrong."

Emma crumples, and I rush over to give her a hug. "Hey, shh. Everything's going to be all right." I seem to be telling people that a lot at the moment. Eddie, on the other hand, hangs back. He's clearly not in the mood to be comforting other people.

"Let's sit down and have something to eat. Some food will make you feel better," I say, steering Emma towards the living room where Caroline and Sibella are sitting and chatting by the fireplace.

When we walk into the room, Caroline stands. "I'll fetch dinner from the kitchen. Could you please help me, Amelia?"

I'd rather not have any more one-on-one time with Caroline after our last conversation, but I can't exactly say no though, can I? "Sure, I'll be right there." I follow her into the kitchen in silence and start collecting a stack of plates.

As I do, she walks over and places a fragile hand on my arm. "Amelia, I wanted to apologise for the way I spoke when we met. I haven't been quite myself lately."

"Don't worry about it. It's a strange time."

"Thank you, dear. I'm sure I made a terrible first impression, and I very much hope I can dispel it as we become better acquainted. I really hope we can be friends."

Well, that's an enormous relief. I'm at my limit for conflict at the moment. I give her a warm smile. "I'd like that."

She nods. "Excellent. Now, I'm going to go and feed these scamps. I believe Sib has something she wants to say too."

I look up and see Sibella waiting quietly in the doorway. What is this, the kitchen of deep conversations?

"Hello, Amelia."

"Hi, how are you?"

She smiles. "Quite well. Doing what I can to help around here. Which is what I wanted to speak to you about actually."

"Oh?" I ask, arching a brow.

"Yes, as you'll know by now, I've been asked to attend the funeral with the family. I feel dreadful about it given your situation with Ed, but it's what people seem to want me to do. I wanted to make sure you were okay with it, though. I won't be doing anything to make it look like Ed and I are together, but that's obviously not how it will be reported. If it will make you uncomfortable, I'm willing to talk to the planning committee and see if they'll reconsider my attendance."

That's surprisingly thoughtful. She's making me feel bad for thinking she was trying to steal Eddie. I wipe an almost tear from my eye—why is everything making me so emotional lately? "Thank you. I appreciate the gesture more than you know. But don't worry, I'll be fine. Do what you need to do to keep everyone happy."

"Are you sure?"

I bob my head. "Positive."

Back in the living room, Leo has joined us, and we're all sitting on the cosy sofas eating pasta—or, in Emma and Lucy's case, swigging champagne from the bottle—when Emma speaks. "I still can't believe it," she says, shaking her head. "How did they hide this from everyone for so long?"

Lucy nods. "It feels a bit like a bad dream. I expect we'll all wake up tomorrow and realise it never happened."

"You're all so naïve," Leo says.

Lucy blinks. "What are you talking about?"

"Let's not beat around the bush here, kids. We all knew he was a selfish bastard."

Lucy gasps. "Leo! You can't talk about your dad like that."

"Watch me," he snarls.

"Look," Eddie says, "Dad wasn't perfect—he never remembered my birthday and thought having a cold, detached parent was character-building—but I don't think any of us can honestly say that we thought he was capable of something like this."

Leo scoffs. "Just because you didn't see what was going on doesn't mean we were all in the dark."

"You knew?" Lucy asks, her eyes the size of saucers.

"I've known about the affair for years."

Eddie's jaw twitches, but he says nothing.

"I found them together once, years ago, at our place on the Welsh coast. I skived off classes once at that awful military boarding school I went to in Cardiff for a while and took a girl for a drive. Turns out Dad had the same idea. He didn't even try to explain himself, he simply yelled at me to leave and never mentioned it again. I'd bet you anything Helena's known for yonks too."

A heavy silence settles over us all. I steal a peek at Eddie. His face is tight, and he's gripping his glass of beer so hard it looks like it might smash at any second. He exhales slowly through his nose, nostrils flaring. When he speaks, it's slow and quiet. "You knew, and you didn't tell me?"

"Why would I tell you? Despite what your adoring fans say, not everything is about you."

Suddenly, Eddie's expression changes, and his eyes are full of fire. "This isn't about me!" he shouts. "This is about all of us! I can't handle your insecure complaints about not being special enough right now. You're so selfish it defies belief."

"I'm not going to sit here and be insulted by a man who can't make a single decision by himself. You're a joke. I'm leaving."

Eddie grits his teeth. "Good riddance. Oh, and make sure that girlfriend of yours doesn't leak any of this disaster to the tabloids. That's the last thing we need right now."

"Kayla would never do that."

Eddie gives a joyless laugh. "Well, it looks like there's something I know that you don't. How the tables have turned."

"What are you on about?"

"Kayla. She's been leaking stories about Amelia and me to the press for months."

"I don't believe you," Leo says through clenched teeth.

"She did," I say. "She took me out to lunch to set me up and had a reporter catfish my flatmate so he could rifle through my things."

He scoffs. "That's ridiculous! You're making it up."

"I can show you proof if you'd like. But believe it or don't believe it, I don't care," Eddie says. "It's true either way."

Leo stands and marches towards the door. "You're jealous of our relationship. It's pathetic." Stopping at the door, he fixes me with a stare. "And you. Careful what you say about my girlfriend. If I get so much as a whiff of you trying to turn people against her, I'll have you fired from the foundation immediately."

A few seconds later, the door slams, and Leo is gone. It's times like these I really wish he wasn't my boss.

Emma puffs out her cheeks. "Well, that was quite the exit, wasn't it? Really knows how to put on a show, our Leo does."

"He's always had a flair for the dramatic. Remember when he was ten and had a trumpeter follow him around all summer playing fanfares every time he entered a room?" Lucy said.

Emma giggles, but Eddie is silent. She reaches out and pats him on the shoulder. "Don't let him get to you, love. He's dealing with things in his own way. We all are."

"His way *is* slightly more reminiscent of a disaffected teenager than ours," Lucy adds.

Emma takes a swig of champagne. "He's an officious git sometimes, but he's our officious git. He'll come back when he's ready."

Eddie's lip curls. "This whole situation is a catastrophe. Trust Dad to make a tremendous mess and leave us to clean it up."

CHAPTER 12

"REMIND me again why you're sitting on a second-hand sofa in my living room watching Albert's funeral and not in the front row at Westminster?"

"You know full well why I'm here and not at the funeral in person, Penny."

"I do, but I want you to say it out loud and hear how it sounds."

I grit my teeth. "I'm here with you because the official palace line is that Eddie and Sibella are still together and I don't exist. Also, because you're my best friend and I miss hanging out with you and sitting on sofas with mystery stains on them like a normal person. All the furniture at KP is abnormally clean."

"Full-time housekeepers will do that," Penny says, shrugging. "But this isn't about furniture, it's about you and your relationship. Obviously, I like Edmund a lot, but I love you more than ice cream and always want what's best for you."

"Do you really love me more than ice cream? Even the addictive white chocolate and salted caramel stuff from that fancy artisanal gelato place in Soho?"

"Absolutely." She bites her lip. "I don't recommend asking me when I'm hungry, though—you might not like the answer."

"I'll keep that in mind."

"Make sure you do. But in the meantime, don't try to change the subject. Are you sure you're okay with Sibella being there for Edmund today instead of you?"

I tug on the necklace I'm wearing. "I'm not thrilled about it, but I'll be fine. He's doing what he has to do. Besides, she's only there sitting with the family because the palace asked her to. She even offered to not go to the funeral at all if it made me uncomfortable, even though she probably would have been there even without the whole fake engagement, given how close she and Caroline are."

Okay, if I were being really honest, I'd tell Penny I'm devastated about not being there. I feel awful and utterly helpless not being there and holding Eddie's hand through it. And even though I know Sibella is going out of her way not to make herself look any more like a royal fiancée than absolutely necessary, I'm still hating all the comments from the BBC royal correspondents about how regal she looks.

Penny purses her lips. "Hmm. I hear you, but I don't believe you. Does he really have to pretend that you're not together? I understand there's a lot going on, but he's the king. If he wanted you there, you'd be there."

I look around the tiny living room. I'm convinced it's gotten smaller since I moved out. Smaller and shabbier. I'd never noticed how many cracks there are on the ceiling. "It's not that simple. Yes, he's the king, but unfortunately, he can't do whatever he likes. There are protocols and advisers and expectations. I can't expect him to stand up to all of that to make me happy."

"Maybe that's exactly what you *should* expect. You're smart, funny, hard-working, and have the biggest heart of anyone I know. You deserve to be happy. I don't care what you say—I refuse to believe this is the life you pictured when you decided to give him another chance."

I sigh. "You're right. It's not what I wanted, but it's what I can have for now. And it's temporary. It's not like I'm going to be hiding in the KP basement forever."

"I should hope not. But if you were going to be held hostage and forced to live in a basement, there are worse basements you could choose. Still, not how a future queen should be living."

I shudder at the word "queen." "Don't jinx me by talking about me being queen. We still don't know if Eddie even wants to get married."

"Let's get real here, Mils. This is not a relationship with Dave from the pub. Eddie's the *king*. In his family, having a long-term live-in girlfriend isn't an option. All these protocols and traditions you're talking about mean you won't have a real role in his life unless you're his wife. So if you're not moving towards getting married, what are you doing?"

"I wish I knew."

Two days after the funeral, I'm sitting in the dining room at Wren House staring out the window and shuffling eggs around my plate while Eddie sits across from me working his way through the morning news briefing. I can't stop thinking about Isla. I found it incredibly hard not being able to be at the funeral, but I can't even imagine how it must have made her feel—upset she couldn't be there to farewell her father, angry she never got to have a relationship with him, rejected by her family? Or maybe a combination of all the above? I wonder if Eddie has stopped to think about how she's feeling. It's one thing for the palace to ice me out, but I can't stand by and watch someone who is actually family be rejected.

I clear my throat. "Hey, Eddie?"

"Mm," he says, looking up from his iPad. "What's up? Is it something more interesting than changes to European coal export levies? Please tell me it is."

"What happens if it's not?"

He presses his lips together. "I expect I'll lose the will to live, crumple to the floor, and not move again until I get hungry or Henry sends a security contingent to drag me to a meeting."

"Well, probably best to avoid that if we can."

"Quite right," he says. "Hence the plea for stimulating conversation."

Seems like he's in a pretty good mood. Fingers crossed mentioning Isla doesn't kill it.

"I've been thinking about Isla . . ."

Eddie shakes his head sharply. "No, sorry, not what I was after at all. Can we please forget you said that? You can start over with some kind of witty observation about a television show. Or horses? Surely you've got something entertaining to say about horses now that you live at a house with stables."

"Wait," I say, blinking. "We have horses?"

"We certainly do. Where did you think the horses the guards patrolling the courtyard ride came from?"

"I'm not sure. I guess I thought they rode them to work?"

Eddie whoops. "You thought guards were bringing horses with them on the Tube in the morning and trotting down Kensington High Street to get to work?"

"Well, when you put it that way, it doesn't sound super likely. Don't think you can distract me with horses, though—I will go for a walk to find the stables later, but right now, I want to talk about your sister."

"As I believe I've told you before, she is *not* my sister. She's an acquaintance who I had nothing against until I found out she ruined my family."

So much for that good mood. "You know Isla didn't have any choice in this either, right? This was all your dad and Soph."

Eddie clenches his jaw.

"Look, I know none of this is easy," I say. "And I didn't exactly get along with your father, but Isla is innocent in all of this, and she's technically your sister—well, half-sister. It was also your father's last wish that you let her be a part of the family. Maybe it would help you get through all of this if you tried to get to know her better. It might give you some closure."

Eddie snorts. "Dad was having an affair for who knows how long and had a secret love child. I'm not exactly rushing to follow his suggestions about how to manage our family. Last wish or not, I'm not doing it."

"That's a fair point. But can you listen to me, though?" I lean over the table and stroke his forearm. "This whole situation has caused so much pain. It's tearing your family apart. First your mum and your aunt, now you and Leo. I've never seen you as angry as you were with him the other night. It's breaking you."

"That's not my fault."

"It's not, but you can change it. Why not take something positive out of this whole disaster and expand your family? Being with you over the last few months, I've seen first-hand how important your circle of family support is when you live such a strange, high-pressure life. You're so lucky having everyone here. I'd love to have my parents and sister next door—well, most of the time, anyway. Family is everything. Why wouldn't you want more of that?"

Eddie closes his eyes and shakes his head. "I can't do it. I can't see her; I can't talk to her."

"I get it, it's all so new still. You might have to give yourself some time to adjust."

"No. I want nothing to do with her. Not now, not ever. When I think of her, all I can see is my selfish father."

With that, Eddie drops his head and returns to reading his briefings. When he'd rather study coal export trends than talk about something, you know things are grim.

AFTER BREAKFAST, I call my security guard Michael and ask him to bring a car around. Given I'm not officially meant to be living here, I'm still using private security and going to the office when I can. As the head of the legal department, I can get away with working from home a day or two each week without raising suspicion, but I still need to show my face most days.

In the car on the way to work, I get a news alert on my phone. The headline screams at me. *ALBERT'S LOVE CHILD SHOCK, SECRET DAUGHTER SET TO SUE.*

Well, this can't be good.

Today The Sun *can exclusively report that the late King Albert had a secret love child, none other than the thirty-two-year-old Lady Isla Barrington.*

Lady Barrington, the daughter of King Albert and Lady Sophia Sumner-Jones, is a firm fixture on the London social scene. She grew up in ritzy Mayfair and attended Downsfordvale Academy where she rubbed shoulders with the country's elite—including half-sister Princess Caroline and cousins Princesses Emma and Lucy. A source close to the family revealed exclusively to The Sun *that the shocking news came to light after the late king's will was examined. The will left millions of pounds of prime country real estate to Barrington, blindsiding Queen Louisa and the late king's legitimate children. The king's dying wish was that Barrington be elevated to princess and live as one of his children.*

The insider confirmed that the family has completely frozen out Barrington on the orders of the newly minted King Edmund. But in what's likely to come as a tremendous blow to the family, she's not going down without a fight. She's been spotted over the last few days meeting with her high-powered legal team, who are rumoured to be in the final stages of preparing a case against the family. Sources say that Barrington is livid with the way she's been treated by the new king and is planning to sue for the right to use the title of princess and for a significantly bigger slice of King Albert's estate. The case is set to air the royal family's dirty laundry on a scale never seen before.

More to come.

By the time I finish reading the article, I've had at least twenty additional news alerts and messages come through. On some level, I knew the news about Isla probably wouldn't stay quiet for long, but this is much worse than I'd ever imagined. If she does sue, who knows what sort of sordid details about the family will come out? It will devastate Eddie and the others. I quickly try to call him to make sure he's okay. The call goes straight to voicemail, but a message from him pops up.

Eddie: *Take it that you've seen the news. In crisis meetings, will call when I can.*

Me: *Don't worry about calling, I wanted to make sure you're all right. I'll make a quick appearance at the office and then come home. See you there when you're done with meetings.*

When we arrive in the office basement, Michael stops in front of the lifts and hops out of the car to open my door. "Pick up at six, ma'am?"

"Change of plans, actually. I'll only be staying for a couple of hours. Can you be back at eleven?"

"Of course, ma'am," he says before pausing for a beat. "I expect there's a bit to discuss at home."

WHEN I EMERGE from the lift, the office is abuzz. There are groups of employees huddled around the floor, either chatting feverishly or simply looking stunned.

"See the news, Amelia?" a man called Fred from accounting

asks as I walk by. I nod, unsure of what to say. "Dodged a bullet not marrying into that family, didn't you?" he says before laughing awkwardly. A woman standing next to him slaps his arm. "Er, sorry about that," he says, scratching the side of his nose. In retrospect, I'm not convinced making an appearance at work was such a great idea after all. Block it out, Amelia. Just block it out.

At my desk, I try to catch up on emails, but after reading the same line in a project update four times, I give up on getting any meaningful work done. It's a common theme lately, even without the drama of this morning's news. There always seems to be distractions at the moment—finding out about Isla, the funeral, the articles about Sibella, coronation plans. It's endless. Although the royal family and my job are inextricably linked, the closer I am to the family, the less work I seem to be able to get done.

I can see there are still people crowded around the floor outside my office, so I decide to at least sort through my inbox and flag the emails I need to do something about later. You couldn't pay me to walk back out into the middle of those conversations after Fred's comment. I don't even want to think about how people would look at me and the comments they'd make if they knew Eddie and I were back together. They'd probably think I should quit or focus on PR appearances like our CEO William had tried to make me do not long ago when there were stories about Eddie and me everywhere. A heavy feeling settles in the pit of my stomach. I hate being kept a secret, but in some ways, it's a relief. When the world finds out we're together again —for good this time—things will change, and I'll be back to being the centre of attention.

A while later, William walks across the floor to a meeting room, glaring at people as he goes. Everyone seems to take the hint and retreats to their desks to look busy. I check the time—quarter to eleven, probably as good a time as any to disappear. I call Michael to ask if he can get the car to come to collect me a bit early and find that it's already downstairs, so I gather up my papers and jump into the lift to the basement.

On the way back to KP, I send Eddie a quick text.

Me: *Heading back now. Any idea how long you'll be in meetings for?*

A few minutes later, a reply flashes up on my screen.

Eddie: *It's going to be a long day. Would you mind popping by the office when you get here? Could do with some backup.*

I know I'm the one who has been pushing to be more involved in palace life and more visible with the courtiers, but I'm not sure this is a meeting I want to be involved in. Eddie isn't known for his great ability to ask for help when he needs it, though, so if he's asking, things must be bad.

"Hey, Michael? Can we please head to Edmund's office instead of home?"

From the rear seat, I see Michael nod. "Certainly, ma'am."

When we pass by the guardhouse at the entrance to KP, instead of driving straight ahead as we usually do to get to the cottages tucked away at the back of the grounds, we turn right and drive to part of the main palace building known as the State Rooms. This section of the palace sits next to Queen Louisa's expansive home at Apartment 1A and houses a series of offices used by the family and their advisers, as well as immaculately restored seventeenth-century rooms that are open to the public.

Our driver drops Michael and me at the rear entrance to the building. We walk down the oak-panelled hallway until we reach Eddie's private office, which now bears a large plaque with the letters "ER" in elaborate script. The initials stand for Edmund Rex (rex being Latin for king, of course) and are known as Eddie's royal cipher—basically a fancy monogram. It used to have a smaller plaque saying, "HRH Prince Edmund, Duke of Southampton," but soon after King Albert died, the old sign was dispensed with in favour of the cipher. I like to imagine that when a monarch dies, there's a team of palace handymen who run around the country at night replacing all traces of the old king or queen left on street signs and postboxes. Having seen how this family operates, it's entirely possible there is.

I knock on the door and am greeted by a petite woman with a mop of tightly set white curls. Sylvie is Eddie's personal assistant and handles the day-to-day secretarial duties like managing his calendar and responding to the many invitations he receives, while his private secretary Henry has more of a strategic advisory role—he's effectively the CEO of Team Edmund. Like a lot of people around here, both have been working at the palace since long before Eddie was born.

Sylvie ushers me into the small antechamber where her desk sits, topped with a china teapot and vase of irises. The door to the main office is ajar, and I can hear raised voices.

"Sounds like things are going well in there," I say sarcastically.

Ever the professional, Sylvie simply purses her lips as she pushes the door open for me.

Walking into Eddie's office, I'm confronted by a scene that reminds me of the will-reading debacle. Queen Louisa is sitting by the window sobbing loudly while Leo and Kayla try to comfort her. Princess Helena is on the opposite side of the room, steadfastly avoiding eye contact with the queen. A team of half a dozen courtiers, including Henry and Eddie's head of HR, Charli McRowan, are standing in the centre of the room bickering. Eddie, meanwhile, is sitting behind his desk at the far end of the room, head in his hands. Is it too late for me to back out of the room without anyone noticing?

"Save your justifications. There's no way you're going to convince me we can 'no comment' this disaster," Charli says.

A white-haired man I've never seen before chuckles. "Ms McRowan, as I've said before, the palace has no interest in sullying its reputation by responding to the stories and getting involved in any kind of mud-slinging with Lady Barrington. It's the way things have always been done."

Charli stamps her foot. "Don't you see? It's too late to avoid sullying the palace's reputation. The story is out there, and it's *true*!" She shakes her head. "We need to get in front of it. We need to get Isla onside too. If she goes through with suing, we're looking at a public relations disaster on a scale none of you can even imagine. Staying silent may have worked fifty years ago, but things are different now. We're dealing with a twenty-four-hour news cycle and social media here. We need a fresh approach."

"Charli," says Henry, "we've heard your advice, but I have to agree with Cornelius—we can't add fuel to the fire by confirming or denying anything. What we need to do is work on making sure there is no lawsuit and figure out who is leaking these damn stories. Maintaining a dignified silence in response to rumours has always been our approach, and I see no reason to change that now."

She grits her teeth and turns to face Eddie. "Your Majesty, please. You have to see that I'm right about this. It's not going to go away if we ignore it."

Eddie groans and then raises his head to consider the assembled advisers. He sees me standing in front of the door and gives a tight-lipped smile. "All right," he says, flexing his hands. "It's time to stop arguing and make a plan. I agree with you, Charli, it could cause issues to ignore this . . ."

Henry clears his throat loudly, interrupting Eddie. "Your Majesty, you can't seriously . . ."

Eddie raises his hand to silence him. "Hear me out, please, Henry, I don't personally want to ignore the story, but my ultimate duty is to the Crown. Cornelius has been head of public relations for Buckingham Palace for an inordinate amount of time—if he says the best thing for the monarchy is to stay silent, then I have to take his advice."

Cornelius smiles smugly. "You've made the right choice, sir. It's the way things have always been done."

Charli huffs. "All right. Well, if we're going to take the silent approach, then we need to do it properly. We need to make sure no one says anything, and no one speaks to the Barringtons and gives them any ammunition to take to the press."

"Couldn't agree more," Henry says, puffing out his chest.

"Who cares if anyone talks to her? Caroline can go and have a slumber party with her for all I care," Leo shouts. "The real point is, how do we stop her from taking our bloody money? I spend at least two weekends a year in at the house he left her in Derbyshire. There's no way I'm letting some interloper lock me out."

Henry rolls his eyes. "Rest assured, sir, Alfred and his team are exploring all options to contest the will. In the meantime, we should be more concerned about the press leak. We should launch a full investigation immediately to root out the traitor."

Queen Louisa sobs loudly and blows her nose. "Who would do this to us? Only our closest family and staff know all the sordid details. I can't imagine any of them betraying us."

I can think of someone in this room who would absolutely sell out the family if it meant the media owed her a favour. I look over and see Kayla shifting uncomfortably in her seat as the queen blubbers. I catch Eddie's eye and try to tilt my head towards Kayla as subtly as I can. A spark of understanding crosses across his face.

He glances at Kayla, who gulps, and then turns to the courtiers. "Team, can you please go and figure out if there's any truth to the rumours about a lawsuit? Call every high-priced barrister in town if you have to. We need to understand what we're up against here."

The staff bow and shuffle out of the room. Kayla stands to leave too, but Eddie gestures for her to sit back down. "I think you should stay for this conversation, Kayla."

"Uh, okay," she stammers.

The room stays silent until the staff have all made their exits and the door is closed behind them.

"Darling, can whatever you want to talk to us about wait?" Queen Louisa says. "I'm utterly drained. I desperately need to lie down."

"No," Eddie says firmly. "It can't wait."

"Why ever not? Haven't we dealt with enough today?"

"We have," he says. "And I'd like to know why we've been put in this position." He fixes Kayla with a stare. "Care to explain?"

Kayla says nothing.

Queen Louisa looks between the two of them, confused. "I don't understand. Why would she be able to explain anything?"

"Because I think she knows exactly how this story ended up in the papers."

Leo jumps to his feet, his face flaming. "Are you seriously saying you think Kayla would leak this to a scummy tabloid?"

"That's exactly what I'm suggesting, brother. I told you she was leaking stories about Amelia and me to the press earlier in the year. She's been selling stories since the moment she met you."

"You're unbelievable, you know that? Just because you won some genetic lottery, you go around thinking you're better than everyone else. I've had it! I'm not going to stand here and let you treat my girlfriend like dirt." He grabs Kayla's hand. "Babe, tell them they're being ridiculous and you would never talk to the press about something this important."

She bounces her foot up and down on the carpet but stays conspicuously quiet. Meanwhile, Eddie pulls out his phone and taps away before offering it to Leo. "Here. Security looked into it and got photos of Kayla meeting with reporters and intercepted her emails. She doesn't need to admit it. It's all there."

Leo slaps Eddie's hand away, and the phone falls to the

ground. "I still don't believe it. I'm sure there's another explanation." He turns to Kayla. "Tell them!"

Kayla looks as if she's trying to fade into the sofa.

"Kayla?" he says quietly. "Did you do this?"

This is so awkward to watch I can barely stand it. But I'm also still holding a grudge against Kayla for the gold-digger stories, so I have no plans to stop watching. As Leo stares at Kayla, she nods, almost imperceptibly. His face darkens. "We're over," he whispers.

"Babe," she says. "Don't let them turn us against each other. I only did what I did because they all treat you like a second-class citizen. We deserve better."

"There is no *we* anymore," he spits.

"Leo! Don't be stupid. Do you think it's going to be easy to find someone else as hot and talented as me? It's not. You're never doing better than this."

He shakes his head. "This isn't about me. You betrayed my family. You're a snake, and I want you gone. Now."

Kayla stands with a huff and walks towards the door. "Whatever. Don't think you can call me tomorrow when you change your mind. I've got plenty of other offers." The door slams shut with a bang, and silence reverberates through the room. Leo stands frozen, staring at the closed door.

"Leo," Eddie says. "I'm terribly sorry, but thank you. You did the right thing."

He spins on his heel and glares at Eddie. "Don't you dare pity me. You humiliated me! Do you have any idea how dumb you've made me look? I'm done being a slave to you." He lunges towards Eddie's desk, picks up a paperweight, and throws it against a wall where it hits a framed photo of Eddie and the national rugby team. The glass in the frame shatters and sprays across the room.

"I'm out!" he yells and storms out of the room.

For the second time in ten minutes, the door slams shut, and the room is plunged into silence. Suddenly, Queen Louisa laughs.

"Well! That was quite a performance, wasn't it? Maybe he should pursue some acting opportunities like his young lady."

Eddie's eyes boggle. "You're not worried he might go and do something ill-advised while he's angry? The last thing we need now is Leo going to Channel Four with some ridiculous exclusive."

"Hardly. Your brother may be short-tempered, but he's not stupid. He knows who keeps him in Krug and Italian loafers."

CHAPTER 13

Everything at KP has been utter chaos since the news about Isla broke earlier in the week. No one has heard anything from Leo since he stormed out. Caroline was meant to be back in Scotland by now, but Louisa is still such a wreck that she's had to stay in the city to keep her company. Poor Eddie is so stressed about the whole thing that he's barely slept. I'm trying to be there for him as much as I can, so I told William I'm sick and need to work from home. There's not much I can do to help the situation, but if I'm at Wren House during the day, at least Eddie has a friendly face to vent to if he gets a break between meetings and engagements. It's not doing anything for my reputation at work, though, so when William called to ask if I was well enough to come in for some important negotiations with a new partner today, I couldn't say no. Videoconferencing is great and all, but it's not the same as being in the room.

When I arrive in the office, things are much calmer than they were a few days ago. Most people seem to actually be getting some work done. Not me, though. I read through my to-do list, trying to decide what to do first, but everything on the list is either complicated, boring, or both. How did I get to the point where I don't want to do any of my work? Maybe I'll have a quick look at some shoes online first.

Half an hour before the negotiations are due to start, Daisy knocks on my door. Meanwhile, I'm still debating if I can justify buying a pair of crystal-encrusted stilettos when I barely leave the house.

"Afternoon. Hope you're all better?"

"Uh, yes, a bit better, thanks. Come in and take a seat."

She walks over and takes a seat in a chair across from my desk before placing a large stack of papers on the desk. "I thought I'd print copies of the agreements for you, given you've been at home without a printer."

"Thanks, I appreciate it."

"So, what do you think about the exclusivity clause?"

I flip through the contract in front of me. It's at least three hundred pages long, and I haven't read a single page. I should definitely have done more prep for this meeting. I'm sure I can bluff my way through it, though. "Hm, what do you think about it, Daisy?"

"Well," she says, thumbing through her dog-eared copy of the contract and rereading a passage. "I realise the foundation is meant to be independent, so it doesn't often enter into exclusive arrangements. But UNICEF is a pretty big deal, and they're offering to put a lot of people and money into projects that we get to choose, so it might be worth it? We can't do a ten-year tie-up, though—that's asking too much. Perhaps we restrict it to exclusivity for medical projects outside of the UK and talk them down to two years so we can get out if things aren't going well?"

"Mm, good idea."

"Are you sure?"

"Yeah, sounds good to me."

Daisy reads back through a dot-point list in her notebook. "I think the liability cap is going to be an issue. They're only offering a hundred thousand pounds, but the projects we're talking about are worth millions. What's the lowest we'd normally accept for this kind of deal?"

I'm tapping a pen on my desk when I realise Daisy has finished speaking and is waiting for me to answer. "Sorry, what was that?"

"What's the lowest liability cap we'd normally accept?"

"Um, I'm not sure off the top of my head. I'll have to think about it."

Daisy's brow creases. "Amelia, I would like to think that we're friends, but you're also my boss, so please tell me if I'm at all out of line asking this. Are you all right? You don't seem like yourself of late. You're generally so on top of everything, but recently you've been a bit vague."

I shuffle my feet under the desk. "I'm sorry. I've been a mess."

"Is it about the king? You didn't break up that long ago. It must be so hard seeing him everywhere."

I suck in a deep breath.

"You don't have to answer," Daisy rushes to say. "Sorry, it's a personal question. Forget I asked."

"No, it's okay. While I've been flaking out, you've been holding the fort here, so you deserve to know why. If I tell you something, do you promise to keep it quiet?"

"Of course."

"It is about the king, but it's not because of the break-up. We're back together. As I'm sure you've seen in the papers, there's been so much going on with the family, which hasn't left me with much time to focus on work. I feel awful. I'm doing what I can, but I've been letting you and the rest of the foundation down."

Daisy's eyes widen. "Wow, I had no idea. No wonder you've been distracted lately! I can't even imagine how stressed he must be at the moment and all the chaos going on behind the scenes."

I give a low whistle. "It's a lot."

"He's lucky to have you there to support him. If there's anything else I can do to help cover for you, I'm here."

"Thank you, it means a lot to me. I'll definitely talk to you if there's anything I need help with. In fact, would you mind taking the lead in this meeting? I'm happy to jump in where I can, but I don't think I've ever been so unprepared for a negotiation."

Daisy leans forward. "Don't worry, I'm prepared enough for both of us."

TWO HOURS LATER, Daisy and I are sitting in the conference room making painstaking progress in discussing each page of the contract.

My phone is sitting face down on the table next to me and starts vibrating with a call. I ignore it and continue discussing insurance requirements with UNICEF's risk manager.

Over the next five minutes, I miss another call and get at least four text messages. I surreptitiously flip my phone over and check who's been trying to get on to me so desperately.

Soph.

It feels like all the air has been let out of my lungs. Time to fake a bathroom break. "All right," I say, standing from my seat, "I think we've made good progress this morning. Let's break for fifteen minutes. Daisy can show you where the kitchen is if you'd like tea or coffee. We'll reconvene at eleven thirty."

I pick up my phone and calmly walk towards the door. As soon as I'm safely out of earshot of the conference room, I break into a sprint, making a mad dash for my office.

When I get there, I slam the door shut and collapse into my chair. I put my phone down on my desk and stare at the screen. Two missed calls, four messages—all from Soph. I'm not sure if I can bring myself to read them, but on the other hand, the only thing more stressful than reading messages from her is knowing there are messages from her sitting there on my phone unread. Until I read them, they could say anything. It's probably not even about Isla. Maybe she's calling about something work-related. She could have quit her job at the King's Trust. Eddie could have fired her. She could be contesting Albert's will and suing for more money. She could be dying.

Okay, Amelia, calm down—that's quite enough spiralling for today. The longer I leave the texts unread, the more anxiety they're going to give me. I already feel like there's an elephant sitting on my chest, so I'm going to do it. I'm going to read them.

I open up my messages, tap into my chat with Soph, and squeeze my eyes closed for a second. Maybe if I wait for a minute before I read them, anything stressful in the messages will disappear. That's how it works, right?

I open one eye and look down at my phone. There's a voicemail notification message I ignore, and three other text messages.

Soph: *Amelia, please call me when you have a chance.*

Soph: *I need to speak to you as soon as possible.*

Soph: *Please don't mention this to Edmund.*

Well, this is exactly what I didn't want to happen. Ever since the Soph and King Albert bomb first dropped, I was worried I was going to somehow end up caught in the middle. I should definitely ignore her call, but I have a lot of sympathy for her and Isla. I know how it feels to be shut out by the palace, and it's not pleasant.

My finger hovers over the call button. I'm due back in my meeting in eight minutes, so it's now or never.

Screw it. Soph and I have been friends for years, and as much as I care about Eddie, I care about her too. Besides, I might be able to help both of them at the same time.

I hit the button, and Soph answers after half a ring.

"Amelia, darling. Thank you so much for calling me back."

"Hi, Soph, how are you doing?"

She lets out a long sigh. "Can I be brutally honest? Fairly awful. Losing Bertie has been heartbreaking, of course, and Isla had no clue about anything until the other day, so naturally she's furious. She hasn't spoken a word to me. Helena won't take my calls, and there's a good chance poor Louisa is going to have someone poison my tea—and I wouldn't blame her either. I'd probably do the same."

"I'm so sorry. It all sounds tough."

"It's hideous, dear, absolutely hideous. Obviously, I've had to resign from my job as well. My life has been positively ripped apart."

"Well, it might be a bit awkward given my connection to the family, but I'm always here if you need to talk."

"Thank you, Amelia, it means the world to me. I know full well this may be too much to ask, but I was hoping you might try to persuade Caroline and the boys to speak to Isla. They're angry and won't listen to me, but I've heard Isla's having a rough trot. I think speaking to them could really help her."

After the last conversation we had about Isla, I've got a pretty good idea how well that idea would go down.

"I have to say, Soph, I don't think Edmund will go for it."

"I won't hold you to anything, Amelia, but I would be eternally grateful if you could try."

Sigh.

"All right, I'll do what I can. While we're speaking, it's not my place to ask, but my curiosity is killing me."

"What is it, dear?"

"What was in the bank vault that Albert left you?"

There's a silence followed by delicate sniffles. "Nothing of value to anyone but Bertie and me. Simply a box of mementos of our time together. Photos and the like. He may have had a reputation for being iron-willed, but he had a soft side too." She sighs. "I miss him terribly."

CHAPTER 14

After work, I bundle into the Range Rover I find waiting for me in the office basement. Before I do anything, I need to talk to someone impartial about this, preferably someone who will have no qualms about telling me if something I suggest is a terrible idea. Time to call Penny.

"Hello, Penny March speaking."

Weird. Did I accidentally turn my caller ID off? "Hey, Pen, it's me."

"Sorry, who is this?"

"It's me, Amelia."

"Amelia, hm. Doesn't ring a bell. Wait, I did know an Amelia once—nice girl with excellent taste in friends. Moved to a palace and forgot all the little people, though. Not sure what happened to her. She might be dead for all I know."

I snort and roll my eyes. "Pen, I saw you two days ago."

"Maybe," she sniffs. "But where were you yesterday?"

"Uh, at work?"

"Likely story. How do I know you weren't hanging out with some exciting new celebrity friends who are far more glamorous than I am and know the difference between a dessert spoon and a grapefruit spoon?"

"Well, given that I'm currently Eddie's *secret* live-in girlfriend, I never leave the house, and no one famous wants anything to do with me, I'm probably not doing that. Also, if I was hanging out with celebrities who have unusually extensive cutlery collections, you would definitely hear about it. Who else would I debrief with?"

"All very good points. So now you've reminded me who you are, how can I help you?"

"Are you free tonight? I was hoping to come by for dinner."

"I'll have to check my schedule. I'm probably busy tonight, but I may be able to squeeze you in sometime next week."

She's really going to make me pay for moving out, isn't she? "Please, Pen, I desperately need my best and most youthful-looking friend right now."

After a long pause, she sighs. "Flattery will get you everywhere, my dear. Come on over."

WHEN WE PULL up in Camden, Michael gets out of the car first to scope out the street and then disappears inside to sweep the flat. Even though Eddie and I aren't publicly dating at the moment, ever since he became king, my security has increased. Michael checks every room before I enter to make sure there are no bugs or bombs, and he often wants to bring a second guard along if I go anywhere other than work. For the most part, it means it's easier to stay in. Running down to the supermarket when I realise I'm out of milk like a normal person is well and truly a thing of the past. I don't even want to think about how much worse it will get when we make a public announcement. The whole thing is a colossal headache. Luckily Eddie is so dreamy.

A few minutes later, Michael reappears and raps sharply on

the driver's window. No sign of paparazzi or would-be assassins, so I'm free to go. I skip up the steps and knock on the door. When Penny sees me, she sweeps me into a giant hug. Looks like she's not holding the less frequent visits against me too much. "So much for playing it cool there, Pen."

She squeezes me harder. "Lady, I missed you way too much to play it cool."

"Again, we saw each other two days ago."

She releases me and waves her hand around. "Details, details. I'm used to you being here all the time."

"Well, at least you make me feel wanted."

"You're always wanted here. Come sit down. I've got ice cream and more doughnuts than I should eat alone if I want to be able to look myself in the eye tomorrow."

I plop myself down on the sofa while Penny rattles around in the kitchen, collecting our bowls of diabetes.

"What brings you here tonight?" she calls out from the kitchen. "Are you not feeling wanted at home? Say the word, and I'll give our Edmund a right talking-to. He may have his face on postage stamps, but that doesn't give him the right to ignore a stone-cold fox like you."

I smirk. "Don't worry, I'm perfectly wanted at home. No need for you to defend my honour. It is about Eddie, though."

"Oh?" Penny asks, making her way back from the kitchen and handing me a bowl. "What's he done today?"

"It's nothing he's done. More something his dad did."

Her eyebrows shoot up. "Is it about the Isla situation?"

"Yup. What a debacle."

"Such a scandal! When did Edmund find out? How did everyone react? Tell me everything! I need the inside scoop on this."

I hesitate. "I don't know if I can tell you about what's going on at the palace. It's all extremely confidential."

"Understood," Penny says, miming zipping her lips closed.

I definitely shouldn't be talking to anyone outside of the family about this, but I need an opinion from someone who isn't as emotionally invested in the situation as they are. "I'm serious, Pen. I don't want to play the 'I swore you to secrecy about the dating a prince thing and then you accidentally told a reporter everything' card, but I need to be absolutely sure nothing I say will leave this room."

Penny's face falls. I hate reminding her of the awful day when she found out she had been unknowingly dating an undercover reporter who was using her to get stories about me, but this is potentially country-changing information.

"Mils," she says, lip trembling, "you know how terrible I feel about that. I'm completely paranoid about your privacy after everything that happened. I'd never risk saying anything after what happened last time."

"I know you wouldn't, but I need you to understand how serious I am about keeping this under wraps," I say, wrapping an arm around her. I close my eyes and hum. "Where do I start?"

"Probably at the beginning. You're meant to be the smart one here. I shouldn't have to tell you these things."

I roll my eyes. "It was a rhetorical question, but thanks anyway. Back to my story. Did I ever tell you Soph came to visit me when Eddie and I were broken up?"

"No, you didn't."

"Right. Well, she came to try to convince me not to give up on Eddie so easily. She told me she'd been in love with Albert since she was a teenager—he wanted to marry her, but she was scared of what being with him would mean, so she said no."

Penny lets out a low whistle. "I never knew that! So when was the affair?"

"They'd been having an affair for decades, basically from the start of his relationship with Louisa. They were still together when he died."

"No!"

I nod slowly.

"This is some steaming hot tea you're spilling here. There would be so much scandal if this got out. It's being sold in the papers as a short-term fling back in the eighties, not something that had been going on for forty years. So, how have they all been keeping this quiet for so long? I never picked Louisa for someone who would sit by and watch while her husband went around with someone else."

"It's easy to put up with something you don't know about."

Penny grips my arm, and her eyes widen. "Wait, she didn't know?"

"Nope, the whole family only found out when we were at Albert's will reading and his lawyer announced to the whole family that he left a bunch of money and fancy houses to Soph and their illegitimate daughter."

"What a way to find out."

"It's a nightmare. It's completely ripping Eddie's family apart, and somehow I've found myself right in the middle of it."

"Because you already knew about Soph and Albert?"

"Not just because of that," I say, grimacing. "Soph called me this afternoon. She wants me to talk to Isla and try to get Eddie to meet with her."

Penny gives a bark of laughter. "Fat chance of that happening!"

I hum noncommittally.

"Oh my god! You're thinking about helping her. Why would you do that?"

"I feel like I owe it to Soph. We've always been close. Besides, if it wasn't for her, I would never have met Eddie in the first place, and I probably wouldn't have gone back to him after we broke up. I also feel a connection to Isla as a fellow palace outcast."

"I get that, I do. But how would Eddie react to you going

behind his back like that? I assume he's not thrilled about the whole situation."

"He's livid and wants nothing to do with Soph or Isla."

"Right, well, there's your answer. Pick your side, block her calls, and move on."

"I could do that . . ."

Penny fixes me with a sceptical stare. "Why would you not?"

"As I said, I owe Soph a lot. But it's not only about that. I really think Eddie should talk to Isla. Living at KP, I've come to understand more than ever how isolating his lifestyle is. Family is so important to him, and I think he should take this as an opportunity to add another sister to his support team."

"Sheesh. I'm not sure about that at all. It's not like she's some long-lost relative he's been dreaming of being reunited with. This is some potentially life-ruining stuff here. You can't expect him to go with it and play happy family."

"He was pretty aggressively against the idea when I raised it with him, but I'm convinced it could be good for him. Sometimes he and his family are so guarded they don't let anyone in. Look at how Henry has been treating me—all I want to do is help, and he's outright rejected me. I don't want that to happen to someone else too."

"If you've suggested talking to her and he's not into it, you've gotta leave it alone. He's a grown-ass man who runs an entire commonwealth. Trust him that he knows what he wants."

"I know he's an adult and he can make his own decisions, but . . ."

She drops her head to her chest and groans. "You're going to decide you know better and try to convince him to talk to her anyway, aren't you?"

I gnaw on my fingernail.

Penny shakes her head. "What is it with you lawyers? Are you missing the gene that lets you admit when you're wrong?"

"Wrong?" I say with a shrug. "Never even heard of it."

CHAPTER 15

TWO DAYS LATER, I've spoken to Soph about organising a meeting with Isla, and I am walking through Hyde Park to her flat in Mayfair. I didn't realise until Soph sent me her address that Isla lives right across the park from KP. Granted, it's an enormous park, and it takes half an hour to walk from the palace to the other end, but it still seems odd that she's basically been next door the whole time. When I emerge, I cross over into Green Street and gaze up at the brick and stone terraces that line the street. Built in the eighteen hundreds, the terraces are five or six storeys high, with ornate facades and cute attic dormer windows. They cost an absolute fortune.

I find the street number Soph sent me and check her instructions. Isla is in a flat spread over the lower ground and ground floors of a stone-fronted terrace, so I open the iron gate and walk down the steps towards her shiny black door. Before I knock, I glance around the street to make sure there are no photographers hanging around. Henry and Charli may team up to murder me if I were spotted visiting. On the plus side, being united against me could do wonders for intra-palace relations—wanting to throttle me might be the first thing they ever agree on. No one seems to have taken any notice of me, though, so I rap on the door with the heavy brass knocker. A moment later, the door opens, and a blond woman in her thirties opens the door. Isla's flatmate, maybe?

"Hello."

"Uh, hi. Is Isla here?"

"She is. Please come through."

The woman holds the door open and gestures for me to enter. I walk into the hallway, and she closes the door behind me. "I'm Amelia, by the way. Nice to meet you."

The woman nods. "Charlotte. Isla is upstairs. Please follow me."

She leads me along the hallway and up the stairs to a white-panelled reception room with dark herringbone floors and navy velvet sofas arranged around a fireplace. In the corner, a slight figure sits with her back to me, looking out the window.

Charlotte clears her throat, and Isla turns around. Her face is blotchy and stained with tears. "Thank you, Charlotte. Can you please bring us some chilled water with lemon?"

"Of course, ma'am."

Maid, then, not flatmate. I didn't expect that. Not even Eddie has a full-time maid—sure, he has full-time palace staff for the business side of things, and a couple of maids who visit for an hour each morning to clean the house, but he doesn't have anyone waiting around at home to bring him lemon water.

Isla stands and blots at her eyes with a handkerchief. "Amelia, thank you for coming. It's lovely to finally meet you."

"It's good to meet you too. I've heard so much about you from your mum."

She gives a weak smile. "And from the papers lately, I'm sure."

"Yeah, them too. I try not to put too much stock in what I read these days, though."

"I recommend not believing a single word you read in the

British tabloids. They're not widely known for their journalistic integrity."

I shrug sympathetically.

"Sorry, enough of my ramblings. Shall we go and sit in the garden? It's sublimely peaceful at this time of day." Isla walks over to the large bay windows at the far end of the room, and I realise one window is a door. She opens it and leads me down a set of stairs into a large garden surrounded on three sides by the backs of the nearby terraces, and a large brick wall on the other side. Isla walks to the centre of the garden and sits on a park bench by a pond. As she does, Charlotte appears and places a heavy silver tray of water and finger sandwiches on a small table next to the bench.

I follow and take a seat next to Isla. "Is this one of those secret city gardens, like Hugh Grant breaks into in *Notting Hill*?"

"It is. Only the ground-floor flats on this side of the road have access—there are eleven apartments in total that have keys. It's quite the perk. I do wish they'd never made that film, though—over twenty years later and we still get someone trying to scale the garden wall every second week. It's such a headache having to constantly call ambulances when they fall."

"I can see why they'd try. It's lovely here." As I breathe in the fresh air and scent of roses, I'm struck by the fact that less than a year ago I was living in a postage-stamp-sized flat in Camden and didn't know anyone who could even dream of living in a place like this. It's hard to believe this is the same London I've lived in for the last four years, but in Eddie's world, this kind of luxury seems to be par for the course. "So," I say, taking a sip of water, "your mum said you wanted to talk to me about Eddie."

She closes her eyes and exhales. "I do. I'm hoping you can help me plead my case to him."

"Plead what case? Because to be totally upfront with you, I've already spoken to him about it, and he's been clear he has no interest in talking to you."

Isla sniffs.

"If this is about you wanting Eddie to let you call yourself a princess, I can tell you right now that it's not going to happen. So I'd give up on that dream now unless you're actually willing to sue him over it."

She sniffs again. "I thought you said you don't believe everything you read in the papers."

"I don't, but when I have no other information available to me, I start to consider there may be some truth in it."

At that, Isla sobs violently. Either she really wants to be a princess or is really insulted by the idea. "I'm sorry," she says between tears. "I'm so emotional these days." She pulls out her handkerchief and madly tries to dry her eyes, but she's crying faster than she can wipe away the tears.

"Hey." I put my arm around her shoulder. "It's all right."

"It's not all right." She shakes her head back and forth, tears still streaming down her face. "Everything is a disaster."

I pat her back gently and try to get her to drink some water. After a few minutes, the tears have mostly stopped.

"I'm sorry, I'm a right mess at the moment. I can barely get out of bed. I cry every day. I just . . ." She trails off and takes a big gulp of water.

"It's okay. You don't have to explain yourself to me."

"I want to. That's why I asked to see you. Two weeks ago, I found out my father isn't my father, and my real father is dead. And my parents' marriage was a lie. My entire universe has fallen apart. I don't know who I am anymore, and I feel like I can't trust anyone."

"That sounds very difficult."

"It is, and no one understands. Edmund, Leo, and Caroline are the only people who possibly could. All I want is to speak to them. I need to talk to someone who understands. I've tried to get on to them, but they won't take my calls." She blows her nose and wipes away a fresh stream of tears.

"They've been told by the palace not to speak to you, but even if they hadn't, I'm not sure they'd want to. They've all been having a pretty terrible time too. Eddie is so stressed already, and these stories about you trying to overthrow the monarchy have put him over the edge. It doesn't help that the media team has banned him from making any kind of statement, so he has to suck it up and let rumours run wild."

"Please trust me, this is not about wanting to be a princess. Why would I want to be a princess when I already have all the money and none of the responsibility? I don't want to be alone in this horrid situation." After speaking, she dissolves again into deep sobs.

"I understand," I say. "Your situation is completely different than mine, but I know what it feels like to be rejected by the palace and family. Eddie and some of his family have embraced me, but there are people in the palace who are absolutely adamant that I have no place there. It's incredibly isolating."

"It is," she says between sobs. "That's why your help would mean so much to me."

"I want to help you, but I'm not sure if I can."

Once Isla calms down, she decides she needs a nap and makes me promise to consider if I can help connect her with the family.

On my walk back through the park to KP, I call Penny.

"Hey, Mils, how's things?"

"Ugh, complicated."

"You spoke to Isla, didn't you?"

"I visited her at home."

"Oh, Mils. Did she give you puppy-dog eyes and beg you to help her?"

"Something like that. I'm so torn. I know Eddie doesn't want to talk to her, but I feel so bad for her. She's so upset and wants to be with her family. I'm not sure how to fix it."

"You know this isn't your problem, right? You don't have to fix it."

"Maybe not, but I can't see a problem and do nothing about it."

"I don't know if you called just to rant or if you wanted advice, but I'm going to give you some advice anyway. If you're going to involve yourself in this disaster, don't do it alone. You should talk to Lucy and Emma about it before you do anything else. They've known Eddie much longer than you have and understand how the family dynamics work. They might be able to stop you from completely blowing up your relationship."

"I wasn't asking for your advice, but I will begrudgingly accept it. At the very least, talking to them will mean I don't have to deal with the stress of this alone. And I can blame them if it all blows up in my face."

"Always gotta have somewhere to shift the blame, babe."

I laugh. "Thanks, Pen. The weight in my stomach is getting lighter already."

"Good. Well, off you go, phone a friend. Promise me you'll come by for dinner this week and tell me everything."

Looks like I'm going to Ivy Cottage.

WHEN I GET to Ivy Cottage, the lights are off. I knock on the door but can't hear any signs of life inside. After waiting a couple of minutes, drumming my fingers on the door frame, I turn to leave. As I do, the door creaks open and reveals Emma standing inside, rubbing her eyes.

"Sorry, were you asleep?" I check the time on my phone, and my forehead wrinkles. "It's four in the afternoon. That's a late start to the day, even for you."

She gasps and clasps a hand to her heart. "Excuse you! I've been up. I popped down to the shops early this morning to do some shopping. The new Valentino collection is out today. I could have had them send some pieces over, but I love the rush of beating someone to the last skirt. Obviously, I deserved a nap after all the excitement."

"Obviously," I say, nodding.

"Is that really what you think of me, though, that I lounge around sleeping until after midday? I'm insulted. You should know I only do that on special occasions. Like weekends, and Tuesdays. And sometimes Wednesdays and Thursdays. Mondays and Fridays, though, I'm up at the crack of dawn without fail for my Pilates classes."

"Em, we do those classes together. They're at eight o'clock in the morning, and you miss at least half of them."

"I know," she says, fanning herself. "We should reschedule them to a more civilised time."

I roll my eyes and start fiddling with my sleeve.

She cocks her head. "What's up, love? You look particularly on edge today."

"Can I talk to you about something?"

"Always, my dear. Oh, is it something juicy?"

I chew my bottom lip. "Well . . ."

"Wait!" Emma says, throwing her hands up in the air and looking alarmed. "Don't tell me now. Come in first. If it's something scandalous, I'm going to need to be sitting down with a cup of tea to enjoy it properly."

In the kitchen, Emma assembles a tray of tea and snacks. "Is this more of a chocolate conversation or a biscuit conversation? Actually, it doesn't matter. I'll get some of everything."

I love Lucy and Emma like the completely eccentric cousins I never had, but sometimes they're high maintenance even for people who live in a palace. It takes almost fifteen minutes for Emma to be satisfied that she's curated an appropriate gossip-snack selection and allowed her tea to steep for the optimum amount of time.

Finally, we settle down on the sofa, and she takes a long sip of tea from an heirloom china cup decorated with a delicate floral pattern. "Mm, perfect. Okay, time for you to spill."

"Is Lucy here, by the way? I'd like her take on this too."

"No, she's out cutting a ribbon somewhere. A charity for horses with limps, or children with limps learning to ride horses? Something horsey. Whatever it is, I'm sure she's mainly involved because she loves an excuse to wear jodhpurs. You'll have to trust my impeccable judgement for now."

Why did I think this was a good idea again? I take a deep breath and clasp my hands together in my lap. "So," I say, looking down and pulling at the sleeve of my shirt, "I spoke to Isla today."

Emma splutters and tries to choke down a mouthful of tea. "You didn't!"

"I did. I saw her actually. Soph called me the other day and told me how much Isla's been struggling with the news. Soph asked me to go and visit her, and I didn't feel like I could say no."

"How was it?"

"It was okay—seriously awkward to start with, but that's to be expected."

"Did you ask her about the reports? Is she really going to sue poor Ed?"

"She says she has no idea where the story came from, and she'd never even considered it. She's not interested in having another title. All she wants is to spend time with you all and to have the support of people who understand what she's going through."

Emma taps her long nails on her teacup and purses her lips. "You believe her?"

"Maybe I'm being naïve, but I do. She was so emotional when we were talking. I'm not convinced she could fake that. You know her. Do you think she'd be able to manipulate me like that?"

"I don't know her all that well. We've obviously spent time together other the years, given how close Soph and Mummy are. We also went to school together, and even though she's a few years older than me, you gain a certain level of knowledge about the people you're trapped at a boarding school in the middle of nowhere with for years. I've never known her to be a dishonest person. She's never been part of the crowd who are obsessed with their own titles and bank balances either. She spent most of her time at school in the library or the stables."

"So you don't think she wants anything from the family?"

"If that's what she told you, I'd be inclined to trust her. Lord knows she doesn't need more money. Her grandfather has one of the largest private landholdings in the country. She'll barely even notice the extra house Uncle Albert left her."

"All right, sounds like we can probably take her at her word."

Emma places her teacup down on the table and turns to face me. "What do we do now? I assume you haven't told Eddie about any of this."

"No, I didn't tell him she'd reached out or that I was going to see her. I'm completely wracked with guilt about it. Do you think I should come clean?"

Her jaw drops, and she clutches the side of the sofa. "Tell Eddie? No, no, no. That's the last thing you should do. We've all heard how he feels about the situation. You need to decide what you want to do, though. Do you want to help Isla, even if it upsets Eddie, or do you want to let it go and keep the peace?"

That's the question, isn't it? Am I willing to create drama in my relationship to help a woman I barely know? It seems like it should be a no-brainer—our relationship has been up and down lately, and I've been desperate to fix it. If you'd asked me a week ago if I'd risk upsetting him again over the issue, I wouldn't have hesitated in saying no. But Isla seems so lost and so hurt—she needs this family, and deep down, I still think letting her in would be good for Eddie too. "I'd like to help her. Or try at least."

"Well," Emma says, clapping her hands together. "Then we need a plan."

"Any suggestions?"

"I'm glad you asked. Meddling in family politics is one of my specialties."

I shake my head and chortle. "Somehow that doesn't shock me at all."

"Nor should it. I own who I am. Anyway, we need a way to get Eddie and Isla together in person. We need to *Parent Trap* them."

"You don't think it would be better for us to speak to him about it all and try to convince him to call her?"

"Oh, Amelia." Emma tuts and pats my knee. "You're clearly new to the scheming business. There's no point trying to have a rational conversation with dear Ed about this—you've already tried that, remember? No, what we need is a good old-fashioned ambush. With cocktails. We'll invite them both here for dinner and force them to talk to each other. If he sees her in person and sees that she's genuinely as upset about the whole drama as he is, he might come around."

"Are you sure that's a good idea?"

"As I said earlier, you have to trust my judgement."

I take a moment to drink in the sight of Emma sitting there in her living room, struggling to choose between a shortbread and a chocolate-coated shortbread while wearing an enormous, jewel-encrusted turban and a bathrobe made entirely of an assortment of multicoloured feathers. "No offence, but I don't trust your judgement at all."

"I am exceedingly offended by that. Do you have a better idea that isn't just trying to talk to him again?"

She's got me there. "No, I don't."

"Excellent," she says, plucking a biscuit from the tray. "Dinner it is then. Thursday at six. You invite Isla and Eddie, and I'll take care of the rest."

"The rest? What else is involved in this plan?" I only agreed to this a minute ago, and I'm already regretting it.

"The dinner, obviously! And drinks. Lots of drinks." She places the biscuit in her hand back on the tray and takes a chocolate-coated shortbread instead. "Family politics always require drinks."

CHAPTER 16

A BIT after six o'clock in the evening, Michael drops me off outside Ivy Cottage. Having had a few days to consider it, I'm not super confident this dinner was a good idea after all. Too late now, though. What's the worst that could happen? Actually, perhaps best not to think about that. Let's just hope for the best instead. Lucy opens the door holding a cocktail, and I can hear music playing in the living room. She kisses me on each cheek while balancing her glass in the air. "Hello, darling! How's your day been? Still persisting with this whole job business?"

"Yes, I'm still working. I've come straight here from the office actually."

"Weren't you there when I tried to call you this morning?"

"Yes, I went in at nine this morning."

"You were there for nine hours in one day?" Lucy asks, fanning herself with her non-cocktail-holding hand. "Come in quickly, dear. Sounds like you're the one who needs a drink."

As we walk through the foyer, Lucy shouts out, "Emma! Fix poor Amelia a drink immediately. She's been in one of those ghastly office places again!"

We walk into the living room, and Emma thrusts a drink into

my hand. Across the room, Caroline and Isla are sitting by the window, deep in conversation.

Caroline looks up as I walk in. "Hello, Amelia. Come and sit with us."

"Hi there," Isla says, smiling.

True to her word, Caroline has been making an effort to get to know me after her initially icy reception. I'm still a bit wary of her, but I'm trying to lean into it. "Hey, Caroline, how was your day?"

"Not entirely awful. I can't stand being cooped up here in the city, but Mummy still needs me here. I've spent most of the week in her sitting room listening to her alternate between being devastated about Daddy being gone and furious at him for leaving her in this position. She's been in floods of tears."

"I'm sorry, that's so hard."

Caroline nods heartily. "It's jolly hard work keeping up with her. She's giving me emotional whiplash. I'd rather be tucked away on a mountainside at home."

"I'm sure she appreciates the support."

She scoffs. "I should hope so." She leans in and lowers her voice. "Speaking of support, I thought you might be glad to hear Sib is on her way back to the country tonight. After your talk the other week, she decided it may be easier for everyone if she wasn't seen to be staying here now that the funeral is over."

Well, that's a relief. Eddie may not have publicly called off their engagement yet, but at least there won't be paparazzi photos of her coming in and out of the palace anymore.

"Thanks, Caroline, I really appreciate it. I know having her here at the moment meant a lot to you."

She shrugs. "It was good to have her here, but I'm a grown woman. I can take care of myself—and Mummy, apparently."

My phone beeps.

Eddie: *Walking over from the office now. See you in five mins.*

I clap. "Okay, ladies, he's on his way." I turn to Isla. "Are you ready?"

She chews her bottom lip. "I think so. I do hope he won't be too put out by me surprising him like this."

"Look, I'm not going to pretend that he's going to be excited to see you, but I'm sure he'll come round."

"But don't worry, love, he'd be bonkers to not want to get to know you better," Lucy says.

"Don't take it personally if he reacts badly. He can be a bit of a git sometimes," Emma adds.

Caroline smirks. "He is, on occasion, a class-A bonehead."

Isla titters nervously. "Do we get to call the king names?"

Emma pats her knee. "Of course we do, darling, we're his family. If we don't keep his ego in check, who will?"

Just then, the doorbell rings, and all of our heads snap up.

Lucy grins. "Ladies, it's showtime." She jumps up from the sofa and bounces towards the door. From my seat in the living room, I can hear the door open and Lucy greet Eddie warmly.

"Edmund dear, thank you for gracing us with your presence."

"Good to see you too, Luce. What's for dinner?"

"It's obnoxious canapés night—everything is miniature, imported, and full of ingredients with names I can't pronounce. You'll love it. The gruyere and jicama croquettes are to die for."

Eddie's laughter fills the room as he appears in the doorway.

I smile over at him. "Hey, Eddie."

He returns my smile and walks towards me. A few steps into the room, he does a double take and freezes.

Isla smooths her skirt and clears her throat. "Hello, Edmund. It's good to see you."

The silence is deafening. Eddie's jaw is clenched, and his nostrils are flaring. Now, I'm not a body language expert, but this isn't looking good. After what feels like hours, Eddie speaks. "What are you doing here?" His voice has an icy edge to it that I'm not used to.

Isla's eyes dart around the room, from Eddie back to Caroline and me sitting on the sofa. "I'm aware that I'm likely the last person you were hoping to see, but I believe we should talk."

His eyes narrow. "Oh, you think we should talk, do you? Who are you to tell me what I should do?"

"Eddie," Lucy says, touching his arm. "Be reasonable. Poor Isla has been through as much as the rest of us and wants some support from her family to get through it."

He snorts. "Her family? I don't care what any DNA tests say—we are *not* her family. I expressly told you all I had no interest in speaking to her, and yet you bring her here behind my back. Unbelievable." Eddie turns back to face Isla. "Get out."

"Come off it, Edmund," Emma scoffs. "In case you haven't noticed, this is our house, and Isla is here as our guest. You can't ask her to leave."

"In case you haven't noticed, I'm the king! You're living in *my* palace!"

Before things can escalate any further, Isla interrupts. "It's all right, I'll leave. I don't want to upset anyone by being here." With that, she picks up her handbag and practically sprints out of the room.

The door clicks shut behind her, and Eddie glares at Lucy, eyes bulging. "Why on earth would you do that? I have never felt so betrayed." Without waiting for a response, he rounds on me. "And you! I expect these kinds of stunts from the others, but what were you thinking? I thought you were better than this."

Lucy and Emma edge towards the door. "Sounds like you kids need to talk, so we're going to make ourselves scarce. Cousin, don't say anything you'll regret. If it comes to choosing sides, know that we're choosing Amelia."

Caroline jumps up and hooks her arm through Emma's. "Let's go to Mummy's." The door slams behind the three of them.

Thanks for abandoning me, guys. Thanks a lot. "Eddie, I'm sorry. I know this isn't what you wanted, but I still think you should give her a chance. She's not the one who hurt you. Her intentions are good, and I think she deserves a chance to show you that."

He scrunches his eyes closed and grabs at his temples. "I'm not interested in her intentions! I can't believe you'd do this to me. You blindsided me!" He sits back and pants, a vein visibly throbbing in his neck.

"I'm done with this conversation," I say, standing to walk towards the door. "I've told you where I'm coming from, and I'm not going to sit here and be yelled at. When you're ready to discuss it like grown-ups, I'll be at home."

He sighs deeply, his face slowly relaxing as if he's counting to ten. When he speaks again, there's a softness and a vulnerability in his voice. "Amelia," he says, reaching out to take my hand. "Please don't walk away. We need to talk about this. *I* need to talk about it. I refuse to be like one of those couples in movies who create infinite problems for themselves by not communicating."

I shake my head. No matter how frustrated I am by this whole situation, I can't get away from the fact that he's right. "All right, let's talk."

He pulls me down to sit next to him and interlaces his fingers through mine. "I'm sorry I got angry. I want you to know that it's not really about you. You may have noticed that things haven't been going terribly well for me lately—my father died, I got thrust into an incredibly stressful new job, and then it came out that my father had an illegitimate child who may or may not be trying to sue me. I'm completely at sea here, and I need help. You're the life raft I'm clinging to, and I need to feel like you're on my team."

As he speaks, I can see the pain in his eyes, and my heart breaks for him. I reach out and stroke his cheek. Everything I've done has been with his best interests in mind, but is it my place to decide what those interests are? I don't want to be another Henry trying to control his life. "Eddie, I need to apologise. I've been trying to do what I thought was best for you, but I realise now that I've been going about it the wrong way. I'll always give you my opinion, but from now on, I'll make sure I don't ignore yours."

"You'll stop talking to Isla?"

"I still don't agree with freezing her out, but I'll respect your decision. I get that this isn't about me, and I overstepped. You won't hear me mention her again."

"I appreciate that."

I squeeze his hand. "What can I say? I'm a really big person."

"That's all part of what makes you so special. While we're having this conversation, is there anything else you'd like to bring up? I know I've been distracted and busy lately, but something seems off with you too."

I hesitate and study Eddie's face. His eyes are soft, and the tension in his jaw has dissipated. He looks much more relaxed now than he did before. The last thing I want to do is ruin that by raising new issues. But he's right that there are things that have been bothering me, and maybe there's no time like the present to lay them on the table.

"Earth to Mils." He waves his hand in front of my face. "What's going on in that pretty head of yours?"

"Are you sure you want to hear it?"

"Absolutely. I wouldn't ask if I didn't want to hear the answer."

"Well . . ." I trail off.

He rubs my knee. "What is it? Have you been trying to find a polite way to tell me I snore? Do you secretly hate my new pancake recipe? I should never have added the dash of lemon zest."

The corners of my mouth pull up into a weak smile.

"Come on, Mils, whatever it is, I can take it. If it looks like I'm crying, ignore it. I probably have something in my eye."

I count to three as I take a breath and brace myself. I'm not sure if I'm going to like the answer to my question, but it's come to the point where I need to know. "Eddie, what are we doing here?"

A deep crease appears between his eyebrows. "What do you mean, what are we doing?"

"I mean, when are you going to let palace aides stop running our lives and go public with our relationship? I love you, and I love living here with you, but I feel like you're ashamed of me. When I chose to be with you and move in here, I wasn't expecting to have a committee of middle-aged men controlling my life."

Eddie looks at me but says nothing.

"I might have totally misread the situation, but in Kenya, it seemed like you were going to propose. Then we came home and people thought you were still engaged to Sibella, so I didn't mention it again. But that was almost two months ago now, and you've never said anything. So I've driven myself crazy trying to figure out if I imagined the whole thing or if you really do want to marry me."

A grin splits his face, and warmth radiates from him. "Of course I want to marry you. I would never have asked you to move in with me and be my partner in all of this madness if I didn't. If you haven't figured that out, you must be rather less intelligent than I'd assumed."

"You mean it?"

"I've never meant anything more. You're right, I was planning to propose that night. I had a ring in my pocket and then, well . . ." He hangs his head.

"Everything changed," I finish for him. "So, where does that leave us now?"

"I still want to marry you," Eddie says, his expression steely. "But things are complicated. This isn't a fairy tale where we can get married and have a neat happily ever after moment. After losing Gran and then Dad in quick succession, everything feels like it's in flux—not just for me, but for the country, and I have to consider what's best for the monarchy as a whole."

"But isn't the best thing for the monarchy for you to be happy and be the best version of yourself?"

Eddie slumps against the back of the sofa. "I wish it were that simple. Announcing I was engaged for the third time in a year could completely undermine the image of stability I'm trying to portray. I can't in good conscience do something I know may cause issues for the palace. No matter how desperately I want to." He sits up straighter and takes both of my hands in his. "I will marry you, Amelia, but not yet."

I know he's worried about what people will think of him appearing to change his mind so quickly, but I don't agree that us getting married would bring down the Crown. I can see, though, that I'm not going to convince him. His sense of duty won't allow him to put his interests first. "Can we at least talk to them again about making the break-up with Sibella public? I can't handle walking around in a world where everyone thinks you're with someone else."

He lifts our clasped hands to his lips and kisses my hand. "I'll work on it, I promise."

I hope he does because a future of skulking around the palace while Sibella attends official events is no future at all.

CHAPTER 17

LYING in bed one Saturday morning, I have one of those moments when you suddenly realise mid-dream that you're awake. One minute I was sitting with Penny in a fancy café overlooking the Eiffel Tower, wearing a stripy shirt and eating what looked like a tasting platter of artisan doughnuts, and the next I'm here trying to figure out why I'm awake and, more importantly, why more people don't serve doughnut-tasting platters.

A flock of birds cheep furiously outside the window. Well, that answers the question about why my dream was cut short. I sleepily open my eyes and see faint sunlight peeking through the shutters. I grab my phone off the nightstand and check the time. Six forty-five. Damn it! I could have slept for at least another hour. But I'm awake now, so I may as well get up.

I swing my legs over the side of the bed and peel myself out from under the covers. The room is quiet, and Eddie's side of the bed sits empty. Waking up alone is nothing new. Ever since he became king, his days have been getting busier and busier. He's been getting up by five most days and heading to his office over at the other end of the palace to try to catch up on briefing papers and foreign news before he gets sucked into a vortex of meetings and appearances for the rest of the day. I'm sure in part he's doing it so he can make it home for dinner with me on days he doesn't have a dinner party to attend, and I appreciate it, but I also miss waking up and seeing him lying there looking all cosy and peaceful.

After a quick shower, I head downstairs in a robe to have some breakfast. I should probably get dressed before going downstairs—living in a palace, you never know when a maid, security guard, private secretary, or royal dog walker will let themselves in. Luckily, there's no one downstairs to judge me on my loungewear anyway. What there is, though, is a card on the dining table with my name on it. I flip the envelope over and see it's been sealed with a dollop of red wax, embossed with Eddie's personal coat of arms, a shield featuring a dove and a dragon with its tail wrapped around a sword.

Amelia,

I'm sorry to let you wake up alone yet again. Today it's for a good reason, I promise. I may not be able to show the public how much I love you yet, but I can show you. I've done a deal with the devil and traded my soul for almost a full day off work (I may also have had to feign some severe intestinal issues). Michael will be by at eleven to collect you. In the meantime, there's a frittata for you in the fridge, and the new romance novel you mentioned wanting to read the other day is waiting in the living room.

See you soon,

E

Breakfast foods, reading material, and a mystery outing? This was a day worth waking up early for. A whole afternoon together also sounds like exactly what Eddie and I need—an opportunity to properly reconnect, and a chance for me to talk to him about how much I'm struggling with all the changes and uncertainty in my life at the moment. We've had so many conversations lately about the issues he's dealing with, but other than our one conversation about getting married, we never seem to have time to talk about my issues. I guess they never feel like a high enough priority to spend our limited time on.

After a few hours curled up in the corner of Eddie's linen sofa losing myself in a new love story, I decide I should put on some actual clothes before my car turns up. As I'm getting dressed, my phone buzzes.

Isla: *Hello Amelia, I'm terribly sorry about the drama I caused the other night. Can we go for coffee soon to talk?*

Nope, no way I'm going anywhere near this again. Not when things with Eddie feel like they're getting back on track.

Me: *Hi Isla, don't worry, it wasn't your fault. That said, I don't think we should speak. I don't want to do anything that might upset Eddie. Hope you understand.*

I'm zipping up my jeans when the doorbell rings, followed by three sharp raps on the door. As I bounce down the stairs, I see a reply from Isla come through.

Isla: *Of course. I appreciate all your efforts. Thank you for trying to help x*

Well, that's a relief. One thing crossed off my list of things to worry about. I step outside and see Michael waiting. "Morning!" I say, beaming.

He gives a small nod. "Good morning, ma'am."

"Where are we heading?"

"I'm afraid I'm not authorised to tell you that."

I pout. "Really? I won't tell anyone you spilled the secret, promise."

He silently shakes his head as he holds the door of the Range Rover open, waiting for me to climb in.

"Ugh, fine. I respect your professionalism, even when it's inconvenient for me."

Soon we're speeding away from London down the M4.

Shortly after eleven, we pull off the motorway and drive down a dusty road surrounded by rolling green hills.

"Are we almost there?"

"Nearly, ma'am," Michael responds as we turn down a small laneway.

We finally pull up on a gravel driveway in front of a small Tudor-style cottage with whitewashed walls and a thatched roof. I have no idea what Eddie has planned, but I'm here for it. Stepping down from the car, I scan the area for Eddie, but there's still no sign of him. There is, however, a woman standing in front of the cottage holding a large box. I smile at her, and she bobs her head.

"Ms Glendale, welcome."

"Hi, thanks for having me."

"It's a pleasure, ma'am."

"If you don't mind me asking . . . where are we?"

She claps her hands in front of her. "I'm afraid I'm not authorised to tell you that."

"Huh. I seem to be hearing that a lot this morning."

Standing in the background, Michael makes a noise that sounds suspiciously like a snort of laughter.

The woman walks towards me and holds the package out towards me. "If you'd like to head inside, ma'am, His Majesty has asked that you dress for the occasion."

I glance down at my T-shirt, jeans, and sneakers. Hm, maybe I went too casual. My head snaps back up, and I see the woman is looking at my outfit disapprovingly. I should probably take the box. Inside the cottage, I'm directed to a small bedroom where I close the door and place Eddie's gift on a bench at the end of the bed. I carefully pry the lid off the box and hold my breath.

Oh. It's very . . . yellow.

I take the clothes out and lay them on the bed—a fifties-style pastel yellow circle skirt, a white cap sleeve blouse, a pastel yellow cardigan, a string of pearls, and white brogues. I'm not sure what I was expecting, but this definitely isn't it. I do love a good full skirt, though, so why not? When I emerge from the cottage, I look every bit the fifties housewife. I'm still not entirely sure why, but I'm surrendering to the experience.

The woman from earlier is standing in the drive. "Good morning again, ma'am. If you'll please, could you make your way out to the garden?" She gestures to the side of the cottage. "Down the path to the right."

"Of course, thanks."

Rounding the cottage, I catch sight of what looks like an old-timey carnival. There are carnival games, a Ferris wheel, a merry-go-round, and snack stands. All around me, music is playing and lights on rides are flashing. There are no people, though. I'm looking around, struggling to figure out what's going on when I see him. Eddie is walking across the field towards me, wearing tight black jeans, a tight black T-shirt, and a black leather jacket, and his hair is slicked back. I'm so confused right now. Confused, but not necessarily in a bad way—it's definitely not his normal aesthetic, but the leather and tight everything is definitely working for him. And me.

Eddie beams as he sprints the last few metres towards me, lifts me up, and spins me around. Placing me back on the ground, he leans in and kisses me hard on the mouth. "I'm so glad you made it."

"What is this place?" I ask, gazing around in wonder. I flick my eyes back to Eddie, and suddenly it clicks. "Wait! Are we in *Grease* right now? I love *Grease*!"

His face breaks into a huge puppy-dog grin, and he gurgles with laughter. "I know you do."

"You built the carnival from the end of *Grease* for me?"

"I wasn't out here personally assembling fairground attractions, but yes, I organised it. You've been having a rough time lately, and we haven't been able to spend nearly as much time together as either of us would like, so I wanted to do something special. Just for us."

"Well, it's pretty amazing." I lean into his shoulder. "You're pretty amazing."

He kisses the top of my head. "I'm so pleased you like it."

"I love it. And you've obviously gone to a lot of effort to organise this, so I don't want to be picky, but . . . if this is the carnival at the end, shouldn't I be in leather too?"

"Technically, yes, but I find that part of the movie highly problematic. Sure, Olivia Newton-John looked smoking in those pants, but why should she have to change for a man? What kind of lesson is that? I love you exactly how you are, no leather or ill-advised cigarettes necessary."

Swoon.

"I love you too. Even in this leather." I bite my bottom lip. "Maybe especially in this leather."

Eddie's face glows. "Who knew you had such a thing for bad boys?"

"What can I say, Travolta? You make bad boy look good."

We spend the afternoon riding fairground rides, throwing balls at clown heads, and eating balls of fairy floss the size of my face. It's way too perfect to ruin with my sob stories about being rejected by Henry and not knowing what I'm doing in my life.

After a couple of hours, Eddie takes my hand and leads me down another gravel path. Soon we come to a convertible hot rod with flames painted down the sides. He's really committed to this *Grease* bit. He opens the door and gestures for me to get in.

Tell me more, tell me more, like does he have a car?

"Where are we going now?" I ask as I climb in.

"If I told you, that'd ruin the surprise now, wouldn't it?"

I roll my eyes. "Does everything have to be a surprise today?"

Eddie closes my door and walks around to jump into the driver's seat. He gives me a devilish grin. "I'll let you in on a little secret. I mainly kept the plans for today a surprise because you're always so on top of everything, I know it drives you crazy when you're not in control."

I playfully slap his arm. "That's so evil. What's next? Are you going to break into my office at night and move the things on my desk *just* enough that I can tell something is wrong but can't figure out what it is?"

He shrugs. "I wasn't planning to, but now that you suggest it . . ."

"You're lucky you look so good in that jacket. If you didn't, I might get out of this car and never come back."

"I don't know, Mils," he says, scratching his jaw. "I'm not entirely sure that's true. I think you enjoy living at KP too much to leave me. You couldn't give up the hand lotion."

"The lotion is incredible, I'll give you that. I've never seen a house that has expensive lotion plumbed into the bathroom before."

"All part of my elaborate plan to buy your love. Anything for my future wife."

As long as I live, I'll never get sick of hearing him call me that.

"Aw, you don't have to buy my love—you're way better than any skincare product. Don't get me wrong, though, we should definitely keep the lotion too. My hands have never been softer."

We both laugh as we drive down the road towards some woods. Moments like these—when it's the two of us, and things feel relaxed and light—they're like pure sunshine. They warm my heart and leave me feeling all bubbly. But they're bittersweet too, these perfect little slivers of time. They remind me what life might be like if things were different. If Eddie weren't King Edmund and was some guy I'd met at work—an accountant or a project manager. That said, I shouldn't complain about the whole king thing too much. I'm pretty sure an accountant wouldn't be recreating movie sets for me.

After driving into a heavily wooded area, Eddie turns down a narrow laneway, and we emerge into a clearing. There are glowing lanterns strung through the trees, and at the far end, there's an enormous movie screen. In the middle of the clearing, I see a tartan picnic blanket, a large wicker hamper, and stacks of pillows and blankets.

Eddie turns to me as the car comes to a stop. "Movie night?"

Soon we're cuddled up in a nest of pillows on the ground, watching the waves roll onto the sand in the opening scenes of *Grease*. When the opening credits appear and Eddie sings along to "Grease is the Word," I clutch at my heart. "You know the lyrics to all the songs, don't you?"

"I learnt a few things growing up in a palace full of women who refuse to relinquish control of the remote."

I turn to face Eddie and run my fingers through his hair. "Have I told you lately how great you are?"

"Not recently enough. It's been at least two hours by my count. You may want to work on that."

I kiss his temple softly. "Yes, Your Majesty."

We sing our way through the movie, and he wasn't kidding—he really does know all the words. He does a pretty mean "Greased Lightning" dance too. Be still my heart. When the movie ends, I lie nestled into his chest and close my eyes, drinking it all in.

"Have you had a good day?"

I hum happily and open my eyes to gaze up at him. "The best."

"You deserve the best. I know being part of my world isn't necessarily easy. I hope I can do enough to make the inconvenience worth it."

"You don't need to apologise for your life—it's all part of you, and you're the one that I want."

Eddie wraps his muscular arms around my waist and, in one

swift movement, pulls me into his lap. "Has anyone ever told you that you're incredibly sexy when you're quoting *Grease*?"

With one hand still gripping my waist and one tangled through my hair, he kisses me with a new level of intensity. And, well, it's electrifying.

CHAPTER 18

On Monday, I'm woken by a delicious smell. Mm, what is that, pancakes? No, waffles. Definitely waffles. Well, if that's not worth getting out up for, I don't know what is.

In the kitchen, two places are set at the island, alongside a vase of flowers and a platter of waffles, bacon, and berries. Meanwhile, Eddie is floating around the room, wearing an apron and singing an adorably off-key version of "Mr Brightside" to himself. I stand quietly in the doorway, taking in the scene.

Eddie spins around, drumming on the bench and coffee canisters with a wooden spoon. As he finishes signing, he sees me and winks. "Good morning, my love. How long have you been standing there, scarily watching me?"

"Would you describe it as scarily? I'd prefer to say I was simply admiring you in a loving and not at all threatening way."

He takes another waffle from the iron with tongs and adds it to the pile. "You say tomato . . ."

"Whatever you call it, I wish I'd been here longer. I love the first verse, and I missed it."

"I'll keep that in mind next time we have a palace karaoke night."

"Is palace karaoke a thing that happens?"

Eddie pulls the apron over his head and tosses it onto a stool. "It's not, but perhaps it should be. I'll have Henry add it to the agenda for our next strategy meeting."

"Addressing the big issues. I approve. Speaking of things I approve of," I say, gesturing to the breakfast spread, "what's the occasion?"

"Do I need a reason to make my beautiful girlfriend breakfast?"

"No, but everyday breakfast doesn't normally come with a floor show. I haven't seen you this energetic in weeks."

I take a seat at the island and start piling fruit and maple syrup onto one of Eddie's perfectly crispy waffles. How does that man manage to be this attractive and such an excellent cook? I swear, it should be illegal. No woman could resist that combination.

"I am feeling rather chipper this morning, and for good reason—it's an important day."

"Oh, what's happening? I didn't think you were sitting for your official stamp portrait until next week."

He chuckles. "Believe it or not, today I'm doing something even more important than putting my face on your phone bill. Today I'm telling Henry to put out a statement confirming that Sibella and I are no more and that you and I are back together."

I drop my fork with a clang and grin. "Are you serious?"

"I am. It's time people know the truth."

I jump up and throw my arms around his neck. "Thank you. I know your team aren't going to be happy, but we can get through whatever they throw at us together. Officially."

Eddie leans down and kisses me. When we break apart, he holds me close and whispers in my ear. "I love you, and I can't wait for everyone to know it. Again."

~

After breakfast, Eddie gets dressed in his work-from-home—or in his case, palace—uniform of dark jeans and a soft blue Henley shirt that is just tight enough to show that even though he's retired from the army, he hasn't given up the workouts. I'm sitting there on the upholstered linen bench at the end of the bed, ogling his biceps, when I realise he's talking to me.

"Hello?" he says, waving a hand in front of my face. "Earth to Amelia."

"Sorry, I was distracted."

"Is everything all right?"

I stand up next to him and slowly run my hand down one of the muscles in question. "Everything is great. I was lost in thoughts about your arms. How on earth do you find time to find time to exercise so much?"

He grins and shamelessly flexes his bicep under my hand. "Oh, you know, healthy body, healthy mind, and all that. Perhaps I can give you a demonstration later—for educational purposes, of course."

I murmur approvingly. "That's an excellent idea. I'm sure I'd find it quite enlightening." I wrap my arm around him and kiss the side of his neck. How does he always smell as good as he looks?

He sniggers and presses his palm to my chest, putting some space between us. "Mils, now you're distracting me. I've got an important job to do this morning. We can do this later."

"Fine," I huff. "You're no fun anymore."

He smiles briefly before his face turns serious. "Would you mind coming with me to see Henry? I'm rather nervous. I don't expect he's going to take it particularly well, especially with everything else going on. As much as I want to sort out this mess I've gotten us into, I'm concerned he'll find a way to talk me out of it."

"Oh, sure, that should be okay. Let me check my calendar." I open up the calendar on my phone and see I have a full morning of meetings. A couple of them are internal catch-ups with team members I can easily reschedule, but the first one is an important discussion with the CEO of a bank looking to work with us to expand our immunisation program into South East Asia. The project is my baby, and I really don't want to miss it. But then I look up at Eddie, and he's chewing his lip and gazing at me with those big, shining eyes of his. How can I say no to that face? "Sure, I can skip work this morning. Let me text Daisy quickly and ask her to cover me in meetings, and then I'll get dressed."

Soon we're walking across the grounds to Henry's office in the State Rooms. I've never been to his office before, so when his personal assistant opens the door, I'm surprised to see it's a similar size to Eddie's, perhaps even bigger. I guess it makes sense—in an institution as old as this, everything is hierarchical, and you can tell exactly how important someone is by the size of their office. Even though we can see Henry sitting at his desk through the cracked door, his assistant asks us to wait in the outer room where her desk sits. That's some power play right there.

A few minutes later, Henry appears in the doorway and bows to Eddie. "Good morning, Your Majesty." He turns to me and sneers before addressing Eddie again. "Please come through, sir." We both stand, and Henry clears his throat. "Ms Glendale, the king said he had an important matter to discuss with me, so perhaps you would like to wait here. Or, better yet, perhaps you should take a walk through the grounds."

Eddie grasps my hand. "No, I want Amelia to be here for this."

Henry starts. "Are you sure, sir?"

"Positive," Eddie says as he leads me through the door into the office where we take our seats next to each other on the large leather chairs that sit across from Henry's desk. He follows us in and sits down, checking his phone for a minute before glancing up at Eddie. He's really trying to show people who's in charge around here today, isn't he? "So, sir, is this about the approach to the unpleasantness with Lady Barrington?"

"No, it's not. While I don't necessarily agree with the approach there, I've taken your advice on it, so there's nothing more to discuss right now. I actually wanted to speak to you about Amelia."

Henry's arched brow shoots up. "Go on, sir."

"Well," Eddie says, squeezing my hand, "I've been considering it, and while I obviously understand the reasons you advised against notifying the public of the end of my engagement to Sibella and of my renewed relationship with Amelia, I think it's time to put an end to the charade. It's not fair to Amelia to be hidden away like this. I know the press are likely to have a field day at my expense, but this is incredibly important to me."

Henry taps a pen on his large mahogany desk. "You realise, of course, sir, the press won't simply be attacking you over your flip-flopping. They'll be attacking Ms Glendale here too, and the family, of course. I can't agree to the palace releasing a statement. You'll be made a laughing stock—and that's just this time. Imagine how the media and public will react to your next relationship! No, I'm afraid I won't do it."

Bile rises in my stomach. Next relationship? I'm sitting right here. This guy is a real piece of work. Clearly Eddie feels the same because his grip on my hand tightens, and when he speaks again, he's obviously trying not to yell. "I don't know what you think this is," he says, gesturing to our clasped hands, "but I can promise you there won't be any next relationship to announce."

Henry scoffs. "Sir, I strongly recommend you don't make any rash judgements. Why don't we wait a year until the dust has settled after the coronation and see how you're feeling then? You wouldn't want to put Ms Glendale through all the stress of an announcement for no reason."

My blood is boiling. I know Henry doesn't like me, but I can't believe he's talking like this with me in the room. I brace myself for Eddie to explode, but when he talks, he sounds utterly defeated. "I was very much hoping to release a statement and put the whole Sibella mess behind us once and for all." He drops my hand and gazes out the window, glassy-eyed.

Well, that was disappointing. I'm not saying I wanted him to defend my honour by challenging Henry to a duel at dawn, but I wanted him to say something. Someone needs to tell Henry he's being rude and completely disrespectful. I'm about to do it myself when he stops tapping his foot on the ground and clears his throat.

"If I agree to allow you to make an announcement, it wouldn't change anything else we've discussed about your relationship. Do I make myself clear?"

Eddie crosses his arms. "I understand."

He may understand, but I don't. What other things have they been discussing about our relationship? I don't like the sound of that at all.

A beat passes as the men stare at each other, eyes narrowed. Eventually, Henry nods. "The timing may actually be better than I had initially thought—it would certainly draw attention away from the Barrington situation. I'll have a statement prepared for you to review."

CHAPTER 19

"ARE YOU READY?" Eddie asks.

We've finished up dinner with Penny, Caroline, Lucy, and Emma and are sitting around our living room waiting for the statement to be released. It's seven in the evening now, and Charli is due to send the story out to the reputable papers at eight under an embargo that prevents them from publishing anything until the next day. I'm fully expecting a tabloid to pick it up tonight and run with it despite the embargo, though.

"Of course she's ready!" Lucy says. "She's been through this all before."

"True, but Ed was only the heir to the throne then. There'll be much more pressure this time. It gives me hives just thinking about getting that much attention," Caroline says.

"Really?" I ask. "I thought you'd be used to it."

She shudders. "Not at all. Why do you think I live in the middle of the Scottish Highlands where no one can see me?"

"You know who didn't mind the attention one bit?" Lucy asks with a somewhat evil grin. "Henry Cavill. I think he quite liked the publicity boost."

Caroline buries her head in her hands. "Oh, please don't remind me."

Penny squeals. "Oh, I forgot you dated him! Was he as good-looking in real life?"

"He was gorgeous, but I was far more enamoured with him than he was with me."

"We've all been there," Emma says with a sigh.

"Ooh," says Penny. "Do you ever Google-stalk the old celebrities you dated when you were younger to see how their lives turned out? You've got quite a collection of famous exes between you lot."

Emma cringes. "I try to leave the past in the past and avoid reading about men I've dated. Now if I could see articles from the future, that would be quite useful. I would never have thought Taylor Hanson was quite so dreamy if I knew he'd end up having roughly seventeen children."

"You dodged a bullet there, didn't you, Em?"

She rolls her eyes. "Did I ever! The whole Christian family band situation should have tipped me off. Lesson learned, though. Try as they might, those Jonas brothers got nowhere with me."

"Ha. Wait, you didn't really date a Hanson brother, did you?"

"Barely. It was two weeks when I was feeling nostalgic for the nineties. I regret nothing."

"Em, you were barely out of preschool in the nineties!"

"Well," she muses, "perhaps that's where I went wrong. Next time I might stick to a decade I'm more familiar with."

Eddie coughs. "Ladies, as much as I'm enjoying this conversation, can we watch something instead? I know I said I needed you all to help distract me from the impending announcement, but taking a tour of the men who've dated members of my family isn't exactly what I had in mind."

"You're the boss," Lucy says, saluting. "What's it going to be?"

"Something light," he says. "I need some joy in my life tonight.

Bling Empire? I always love a show about people whose lives are somehow more ridiculous than mine."

Lucy shakes her head. "We already finished it, sorry. That Kevin is way too sexy to not binge-watch. I'm not entirely convinced he knows how to read, but who needs literacy when you have a face like that?"

"*Cooking with Paris*?" Caroline suggests.

Emma gags. "Pass. I once got food poisoning at her house in the mid-two-thousands. I don't want to be triggered by watching her cook."

"Note to self: never eat anything Paris Hilton serves you," Penny says.

Emma nods vigorously. "Learn from my mistakes, darling. I was only there because she was dating one of my Greek friends. He always travels with a chef, so I assumed she was the one cooking, but it turns out it was her night off. That's the second lesson you should take from this tale of woe: never spend time with a shipping heir who doesn't have a backup chef."

"Strangely enough, that's not an issue I've ever had to deal with before," Penny says.

"Keep it in mind just in case, darling. You never know when these titbits will come in handy." Emma takes a sip of her drink. "Oh, I've got it! Has anyone seen *Vanderpump Dogs*? It's got a Real Housewife, and it's got rescue dogs finding their *furever* homes. What more could you want?"

"Now you're talking," Eddie says, grinning and reaching for the remote. "You had me at dogs."

After two hours of doggy makeovers and matchmaking, I've almost forgotten why we're all here. Clearly Eddie hasn't, though —he surreptitiously checks his phone ever few minutes. When it finally pings, he almost jumps out of his skin.

"That was Charli," he says. "She's released the statement. It doesn't look like anyone is going to break the embargo and go to print before tomorrow morning, but it may still happen."

I breathe in and out, counting to three on the breath in and again on the breath out. "This is really happening."

"Don't worry," says Penny, squeezing my knee. "You guys are strong. You can deal with anything the media throws at you."

"We're all here to support you too," Lucy adds. "A united front."

"I spoke to Sib today," Caroline says. "She feels terrible about her part in this, so she's happy to do anything that helps—giving a statement, saying nothing, doing something bonkers to create a distraction. Whatever it takes."

Emma rolls her eyes. "You're all getting worried over nothing. It's not even the most scandalous news about our family to come out in the last month. No one will care."

I take another very deliberate breath, hoping to quell the panic rising in my stomach. "Let's hope you're right."

Eddie and I barely slept at all last night. We lay in bed, tossing and turning and obsessively checking our phones for any news. At two in the morning, we made a pact to put our phones on airplane mode and stop looking for articles. We still couldn't sleep, so instead Eddie made us cups of herbal tea, and we curled up in bed together with Poppy at our feet, sipping our chamomile and talking about work, puppies, and everything in between. Waiting for the storm to hit.

We must have fallen asleep at some stage because I wake up in the morning, twisted in blankets and Eddie's arms with a crick in my neck. I extricate myself and grab my phone off the bedside table to check the time. Six fifteen. Well, whatever people are going to print about me, it's at newsstands and on homepages already. I'm about to turn my data back on and see what we're facing when Eddie stirs next to me.

"Mm," he murmurs, stretching his arms wide. "Morning, beautiful. Did you get any sleep?"

"A bit, I think. A couple of hours?"

He plants a kiss on my temple. "How are you feeling? You haven't broken your promise and checked your phone, I hope?"

"Me? I would never."

His eyes narrow. "I woke up just in time to stop you, didn't I?"

I bite my lip. "Maybe."

"Well, I'm glad I caught you. I want to enjoy one last breakfast together before anything changes. Let's head downstairs. There are omelette ingredients in the fridge with your name on them."

"Is there smoked salmon?"

"Naturally. And spinach, feta, Spanish onion, and mushrooms. Plus, I'll be there, and if you're lucky, I'll give you another kitchen karaoke performance."

I tap my chin, thinking for a moment. "All right, you've convinced me. Mainly with the smoked salmon, but the karaoke is quite a draw too. Can I put in a request for some NSYNC?"

His lip curls. "Do I look like a big boy band fan to you?"

"Eddie, you grew up in the two-thousands surrounded by your sister and cousins. I'm going to go out on a limb here and say you spent *a lot* of time listening to boy bands."

"Lucky guess. 'Bye Bye Bye' and breakfast, coming right up."

WE'RE SINGING and dancing around the kitchen together when there's a knock at the door. Eddie freezes. "That's probably Charli with the morning papers."

I gulp as he walks out to answer the door. People love Sibella, and I don't feel ready to see what they say about me stealing Eddie from her. Again.

Soon he walks back into the room with Charli, who is

carrying a pack of newspapers that she slaps down on the bench in front of me.

I wince. "What's the damage? Should I read these or burn them immediately?"

"Hm," Charli says. "I think you're okay to read them. No one has taken a strong anti-Amelia stance yet. Unfortunately, His Majesty hasn't gotten off so lightly."

"Oh no, Eddie! I'm so sorry. I didn't want people to judge you for this."

"It's okay, love, I've been on the receiving end of adverse publicity before. I can handle it. It also helps that most people I meet are prescreened by security, so I rarely have to deal with disapproval in person."

"Still, you don't need to read it."

"Would you like my professional opinion?" Charli asks us.

Eddie nods. "Always. You're the best—that's why I hired you to run my public relations team."

"With all due respect, you also hired me because no one else wanted to run media interference for your brother."

"That was also a factor. But enough about that. What do we do?"

"Sit down, finish your omelettes, choose two papers to read, throw out the rest, and never read anything about your relationship ever again. If you read nothing, you'll drive yourself mad wondering what people are saying. If you read too much, you'll drive yourself mad trying to keep up with all the stories."

I glance at the copy of *The Times* sitting on the top of the newspaper pile. "So you're saying the only way to keep my sanity is to read a normal amount of articles about myself and then ignore them and move on with my life? Sounds like a very sensible and grown-up approach."

Eddie slides the stack of papers just out of my reach. "And what exactly are your chances of sticking to that plan?"

"Hm, slim to none. But I trust Charli, so let's give it a shot. Charli, which ones should we read?"

"Up to you," she says, flipping through the selection she brought with her. "I'd definitely read *The Times*. I also think that knowing you, you'll want to read a tabloid to round it out. Just to see what's out there."

"*The Times* and the *Daily Mail* it is."

I take the two papers Charli is holding out towards me and unfold them. "All right," she says. "I'll leave you two to it. Sir, I'll see you at our press review meeting at eleven." She curtseys and disappears out the door.

Eddie sits down next to me and takes one of the papers. "Here goes."

King Edmund calls off engagement.

Buckingham Palace has today announced that King Edmund has called off his second engagement to Lady Sibella Cavendish. In a statement, the palace confirmed that after the late King Albert's passing, the couple made a mutual decision to part ways but remain close friends. The couple, who had been publicly linked for more than a decade, attracted significant attention earlier in the year when Lady Cavendish sensationally turned runaway bride and left then-Prince Edmund at the altar. Their reconciliation was announced shortly before King Albert's tragic death, and Lady Cavendish was seen supporting the new king at his father's funeral.

The statement went on to confirm that King Edmund has recently reconciled with former love and head of legal for the Prince's Charitable Foundation, Amelia Glendale.

The announcement follows news last month that the late King Albert had bequeathed a significant portion of his estate to secret love child, Lady Isla Barrington. It has been reported that Lady Barrington is preparing to launch a legal attack against the palace, seeking formal recognition of her paternity and the right to use the title of princess.

The abrupt relationship about-face has raised concerns about how the new monarch is coping with the pressure of his new position and the revelations about Lady Barrington. The palace has requested privacy for the king, his family, and Ms Glendale at this time as they face these private matters.

More to come.

"Well, that wasn't so bad. It was all pretty factual, other than the bit about your coping skills. Which, by the way, are excellent considering the circumstances."

"Don't get too excited," Eddie says, handing me the *Daily Mail*. "It's not all quite as restrained."

HEARTBREAK AT THE PALACE—EDMUND DUMPS SIBELLA!

It's Groundhog Day at Buckingham Palace! Only five months after being left hanging at the altar, and two months after announcing his re-engagement, King Edmund has given Sibella the flick. But is it for good this time?

Buckingham Palace has announced that the recently re-engaged couple have called it quits again. While the statement says that the couple made a mutual decision to part ways, insiders claim that Sibella was blindsided by the king's change of heart. His motivation seems clear, though—the palace's statement also confirmed that he is now back together with his post-wedding fling, lawyer Amelia Glendale. Rumours are running wild that the king had been secretly seeing the Australian beauty through his second engagement. Sources say that sick of being hidden away, Amelia gave the king an ultimatum, which didn't end well for scorned Sibella.

With two broken engagements, an aborted wedding, and a rumoured affair in his recent past, it seems that the new king is on a fast track to self-destruction. There is speculation that he suffered a catastrophic mental breakdown following his father's death and is completely unable to perform his role. Palace advisers are scrambling to avoid the full extent of his instability coming to light. Within the palace, there are calls for the king to be placed in an in-patient facility to allow doctors to determine if he will be able to recover or if he will be forced to abdicate. If he abdicates, the country will be faced with its fourth monarch in less than a year and be subject to the rule of the reclusive heir to the throne, Princess Caroline.

Read on for a line-by-line analysis of the hidden meanings in the palace's official statement.

I stare at the paper in my hands and blink a few times to make sure I'm not imagining things. "I can't believe they're saying that you're insane and going to be forced to abdicate."

The kitchen fills with Eddie's cold laughter. "Can't you? Because I can. They're vultures—they'll say anything to sell papers and get clicks. As long as they don't start targeting you, I don't care in the slightest."

"I'm guessing Charli will care."

He winces. "Yes, it's going to cause rather a headache for her. I imagine today's press review meeting will take quite some time, so don't count on me making it home for dinner."

CHAPTER 20

AFTER BREAKFAST, I'm upstairs getting dressed and ready to head into the office. I'm dragging my heels, though, debating between two almost identical black pencil skirts, trying to think of any excuse not to go to work. That might sound like a normal thing to say, but I'm one of those weird people who usually really enjoys my job. What I don't enjoy is people staring at me and whispering—I don't enjoy that at all—and somehow I think there's going to be a lot of it if I leave the house. I could call Daisy and ask her to cover for me, but Eddie will almost certainly be stuck in his office all day, so if I stay here, I'll actually be hiding out and binge-watching something terrible.

As I'm doing some mental calculations, trying to figure out how much time I can spend away from the office without William firing me, my phone rings. Luckily, it's Penny. I'm sure she'll have the answer.

"Hey, Pen."

"Hey yourself, lady. How are you and Edmund going? I thought I'd give you a couple of hours to work through all the news before I called to check in."

"He seems okay, I think? He's much better at ignoring ridiculous public attacks than I am. I'm pretty stressed by it all, so for once I'm trying to do the smart thing and limit how much news I'm reading. I think I'm going to block all the news sites from my phone for a while and assume someone will tell me if anything earth-shattering happens."

"I think that's a fantastic idea. Don't worry, obviously you're my first call if there's a big celebrity divorce or death."

"See, you know what I care about."

"I've got you. I'm hardly going to let you go around living your life and not knowing Ryan Reynolds and Blake Lively have broken up."

"Oh my god! How did I miss that?"

"Calm down," Penny says, cackling. "It was only an example. If they had, I definitely would have led with that instead of asking about your little situation. I have priorities."

"Thank goodness. I would genuinely be so upset about that. It'd be like Ben Affleck and Jennifer Garner all over again. I was a wreck for weeks after they broke up."

"I know, right? I hope you at least learnt from it to never hire a hot nanny."

"Of course, that's Parenting 101."

"Absolutely. Anyway, now I've distracted you, how are you feeling?"

I sigh. "Much better, thanks. I still don't want to make the trip into the office and face the outside world, though. Now the news is out, the attention and photographers and claustrophobia of it all is inevitable. I know I've dealt with it all before, and I've got my strategy for ignoring reporters, but it still makes me anxious."

"Hey, why don't I come with you? I can escort you to work and then go out shopping and come back when you're leaving. You've got Michael for muscle, but I think you could do with some emotional support too."

My heart glows. Sometimes I can be pretty lonely, living

halfway around the world and an eleven-hour time difference from my family and everyone I grew up with, but moments like these remind me that I've created my own little family here too. Even if it is mainly made up of people who are completely nutty. "I'd like that. Are you sure, though? I don't want you to waste your day."

"Of course! I'd do anything for you. Besides, it's an excellent reason to call in sick."

Half an hour later, I hear someone speaking to the PPOs stationed outside the door, and then there's a knock. I open the door to find Penny standing on the front step and usher her inside. She throws her arms around me. "I know I only saw you last night, but it seems like a lot has happened since then."

"It sure does."

"I see your security has stepped up again."

I glance through the window at the imposingly large backs of the two PPOs standing ramrod straight in front of my door. "Yup. The security office decided with the news coming out, there was a higher threat level, so we're under guard twenty-four hours a day. Normally, when we're at home, we don't have anyone here because the grounds are pretty secure, but apparently it's not enough at the moment."

"Wow, that's a bit intense."

"Yeah. Eddie has insisted on my personal security being increased too. Since I've been living here, I've obviously had Michael with me during the day if I go somewhere out of the grounds, and occasionally a second guard tags along. Eddie was worried about backlash against me and paps following me again, though, so from today I have to have a minimum of two protection officers with me at all times. It might be overkill, but if it makes him feel safe, I can deal with it."

Penny tugs at her ear and looks towards the door. "Have you been outside at all this morning?"

"No, not yet."

"Well, you'll see when we go, but I'm not convinced two security guards is overkill. Things are pretty hectic out there."

"I know what it's like. I had photographers following me for months when Eddie and I were first dating, remember?"

"I lived with you at the time and had to battle my way through them on the daily to get to the front door. So yes, I remember. But this is a whole different level. You've got like a Britney Spears number of paps outside the gate. I think I even saw helicopters circling."

I puff out my cheeks. This isn't selling me at all on the idea of leaving the house. "I'm sure things will calm down again soon, like it did last time. It's only the initial rush of interest in me after the news."

Penny looks thoughtful. "Maybe things will be different now that he's king?"

"I'm sure it'll be fine." I hope it'll be fine.

She hooks her arm through mine. "Good, I like to see you being positive about things. In the meantime, while things are crazy, you've got me."

A car horn beeps outside the door. "Ready to go? That's our ride."

Penny winks at me. "Let's do it."

We go outside and climb into the waiting Range Rover. Michael is sitting up front, and one of my new PPOs is sitting behind the driver. I slide in next to him and let Penny have the window. As soon as we sit down, my phone beeps. I look down and see it's a message from Penny.

Penny: *Why didn't you tell me new security is HOT?*

I turn to her and roll my eyes. She taps away at her phone.

Penny: *He looks like Idris Elba, and I approve.*

Penny: *Is it too late to swap seats?*

I laugh and swat at her arm. She quickly sends me a gif of Idris taking a shower, and I break into hysterical giggles. From the ever so slight quirk of his lips, PPO Elba clearly knows something is up but continues to stare straight ahead in silence, like the professional he is.

I'm still laughing when we pass through the palace gates onto the street, and something hits the car's windscreen. My head snaps up, and I see a wall of people in front of the car—cameras flashing, men yelling, people shoving each other. Suddenly, the car jolts to the side, and then back the other way and grinds to a halt. The PPO sitting next to me pushes my head down onto my knees, and Penny screams. "What's happening?"

"We're surrounded," Michael says from the front seat. "I'm calling for police to come and clear the street, but things might be rough for the next few minutes."

I'm not sure how long it is before the police arrive, but it feels like hours. My driver keeps beeping the horn and revving the engine, trying to clear the photographers to no avail. The car is rocking around as it's shoved on all sides. People are smashing their fists on the windows. I'm still folded over with my head in my lap and the PPO crouched over me. I crane my neck to see what's happening outside and see two photographers have climbed onto the car bonnet and are trying to take photos through the windscreen. When I finally hear the sirens approaching, hot tears start rolling down my cheeks. I don't think I've ever experienced such an intense sense of relief in my life. Penny was right. It looks like being with Eddie now that he's the king is a whole different ball game.

After more sirens and shouting, the car finally starts moving again, now with a police car ahead of us and another behind us. I sit up and hug Penny who is shaking like a leaf. Michael turns back to us. "We have police going ahead to the office building to hold back anyone waiting there and seal the basement. We'll be okay now."

The rest of the half-hour drive to the office passes in a blur. When we arrive, I'm thankful to see there are a dozen police officers outside the building, and the waiting photographers have been corralled into pens behind temporary metal fencing. When we pull up, Michael rolls down the window to speak to the police officer, and the car fills with a wall of sound. The police wave us through into the basement, and everything becomes mercifully quiet.

"Will you come up with me, Pen? I don't think I can walk by myself."

"Of course!" She leans past me to look at PPO Elba. "Will you be coming with us? I'm worried some of the photographers might have snuck into the building." Before he turns to speak to us, she gives me an almost imperceptible wink.

Trust Penny—half an hour ago, people were literally trying to break glass to get to us, and she's still focused on trying to pick up. Michael and Penny's future husband usher us into the lift and take us up to my office floor. When we get upstairs, they walk us through the floor to my office and then position themselves discreetly down the corridor—as discreetly as you can position two men the size of brick walls anyway. Penny closes the door behind us, and I immediately collapse into my desk chair. "That was intense."

Her eyes goggle. "Intense? That was insane! I've never seen anything like it."

"Neither have I," I say, shaking my head. "I thought I understood what it was going to be like, but that was something else altogether."

"How are you?" she asks.

"A bit shaken up and overwhelmed. How long is it going to be like this for?"

She puts her arm around me and rests her head on my shoulder. "Oh, honey, I don't know. Not forever, though. It can't be like this forever."

"I really hope not."

"Do you want to call Edmund and tell him what happened? I think he'd want to know."

I shake my head. "I sent him a text in the lift asking him to call me, but I haven't heard back."

"Don't worry," she says, squeezing my shoulder. "I'm sure he'll call when he can. He's probably dealing with a lot today too."

"Thanks, Pen. I'm so glad you're here."

"Are you kidding me? This is giving me way, way better stories for my next date than going to work ever would have. Plus, my next date is hopefully waiting outside that door."

"What happened to Josh?"

"Oh, he's still around," Penny says nonchalantly. "He doesn't look like his biceps might burst through his shirt at any minute, though."

I shake my head. "You're incorrigible. You know that, right?"

She shrugs. "I've been called worse."

A FEW MINUTES LATER, Penny is on her way to the kitchen to get us some water, and I'm still sitting at my desk, trying to regain my nerves, when there's a soft rap on the door. "Come in," I say.

The door creaks open, and Daisy's head pops through the gap. "Morning. Is now a good time?"

"Ah, not really, but come in anyway."

She walks in and takes a seat across the desk from me. "How are you? I saw the news this morning and the pack of reporters waiting outside. I imagine it's been rather overwhelming."

"You can say that again. I definitely underestimated how much attention this would attract."

She smiles sympathetically. "Is there anything I can do?"

"I hate to ask this again, but would you mind covering things for me today? I'm so shaken by the trip here I can't go into a room full of people and put coherent sentences together today."

"Of course, whatever you need. If you can forward through the calendar invites and background material, I'll be there."

"Thank you. I appreciate you stepping in like this. What would I do without you? It's only for today, I promise. I'm also planning to stay here for the day, so why don't I draft the sponsorship agreement I spoke to you about yesterday? At least then you won't have to work late after the meetings to finish it."

She smiles. "Thanks, Amelia. Sounds good."

"Great. I'll send you through the invites and docs you need. Call out if you have any questions."

"Will do." She stands and walks towards the door. "Oh, and Amelia?" she says, stopping in the doorway. "Try not to worry too much. Things will settle down."

CHAPTER 21

BY FOUR IN THE AFTERNOON, I've managed to get my heart rate under control and am engrossed in working my way through the contract Daisy had been responsible for. Working on the task is incredibly calming—focusing on something I know how to do and can work on without having to talk to anyone else is exactly what I need to rebuild some confidence. I'm concentrating so much I don't even notice when someone knocks on the door. So Penny, who has been sitting in the corner catching up on her online shopping, jumps up and opens it. When she sees William standing there, she excuses herself and slips out of the room.

"William, hi," I say.

He strides into the room and stands in front of me. "Hello, Amelia."

"Would you like to take a seat?"

He frowns. "No, no need. I wanted to ask you for an update on the crowd control situation downstairs. The dog and pony show outside has been quite disruptive for the other staff."

"I'm so sorry, William, I didn't expect it to be like this. I haven't seen what's happening out there at the moment, but I'll have the head of our security team call and give you an update."

"See that you do," he says with a sneer. "While I'm here, how was your meeting with the Bank of England today?"

"Uh, I wasn't able to make it actually, but Daisy went along and said the team made good progress."

William looks down at me over his glasses, and his forehead crinkles. "That was an important meeting for us, Amelia. Why weren't you able to attend?"

"I realise how important it was. Today has been a bit of a mess."

He stares at me for a moment before speaking. "I see."

"Daisy is great. She had it handled, and I'll make sure I'm at the next meeting myself."

He makes a harrumph sound. "Well, I have a dinner engagement to get to. Have your security call me." He walks out.

Things aren't going super well today, are they? Penny's head pokes through the door. "Is the coast clear?"

"Yes, we're CEO-less, and judging by how unimpressed he looked, I might be jobless soon too."

"Don't say that! You're great at your job. No one would fire you. Besides, technically, your boss works for your boyfriend's family, so I'm pretty sure it would be a career-limiting move for him to fire you."

"Leo is so temperamental he may fire me himself if he has a bad day."

"Let's not tell William that." She looks at her phone. "Are you about ready to head off? I'm going out for dinner tonight with Josh and some friends, and I should probably have a shower first so people think I'm a grown-up with my life together and basic hygiene standards. I don't want to leave you alone on your trip home, though."

I grimace. "Okay, two things. First, you didn't shower before you came to see me? Second, I know you, so don't think you can fool me into thinking that wanting to drive home with me is some selfless act on your part. I'm well aware it's because you want another shot at sitting next to the new PPO."

"Whoa," she says, throwing her hands up in surrender, "calm down there, missy. Firstly, you didn't even notice until now that I hadn't showered this morning, so clearly, I got away with it. Secondly, I am genuinely worried about you and don't want you to go through another stressful experience by yourself. If in the course of providing emotional support to my best friend in the entire world I *happen* to find myself sitting with my leg against a ball of muscle, that's a bonus."

A laugh bubbles up from my chest. "How do you manage to be both the best and worst person at the same time?"

She shrugs. "It's my special skill. One of them anyway. The others I might save for PPO Elba out there."

"I'm going to pretend I didn't hear that. As a palace-adjacent person, I do not condone sexual harassment. I will let you sit next to him, though."

She claps her hands together and bounces up and down on the spot. "Excellent."

"Give me five minutes and we'll head off. Keep your hands to yourself at all times while in the vehicle."

To my enormous relief, the trip back to KP is fairly uneventful thanks to the police escort—two cars and four motorbikes this time. Still, it's not until we roll past the guardhouse that I feel like I can breathe again. I hop out at Wren House and ask my driver to take Penny home. She pouts at me when the PPOs follow me out of the car.

"Have a great night, Pen. Thanks for today."

"Anytime, love. Say hi to Edmund for me."

I wave as she pulls the door shut, and the car disappears. When I let myself into the house, I hear chatter in the living room. Peeking around the corner, I see Lucy, Emma, and Caroline sitting on the sofa with cocktails. Deep breath. I love them all as if they were my own slightly eccentric relations, but it's been a long day, and they can be a lot.

I plaster on a smile and stride into the room. "Hi, ladies."

Emma jumps up and gives me a hug. "Hi, love."

"How are you?" Caroline asks. "It's been a big day, so we wanted to come by and make sure you and Ed are doing all right."

"I was also hoping you'd have dinner available," Lucy says.

I try not to roll my eyes too hard. Of course she was. Never mind that her mum has a fully staffed kitchen at her apartment less than two hundred metres away. "I survived. Had a slightly scary morning being surrounded by paps trying to get into the car, but it got sorted out. Is Eddie around?"

"No, we haven't seen him yet," Caroline says. "I expect Henry is punishing him for the bad press by keeping him late in mind-numbing political briefings."

I suck on my teeth for a moment. "Right."

"What's wrong, love?" Emma asks. "You're not your bubbly self tonight."

I snort. "I'm not sure 'bubbly' is the way most people would describe me."

"I'll agree you're not always as effervescent as yours truly," Emma says, gesturing to herself. "But you're not normally this depressing."

"I'm not depressing!"

She cocks her head. "Are you sure about that?"

"I am not depressing," I say firmly. "I'm so tired. Today was a lot. The paparazzi were terrifying this morning, but it's more than that. It's trying to adjust to this life and deal with palace politics and work. I think work was actually the worst part of today. I'm so distracted by everything going on here I'm barely getting my job done."

Lucy clucks sympathetically. "It's hard, but you'll get used to it."

"The thing is, you guys were born into this. You've never had this initial rush of media attention or had to figure out who in the staff you need to avoid getting offside. Plus, you don't have to deal with day jobs."

"Excuse you!" Emma cries indignantly. "We most certainly do have day jobs."

"Too right we do," Lucy chimes in.

My lips draw into a line. "What exactly is your job title at the gallery again, Em?"

"I'll have you know I'm the Tate Gallery's *premier* consultant tastemaker."

"Remind me what a consultant tastemaker does again?"

She takes a sip of her drink. "What do I do? What don't I do, darling!"

"Not sure that illuminates things for me, Em. Help a girl out here. Walk me through your standard day."

"Well, if you want to delve into the minutiae, when the team are planning a new exhibit or looking at making some acquisitions, they set up a nice little display with pictures, and I tell them what I like and don't like while I have a cup of tea and people serve me a selection of tiny cakes."

Caroline gives me an amused look across the room, and I try to cover my snort with a cough. "So it's, uh, quite taxing then?"

"Oh, you've no idea! It's exhausting. The pressure of having that kind of power almost breaks you sometimes."

"And how often do you provide the gallery with your taste-making services?"

"Constantly." She mops at her brow. "At least one afternoon a month."

"Hmm. And what about you, Luce? I haven't seen you heading off to the office much recently."

Lucy fans herself. "Well, if you must know, I've given it up."

"You've given up work?" I ask, brow raised.

"Temporarily. Things weren't working out at Sotheby's. I'd grown beyond it, so I decided to take a break to recentre and find a new way to apply my expertise."

"Did you now?"

Emma leans in with a conspiratorial glint in her eye. "What she means, Amelia dear, is work was impeding her holiday plans."

"They wanted me to come in every second week. Every second week! I can't be expected to live with that lack of flexibility. Can you even imagine?"

"Well," I say, rolling my eyes, "I'm expected to work at least five days every week, so yes, I think I can imagine." I'm *expected* to work at least five days each week, but lately I'm lucky to make it into the office twice in a week. Sure, on days I don't go to the office I get work done from home while Eddie is out, but I'm definitely not shouldering my normal workload at the moment. I may as well be a tastemaker.

Lucy's eyes go wide. "Darling, are you still working every day? No wonder you're overwhelmed. Oh, you need to do something about that immediately. I'd recommend cutting down to one day a week at the absolute most."

"I can't cut down to a day or two a week. There's so much to do, and I don't have time to get it all done in five days! The foundation manages hundreds of millions of pounds, supports scores of charities, and has dozens of its own projects on the go at any one time. There's a lot of legal work to do, and I've only got two other lawyers in my team."

Emma titters with laughter. "There's your problem, love! You need an easier job. Why don't you hand the senior lawyer business off to your team and get a nice job like mine that involves a little less stress and a little more tea?"

"It's pretty tempting some days, but I don't want to give up my work. I love my work! It drives me absolutely batty sometimes and is way more stressful than is healthy, but I can't imagine doing anything else. It's who I am." Or at least it used to feel who I was, but now . . . now I'm not so sure. Since I moved in here, I don't know who I am anymore. Some days it feels like all I am is a security blanket for Eddie. And what's going to happen when Eddie and I get married? I don't know when we're going to get married, but I do know that when we do, no matter how hard-working or competent I am, I won't be able to maintain any kind of normal job as queen. It would be impossible. But it's clear that Henry and his crew aren't going to be jumping at the opportunity to give me palace appearance work or patronages, so what will I be doing?

Emma interrupts my train of thought. "If you can't imagine doing anything else, I think we need to work on your imagination," she says with a smirk.

I drop my head and rub my temples. "Can we talk about something other than work, please? I've had a day, and I need a bit of an escape right now." What I really need is my boyfriend, but there's still no sign of him.

Caroline checks her phone. "Hey, Lucy and Em, sounds like some of Mummy's friends who were meant to come for dinner had to cancel at the last minute, so her chef significantly overcatered. If you're still hungry, maybe you'd like to pop by and pick up something to go? There's lobster linguine and something with truffles."

The cousins' eyes light up, and Emma rubs her stomach. "I am rather peckish. Lucy?"

"I've always got room for lobster."

Emma claps her hand onto my shoulder. "Well, darling, sounds like we're going to love you and leave you. Have a good night. I want there to be a sparkle back in your eye next time I see you."

I give them both a hug goodbye, and they sweep out of the room. I collapse back onto the sofa and let my eyes flutter shut, savouring the silence. I'm so relieved they're gone that I forget for a moment that Caroline is still here.

"I hope you don't mind me sending them out. I thought you might need a little space," she says.

I open my eyes and look at her across the room. She's sitting tall, with one ankle crossed behind the other, and is shredding a napkin in her hands. "Thank you, I appreciate it. I appreciate them checking on me and trying to cheer me up too, but I . . ."

"Need a bit of quiet?" she offers.

I nod vigorously. "I really do. There's so much going on in my head right now. If I'm going to find my way through the noise, I need some space to process."

"My cousins are fabulous, but giving people they care about space isn't exactly their forte."

"It is not. Most of the time I love that about them, but today I need to recharge."

The corner of her mouth quirks up. "If you ever want to talk about it, I understand. More than some others around here may. I don't know if Ed has ever told you about my career history?"

"He hasn't," I say. "But if I'm being completely honest, I've read about it."

"Well, you'll know then that I went to university up in Scotland and studied architecture."

"I do."

"I'm sure you're also aware that after university, I came back to the city here and worked at an architecture firm for a couple of years before I moved back up north."

"Mm, to focus on your charity work, right?"

"That was the official story," she says, shrugging. "And it wasn't entirely untrue. I was keen to do more charity work, but it wasn't my primary motivation. I had a bit of a breakdown. I was suffocated by palace life and burnt out by trying to balance it with work. I wanted a normal life so desperately, but I couldn't manage it. Living here, being a working royal, and trying to maintain a career where I insisted on not being given any special treatment . . . it was too much. I got to the point where I snapped. I went from trying to juggle everything to being incapable of doing anything. I had quite a lengthy stay in a mental health facility before I returned to Scotland."

"I'm so sorry. I had no idea."

"It's quite all right, very few people do—Gran absolutely forbade us from telling anyone. I don't tell you this for sympathy. I tell you because I want you to know that I understand the pressures you're going to face on this path. I can see how happy you have made my brother, and I want to do whatever I can to set you up to succeed in this world."

I'm not crying, you're crying. "Thank you so much," I say, wiping a tear from my cheek. "That means so much to me."

Caroline stands and collects her bag. "I'm going to leave you to decompress a tad, but do call if you would like to talk."

"I'll walk you out," I say. At the door, I give her a tight hug. "I'll definitely call you."

CHAPTER 22

I'M TOSSING and turning in bed when I hear a rustling downstairs. It's the middle of the night, and if I wasn't in one of the most heavily guarded houses in the country, I'd be sure I was being robbed. A few minutes later, Eddie appears in the doorway. He tiptoes into the room, using the torch on his phone to light the way. Suddenly I hear a thunk, and he swears and starts jumping around. I sit up and squint through the darkness to try to see what's happening. "Eddie, are you okay?"

"Ugh, I stubbed my bloody toe. Damn, that hurts!" He hops over to the bed on one foot and flops down next to me. "Sorry, Mils, I was trying not to wake you."

I lean over and kiss his temple. "Don't worry, I wasn't really sleeping anyway."

"Rough day?"

"You could say that. It didn't get off to a great start when the car was mobbed by paparazzi who pelted the windows with rocks and looked like they were trying to climb in through the windscreen."

"Amelia!" He pushes himself up to sit against the upholstered linen headboard and flips on the bedside lamp. "That sounds horrific. Why didn't you tell me?"

I shield my eyes from the light. "I sent you a text asking you to call, but you never did. I didn't want to text you about it and worry you."

He rubs his eyes and then scrunches them closed. "I'm so sorry. I had no idea. Security said there had been some photographers waiting outside the gates but it had been handled. They made it sound like it wasn't a big issue—a couple of men trying to get too close to the car. I was planning to call you back the first chance I got, but Henry kept me busy all day and half the night. I feel awful you had to go through that by yourself. You must be so rattled."

"It's okay. Penny came over this morning to offer some moral support and was able to stay with me for the day. I'm glad she did. Work was a bit of a disaster today."

"Poor thing," he says, massaging my shoulder. "Well, I'm glad you weren't on your own, but I should have been the one who was there for you. After all, you're only in this position because of me."

"You've got way more important things to do than babysit me."

"Nonsense, you are important. I can't always be there for you exactly when I would like to be, but I promise you that if there is an emergency and you need me, I will find a way. You need to let me know, though."

"I didn't want to worry you. You have your own dramas to deal with."

"I want you to worry me. We're a team here, Glendale. Best to keep it for genuinely important things, though. I'd rather not hang up on the Canadian Prime Minister so you can show me a cute dog picture."

"But what if it's a tiny dog wearing rain boots? Surely Trudeau would understand."

"Fair point. What kind of monster wouldn't understand the urgency of a dog in rain boots?"

"No one who should be running a country, that's for sure."

Eddie flips off the light and lies down again. "It's late," he says, wrapping his arms around me. "We should get some sleep, but I want to hear all about work and everything else tomorrow. Leave no detail out, especially if it involves canine fashion."

"Got it," I murmur as I lean back into him.

He runs his hand across my stomach and trails kisses down my arm. "I love you, and I'm so proud of you for getting through today. It's not always going to be like this, I promise."

In the morning, we get to talk for a solid forty-five minutes while he skims through the reports stuffed into his daily dispatch box.

"Anything interesting happening at work today?" he asks.

"A few bits and pieces. We're trying to figure out which country to roll the immunisation program out to next. I'm leaning towards the Philippines because their current vaccination rates are some of the lowest in the region, but some of the team are pushing for Myanmar because we've got more infrastructure set up there already, so it would be an easy win. What would you do?"

"That's difficult. Sometimes it can be good to take the easy win, but it sounds like you may have more of an impact in the Philippines. It's hard to say without seeing the comparative cost-benefit analyses, but I trust you, so I think you should review the data, keep an open mind, and then go with your gut."

"Thanks. I'll read through the reports again and see what I think. I'm not the one who gets to decide anyway, but the team asked for my opinion."

"Well, Mils, I'm happy to talk it through if you want to look at the reports together. That's what I'm here for, helping you with the big decisions. Which country do you invest millions of donated pounds in? What should you have for dinner? Are skinny jeans really over?"

I laugh. "Well, don't hold out on me here, Eddie—are they over? I'm planning to go shopping soon and need to know."

"Frankly, I have no idea. But I'm willing to fall down a TikTok hole to find out for you, even though TikTok terrifies me."

"Wow, you really love me."

"I certainly do," he says, pulling his phone out of his pocket. "Should I start watching?"

"Ha, no. I wouldn't do that to you. I'll talk to Penny about it—she's the fashion professional, after all. I'm worried about what kind of can of worms I'll be opening."

"You should be. You may need to purge your closet."

"Let's hope it doesn't come to that. Anyway, not sure how we got onto jeans. What's planned for your day?"

"A visit to the children's hospital in the morning, and then an afternoon workshop with the Climate Change Committee to prepare for my speech at next year's UN climate change conference."

I shrug. "So nothing as important as denim trends."

"No," he says, shaking his head, "nothing that life-changing."

AFTER EDDIE LEAVES for his very unimportant day, my phone pings with a message.

Caroline: *Hi Amelia, I thought you may want some company on the way to work this morning. I can pop by if you do.*

The tightness in my chest loosens a little. If someone had told me the first time I met Caroline that one day I'd be grateful to have her offer to spend time with me one-on-one, I would have laughed in their face. And yet, here we are. Our recent chats have helped me to see our frosty first encounter in a new light, and I'm touched she would offer to put herself in a media-heavy situation for me given how stressful I know she finds them. I quickly tap out a reply.

Me: *If you're sure you don't mind, that would be great.*

Caroline: *See you shortly!*

When I'm dressed and ready to go, I head outside and see my car waiting in front of the house and Caroline walking down the footpath towards me from Queen Louisa's apartment. I wave. "Morning!"

"Hi, love," she says, coming over and giving me a double air kiss. "How are you getting on this morning? Ready to face the world again?"

"Yes." I scrunch up my face. "Maybe?"

"It's all right. If you're not ready today, you can always wait and try again tomorrow. You will have to leave the nest eventually, though. Unfortunately, no matter how many fabulous amenities we may have here at KP, you can't stay inside the gates forever. Trust me, I've tried."

"Ugh, I know. I don't want to go out, but if I put it off until tomorrow, I'm going to build it up in my mind and get even more anxious about it."

Caroline holds out her hand. "Sounds like we're going for a drive then."

"Sounds like we are." I take her hand, and we climb into the car. It's go time. "I thought I had my anxiety about public attention under control. Before the break-up, I'd been doing such a good job of blocking it all out and just focusing on what I was doing—I was a mindfulness master. But this time . . . this time feels different. Now Eddie's king, and the attention is so much more intense than it ever was before. I have coping skills, but they have a limit."

"Don't worry," she says, patting my hand. "I completely understand. You can't cope perfectly all the time." As we approach the gates, Caroline addresses Michael. "Have you had any word on what we're heading into?"

"Yes, ma'am. Similar numbers to yesterday, but police are in attendance, and we have everyone who is on foot corralled behind fences. We don't have a police escort for the drive at this stage, but two of the cars stationed outside the gate are on call to form a convoy if anyone gives chase."

"Thanks, Michael. Sounds good." She turns to me. "If you're going through a high-attention phase, it can help to ask your PPOs to investigate the situation before you go anywhere so you understand what to expect. Easier to control the anxiety if you're not dealing with as many unknowns."

"Smart, thanks."

"Okay, ladies," Michael says from the front of the car. "We're about to open the gates. Everything is under control."

The palace gates swing open, and through the front window I see what looks like hundreds of photographers, reporters, and random passers-by surging against the metal barriers that have been set up on either side of the gates. There are a dozen police officers standing between the barriers and the road. As we pass the pack, I duck my head down, trying to avoid being seen. The noise is overwhelming, but this time no one throws anything at the car and no one tries to jump on us. Baby steps.

Caroline puts a hand on my knee. "Don't forget to breathe."

I draw a deep breath, keeping my head down. "Good reminder. How are we looking, Michael?"

"We've got a few cars and motorbikes tailing us. The bikes are driving fairly aggressively, so I've asked for the police cars to join us as a precaution. Nothing to worry about, though."

I don't sit up again until we're safely tucked into the basement car park at work. "We made it!"

"Good job, Amelia," Caroline says.

"Now I need to deal with the people in the office all day."

"Would you like me to come up with you? I've got an appointment at eleven, but I could stay until then to get you settled."

"No, that's okay. I have to do this by myself. Thank you, though. I may not have been able to make it here without you."

"Anytime, love. If you ever need anything, please call me. It's a crazy world you've decided to join us in. We need to stick together."

As Michael, PPO Elba, and I walk along the corridor towards my office, a sea of heads turns to watch. To their credit, most people whose eyes I catch quickly turn around and pretend to be busy; only a handful of staffers openly stare. Thankfully, no one makes any awkward comments today, but equally no one says hi as I walk past, not even the people who I've worked with for years.

Alone in my office, a wave of satisfaction washes over me. I made it out of the house and all the way to the office without any major incidents. Six months ago, I got a huge promotion and was hitting my stride professionally—I knew what I was doing at work, I was comfortable in the city and in my little life with Penny. Now my heart is so much fuller, but a lot of the time it seems like making it to my desk without crying is the benchmark of success for my day. Somehow I can't help but feel that even though I've gone from living in a cramped flat where the hot water only worked every second day if we were lucky to living in a literal palace, in some ways things are going backwards for me.

I open up my email and start sorting through everything that's come in overnight in an attempt to shake off my introspection spiral. Lucky I do, too, because there's an email from Daisy reminding me we need to finalise the terms sheet for a partnership with Netflix and send it out by the end of today. I'd better get onto that.

I'm finished drafting the terms sheet and running through a final proofread when a news alert from the *Daily Mail* flashes up on my phone *Is the throne set to change hands AGAIN?* Ugh, I was sure I'd blocked these. I clear the alert from my screen. I've got enough stress in my life at the moment without reading ridiculous gossip.

Ten minutes later, as I'm packing up an email to send to Netflix with the terms sheet, project details, and financial contribution tables, my phone beeps again. This time it's a text from Penny.

Penny: *I know you're not meant to be reading news, but this isn't true, is it?*

Below her message, a link to the *Daily Mail* article from earlier pops up. I shouldn't read it, but one article isn't going to kill me, right?

Is the throne set to change hands AGAIN?

According to shocking claims made to this paper, Buckingham Palace is about to be rocked by yet another in a series of devastating scandals.

Only days ago, the palace dropped a bombshell when it confirmed that King Edmund had again broken his engagement to Lady Sibella Cavendish and taken up with lawyer and rumoured mistress Amelia Glendale. Since then, concerns have been mounting about the young king's mental health. Insiders fear that his mental state has been in a tailspin since his father's death and that the palace may soon be forced to have the king declared unfit to rule and oust him from the throne, causing a record-breaking fourth change in monarch in little more than a year. The current heir to the throne is of course the reclusive Princess Caroline, who lives on a ten-thousand-acre family estate in the Scottish Highlands but has recently been seen in and around Kensington Palace, fuelling the rumours that the family are refusing to leave King Edmund unsupervised.

However, as was revealed recently, Princess Caroline is not in fact the late King Albert's second-born child. Lady Isla Barrington was born to King Albert and long-time lover Lady Sophia Sumner-Jones mere weeks after Queen Louisa gave birth to Edmund. As previously reported by this paper, Lady Barrington has been meeting with top barristers and is poised to launch a blistering legal attack on the royal family to secure the right to use the title of princess and her place in the order of succession. Lady Barrington was yesterday pictured walking from her twenty-three-million-pound Mayfair pad to the Blackstone Chambers office of leading constitutional lawyer Lord Dellingworth, KC. If Lady Barrington has engaged Lord Dellingworth, the palace will be in for a fight. The prominent barrister who rose to the ranks of Queen's Counsel (now King's Counsel following the tragic death of Queen Alice) over thirty-four years ago is known in legal circles as the "bulldog of London."

Body language expert Melania James told the Daily Mail that Lady Barrington was using overtly confident gestures which appeared at odds with her usually reserved demeanour. Reviewing an image of Lady Barrington striding towards her lawyer's office, Melania said, 'Isla's posture and hand placement here suggest she wants to send out a very emphatic message that she is not going to back down. Her gait has changed dramatically over recent weeks, now displaying much more regal traits, clearly signalling her intention to claim her place as part of the royal family.'

...

I can't believe they're printing this kind of garbage. Despite having been put in some enormously stressful situations lately, Eddie is one of the sanest people I know. And unless Isla's had a massive change of heart since our disastrous dinner, she's definitely not rushing to call herself a princess, let alone claim the throne and become queen. I know we're meant to be ignoring the press, and I've been trying, I really have, but this is ridiculous. It makes me so angry to see such outlandish lies out there and realise there are people who will believe them. If even Penny thinks there might be some truth to it, what hope does the public have of telling fact from fiction? Henry and Cornelius were set on taking a "no comment" approach, but I'm starting to think Eddie needs to insist on putting out a proper statement and dealing with the rumours once and for all.

I pick up my phone and send him a message.

Me: *Hey, have you seen today's outrageous rumours?*

I don't get a reply straight away, so I assume he's busy. Maybe I should talk to Charli about it. I hit dial, and as I'm waiting for her to pick up, Daisy pops her head into my office. "Hi, were you going to send out the Netflix terms sheet? They were expecting it by four."

I look down at my phone. Four thirty. "Thanks for the reminder, Daisy. I'm on it."

My call goes through to Charli's voicemail, so I leave her a message while I pull up an old email about the Netflix deal and grab the addresses from it to add to the email I had prepared. "Hi Charli, it's Amelia. Can you please call me? I'm not sure that this no-comment business is working."

And send, done. I dust off my hands. Well, I'm glad I got that out. There's nothing else urgent on my list, so I can probably pack up early and deal with emails in the car on the way home. If I get back to KP early enough, I might be able to catch Charli in her office.

I'm piling some papers into my handbag when Daisy's head appears in my doorway again. "Amelia . . ."

"Hey Daisy, I'm heading off. If anyone is asking for me, can you please let tell them I'm on my mobile?"

She doesn't respond. I look at her and see that her face is pale and her eyes are wide. "Are you all right?"

"Did you mean to send the Netflix documents to Amazon?"

My stomach drops. "No! Did I?" I open my sent box and find the email I just sent. My heart races as I peer at the addressees list. Shit, I was so distracted by the news article and trying to call Charli that I accidentally copied the list of recipients from the wrong email. I've sent it to our team, plus a lawyer and some commercial managers from Amazon. At least there aren't any Netflix people on the list, so they don't know about my mistake yet. Acid rises in my throat and my palms start to sweat. "Netflix wanted to keep this deal super confidential for now, didn't they?"

Daisy grimaces. "They did."

Well, this is a problem. "I'll call the lawyer at Amazon I sent it to and ask him to delete it. I worked with him at my old firm, so I'm sure he'll be fine with it, but someone else on the email may have read it by now. Or at least read enough of it to figure out what's going on." I drop my head onto my desk. "I'm going to have to tell Netflix what happened."

My chest is tight as I pick up the phone and dial the number of the lawyer who got the email.

"Hello, Phil Greenwood speaking."

"Oh, hi, Phil, it's Amelia Glendale."

"Hi, Amelia, how are you? I've, uh, seen a bit about you in the news lately."

I bite my tongue nervously. "Yes, it's a slightly weird time."

"That's an understatement. I imagine it must be surreal having people talking about you like that."

"You have no idea. Look, Phil, I'm actually calling about something pretty urgent and super embarrassing. Not sure if you've seen the email I just sent you?"

"No, I haven't seen it yet, sorry. My inbox is out of control."

My shaky breath starts to even out. "That's okay. The thing is, it was actually meant for someone else. Would you be able to delete it?"

"Of course, we've all been there."

"Could you please do me a huge favour and call Richard and Simon from your commercial team and ask them to delete it too?"

"No problem. I'll call them right now. Hope the rest of your afternoon improves, Amelia."

"Thanks, Phil, you're a lifesaver."

I hang up and turn to Daisy. "Okay, now we need to tell

Netflix. I'm going to wait until I hear back from Phil to make sure his commercial guys have deleted it too."

"Do we really need to tell them if no one saw it?"

"I think we do. Even if everyone says they've deleted the email, there's always a chance that one of them had already read part of it and it gets back to Netflix. They'd never trust us again if they heard about it from someone else, but I'm definitely going to chicken out and email them instead of calling."

Just then, I get an email from Phil.

Amelia, have spoken to Richard and Simon and they've deleted their copies too. They thought it was probably a mistake, so hadn't opened any of the attachments. - P

All right, this could've been much worse. Even so, the sick feeling I get from having made a mistake is lingering. I'm a details girl—I triple-check everything and pride myself on never making these kinds of mistakes. The last time I sent an email to the wrong person was seven years ago, and I'm pretty sure I haven't fully recovered from the stress of it yet. This one is going to haunt me.

CHAPTER 23

EDDIE IS out at a dinner engagement, so I spend most of the night sitting by myself on the sofa, wearing sweatpants and eating reheated lasagne, of which I spill way too much on myself. No matter how much things change, some things stay the same. Around nine thirty, I hear a car pull up outside and the crunch of shoes on the gravel path leading to the front door.

"Amelia, are you home?"

"Hey, I'm in the den."

When he strolls in, he looks at me with those warm hazel eyes and flashes a dimple-inducing grin that lights up the room. This. This is why I'm dealing with all the drama and inconvenience.

He drops down to sit beside me and puts his arm around me. "It's good to see you, Mils. It's been a long day."

"Oh, no. Was it the dinner?"

"No, the dinner was bearable enough. I had a lot of frustrating meetings with Henry during the day. He's pushing back on all of my ideas. It's incredibly frustrating."

"Sounds like it. What was the dinner for?"

"It was for an environmental charity that promotes the use of aquaponics. I learnt a lot about how to sustainably produce both seafood and vegetables at home. Fascinating stuff."

"Interesting. Now you just need to find some kind of underground bunker building organisation to get involved in, and you'll be well on your way to being a certified doomsday prepper."

"Excellent idea. We have a significant amount of cellar space here. Currently it's mainly full of seventeenth-century furniture and portraits of wealthy old white men, but it could be much better utilised as canned food storage."

"It's a plan. We'll be able to survive a nuclear winter with the best of them."

"That has always been a great aspiration of mine."

I pat my hand on his chest. "That's why I'm here, kiddo. I'm making your dreams come true one at a time." I nestle my head onto his shoulder. "What kind of fish did they serve, by the way?"

Eddie chuckles. "Actually, they served chicken. Not exactly a ringing endorsement for their product, is it?"

"It is not. We could buy a chicken coop instead?"

"Mm, perhaps. Anyway, enough about me and apocalypse survival. How was your day?"

I study a piece of lint on the couch. "Uh, next topic, please."

"Well, that doesn't sound good. What happened? Was it the media leeches again?"

"No, not really. I mean, there were a lot of people waiting outside, but Michael and the police knew what to expect today, so it was all much more controlled than yesterday."

"So what was it, then?" he asks, massaging my neck.

"I made a mistake at work. I sent a confidential email to the wrong company. I haven't made a mistake like that in years. I called, and the people I sent it to agreed to delete it, but I can't stop obsessing over it."

"I'm sorry. That must have been rather fraught. Has it all been sorted out now?"

"The email thing kind of worked out in the end, but it's not just about that," I say, watching the rain running down the window. "I think part of why I was so shattered by it is that it's not the kind of thing I do. With everything going on, I feel like I'm losing myself."

"Oh, Mils, I'm so sorry. I know life is trying at the moment, but this is a transition period. Life will normalise, and you will find yourself again. I'll be here to support you in whatever way I can, but it wouldn't hurt to organise to talk to someone impartial as well. Therapy is never a bad idea."

I scoff and turn to face him. "Did you not read today's news?"

"No," he says, shrugging, "I didn't. Charli gave me the general gist, though."

"And you don't think me going into therapy would be a bad look if someone found out or it was leaked?"

He shakes his head. "I honestly don't. I find the stigma around mental health very concerning and refuse to accept that maintaining your mental health is something shameful."

"Does everyone in the palace machine share that view? Caroline told me about her treatment and that the palace wouldn't let her tell anyone about it."

Deep lines appear on Eddie's forehead. "I feel dreadful about that for so many reasons. She was struggling so much, and we weren't there for her in the way we should have been." He presses his lips together. "She was subjected to great shame and judgement by a lot of people within the palace—including Gran, unfortunately. Gran was wonderful in many ways, but she saw came from a different era and saw mental illness as a weakness. Trust me when I say I would never allow that attitude to stand in my palace."

I want to believe what he's saying, but based on what I've seen recently, I don't think Eddie would allow anything that Henry didn't approve of. I don't want to cause a fight, but if I don't call him out on these things, who will? I take a deep breath. "Are you sure about that?"

He bristles. "Pardon?"

"You mean well, and you're remarkably emotionally mature for someone who grew up in an upper-class British family, but would you really stand up for Caroline if it happened now?"

"Absolutely."

"You say that now, but what would you do if Henry and his team insisted the issue be covered up? I haven't seen you go against him on anything recently, even on things where I know you disagree with him and the status quo."

He frowns. "I hope you know that if something was really important to me, I would do what I thought was right—regardless of Henry's opinion."

"I wish I could believe that, but I can't. Isn't our relationship important to you? Aren't your charity projects important to you?"

"Of course they are!"

"So why won't you stand up to him when it comes to those issues?"

His voice wavers. "Because I'm scared. I need Henry and the others. I'm nothing without their work behind the scenes."

I take his hand and trace slow circles on his palm. "I know you're scared. But I deserve your support, even when it's scary. Your charities deserve your support. And you know what? You deserve to have the confidence to back yourself and do what you believe in."

"I hope that one day I'll be able to find that confidence. For both our sakes."

"How is Charli feeling about all the press coverage at the moment?" I ask Eddie over dinner one day. "I haven't heard from her in a few days."

"Hm, not amazing. Having papers say I've completely lost my marbles makes her job a tad more difficult than usual."

"I can imagine," I say. Should I risk raising the Isla issue again? It hasn't led to anything good in the past, but people are going to have to talk about her eventually. "I heard there were more articles this week about Isla's supposed plans to sue you. Are Henry and Cornelius still adamant we can't talk to her or put out a statement?"

Eddie places his cutlery down and clasps his hands together. "I've been thinking about Isla quite a bit actually. I feel I may have been a bit too hasty in refusing to have any contact with her. I felt incredibly betrayed by what Dad did, and I needed someone to be angry at, someone to blame. Unfortunately for her, Isla seemed like the easy option."

Well, that's quite a change of heart. I should tread lightly here, though. As much as I still feel the need to be Isla's advocate here, I don't want to risk alienating Eddie over it again. It doesn't matter how much I relate to her or feel sorry for her, she's not worth losing my boyfriend over. "I can see why you'd be angry at the situation in general. None of it is her fault, though."

He stares at the table and fidgets with his fork. "No, it isn't. I should really apologise for the way I treated her at that dinner, but I can't. Henry would never agree to it. I think I exhausted my bargaining power with him when I convinced him to let us announce our relationship. As you pointed out the other day, he hasn't let me have a say on anything since."

"Well," I say carefully, "maybe this is your chance to start doing something about that."

"What if Henry doesn't approve? If I ask his permission to speak to her, and then back down when he says no, I lose even more credibility."

"Now," I say, putting a hand on his shoulder, "this may sound like an Emma-style cockamamie thing to say, but hear me out. What if you call her and don't tell him?"

"Are you suggesting I go behind Henry's back and do something he's expressly advised me not to do?"

"I'm not suggesting you murder a foreign president or anything. All I'm saying is you could make a phone call without running it by a committee. If you want to talk to her, do it for yourself."

He looks thoughtful. "I'm not sure. What if the press found out? It could be a disaster."

"So you make sure it doesn't get out. Going to see her in person risks pap photos getting out, so why don't you keep it simple and call her? No one is going to know if you call her from your personal phone while you're at home."

He rubs his jaw. "That's true, I suppose. I would feel much less stress about the situation if I were able to speak to her and bury the hatchet."

"I think it would be a good thing for both of you."

"All right," he says with a sudden resolve. "Tomorrow morning, I'll do it."

THE NEXT MORNING I wake to Eddie pacing around the room in his plaid pyjama bottoms, clutching his phone.

"All right there, Eddie?"

"Just a tad nervous. What if Henry finds out?"

I laugh. "How is he going to find out? Is he lurking in your closet? I really hope not. I'm not sure how I'd feel about Henry hiding between your coats and watching us."

He taps his phone on his leg. "Let me get dressed and I'll call her after breakfast. As my great-granny always used to say,

'Never have an important conversation without a pocket square and tie bar.'"

I frown. "She probably meant conversations in person."

"True, but we have FaceTime now, so I think we should bring back the discipline of dressing for discussions. I'll be sure to angle the camera to give Isla the best possible view of my tie-related accessories."

"I'm sure she'll appreciate it."

Eddie laughs nervously and finally stops pacing. "Let's hope so. Which pocket square should I wear? Which colour says, 'I'm sorry I blamed you for our father being a deceitful bastard'?"

I walk over to the closet and flip through a selection of colourful silk squares. "Hm. Yellow?" I ask, holding out a piece of canary-yellow fabric. "Yellow feels like a begging for forgiveness kind of colour to me."

He takes the pocket square. "Yellow it is."

An hour later, Eddie has run out of ways to procrastinate, so it's time. "Do you want me to sit with you?"

"No," he says, shaking his head. "I need to do this on my own. I might go and sit in the other room."

"Good luck. Whatever happens, I love you."

"I love you too, Mils. Thank you for being here for me even though I haven't been quite myself lately."

I kiss his cheek, and he walks out of the room. I hope so badly that this goes well for him, and for Isla. They've both been suffering because of Albert's actions, but they can help each other. They can . . . wait, why is he coming back into the room already? "Hey, what happened?"

Eddie slaps his palm to his forehead. "Voicemail."

"Oh. Well, that's a bit of an anticlimax."

"It really was. I left a message and asked her to call me back tomorrow morning. So," he says, grimacing, "can I have another pep talk tomorrow?"

"Babe, I've got unlimited pep-talk capacity. You can have one every day for the rest of your life if that's what you need. But don't expect me to wear a cheerleading uniform. That's a line I won't cross."

"Noted. I suppose I'd best be getting to my first meeting. Can you work from home today? I had a last-minute cancellation, so I have time to come home for lunch."

"That sounds great. I'll be here."

I BATTLE through my morning of work—it's another day where everything on my to-do list sounds awful. I seem to be having more and more of these days at the moment. To avoid reviewing a particularly tedious contract, I spend way more time than I should trying to curate a perfect lunch order. After reading at least fifty restaurant reviews, I decide on a caprese salad and pumpkin ravioli with a burnt butter and sage sauce from an Italian restaurant in Belgravia. Do other people research lunch this thoroughly? I hope so.

The food arrives in time for me to set the plates and serve everything before Eddie gets home. Eating takeaway off real plates—fancy.

"You cooked!" Eddie exclaims as he walks in the door.

"Please, I ordered in."

"Even better," he says with a wink. "This smells delicious."

"It's the burnt butter. Is there anything better than burnt butter?"

"If there is, I'm not aware of it. Perhaps I should task an aide with finding out. It may take several years and many thousands of taste tests, but we'll get to the bottom of it."

"Look at you, tackling the big issues."

We're laughing and enjoying our pasta when there's a knock at the door followed immediately by footsteps in the hallway. I turn around and see Henry striding into the room. His jaw is clenched, and his eyes are bulging.

"Henry!" Eddie exclaims. "What are you doing here?"

"What do you think you've been doing?" Henry yells. As disrespectful as Henry is sometimes, I think that's the first time I've ever heard him speak to Eddie without addressing him as Your Majesty or sir. This must be bad.

"Pardon? I'm having lunch with Amelia. Is that an issue?"

"Don't play dumb," he snaps. Okay, this is escalating.

Eddie plants his hands on the table. "What exactly are you talking about? You're not making any sense."

"You know precisely what I'm talking about. That girl. *Isla*." I can practically taste the venom in his voice when he says her name. "I know you tried to contact her. Why on earth would you do something I expressly told you not to do?"

"Henry, I know you didn't want me to speak to her, but this isn't about work—it's personal."

Henry's face is filled with rage. "Personal! Nothing is personal for you! Everything you do affects the country. Worse, everything you do reflects on *me*!"

"Henry, calm down. I really don't think it should be a big issue."

He slams the table. "I will not be spoken down to! You are an ignorant, insolent young man, and you have absolutely no appreciation of the potential consequences of your actions. Imagine what would happen if the press caught wind of this! Everything I've done to deal with the issue would be undone. The monarchy would be brought into complete disrepute."

Eddie stares at Henry, his eyes wide and hand trembling.

Henry takes the silence as an opportunity to continue his diatribe. "Your grandmother and father would never have let you get away with going around your advisers like this. They would be disgusted."

Eddie's eyes are glazed over. I think he's in shock. I can't let this continue. "Henry," I cut in, "can you lower your voice, please? Then maybe we can have a civilised conversation about this."

"I will do no such thing! I do not take orders from people like you."

Right. Not going to have a civilised conversation then.

"Henry," Eddie says slowly, "how did you know I had called her? Amelia is the only person I told, and I have absolute faith she didn't inform anyone else."

"I know everything."

A wave of comprehension passes over Eddie's face. "You have her phone tapped, don't you?"

"Of course I do," he spits. "I don't trust her at all, so I need to monitor what she is doing. And based on this lapse of judgement, it looks like you can't be trusted to make appropriate choices if you're left to your own devices either. You know *nothing* about how to be king. I have to watch everything you do to make sure you don't destroy yourself and take the entire institution down with you."

I can't believe Henry has been listening to Eddie's personal calls. It's an outrageous breach of his trust. I glance over and see that Eddie's face is drawn, and he's shaking more than before.

Eddie opens his mouth and closes it again. Henry launches into another tirade. "You will never attempt to make contact with that girl again, do you understand? If you do, I will know, and I will never let you out of my sight. It's my duty to do anything and everything in my power to make sure you don't compromise the monarchy. After your father's indiscretions, this institution is on shaky ground, and I refuse to see it destroyed."

When Eddie doesn't respond, Henry slams his fist onto the table. "Do you understand?"

"I understand," he whispers.

Henry sneers. "Good." Then he turns and storms out of the room, leaving Eddie and me in shocked silence.

"Wow," I say a minute later. "Are you okay? That was intense."

"I'm fairly shaken."

I lean over and rub his arm. "I can see why. I can't believe he was talking to you like that. It was so out of line."

Eddie hangs his head and sighs.

"Eddie?"

"Maybe he is right and I shouldn't have tried to talk to Isla."

"What? Don't say that! He was being ridiculous."

"I don't know anymore. He had a point. I'm so young, and most of the time I have no clue what I'm doing. Perhaps I was making a mistake. Either way, I can't reach out to her again. Who knows what Henry would do if I did?"

I grab Eddie's hand and stare at him. "Eddie, look at me." He raises his head and looks at me through watery eyes. "You don't have to listen to him."

"I do. I can't do my job with him. He's got me cornered."

Eddie has always struggled with a level of anxiety and self-doubt, but the combination of being thrown into a role he wasn't ready for and being bullied by a disgruntled adviser has completely decimated what confidence he did have. I wish I knew how to fix it.

CHAPTER 24

EDDIE IS UNUSUALLY RESERVED for the rest of the week. Most evenings he hides away reading papers or sits quietly staring at the TV without taking anything in. Poor thing, he looks so defeated since his dressing-down from Henry. He's really taken all the criticism to heart.

One night over dinner, I decide to try and cheer him up. "Are you excited about your tour to Canada?"

His morose expression is replaced with something more thoughtful. "Excited, and nervous. I've been on tours before, obviously, but this will be quite different. I'm concerned it won't go well. What if everyone sees through me and can tell I don't know what I'm doing?"

"I'm sure it'll be great. Canadians love you. I don't want to minimise the great work you do for charities and international relations, but for a successful tour, you mainly need to smile and look pretty. I have it on good authority that you're pretty skilled at both of those things."

Often in the past, Eddie's anxiety has gotten the best of him, and he's come across as cold and stilted in public. But when he's able to shake his nerves and truly engage with people involved in charities and projects he's interested in, he's magnetic. He's so passionate about the causes he supports, people can't help but be charmed by him. If he can pull it off, this tour might be what he needs to rebuild his confidence.

He twirls his linguine around his plate. "Mm, I hope it will be well received. I wish you could come and be by my side. It would go against every protocol there is for you to come with me, but I'm always so much more relaxed and confident during appearances if I know you're there—that's where the smiles come from. Besides, there are only so many state dinners I can go to without a date."

"Don't worry, I'm sure Trudeau will keep you entertained."

"Perhaps." He grins at me. "He doesn't have your dazzling wit, though."

"That may be, but he does have excellent hair. Will you try to touch it for me?"

He chokes, and his hand flies to his mouth as he spits out the water in his mouth. "I absolutely will not."

"You've tried before, haven't you?"

He places a hand on his heart. "I can neither confirm nor deny that allegation. I can, however, confirm his security officers do keep a rather close eye on me after an encounter in Saskatchewan."

I press my eyes shut and take a deep breath. I want to hold on to this moment forever. Why does someone who I have so much fun with, who makes me feel so complete, have to come with so many complications? Sigh.

"Actually, you may not be able to come on tour with me, but you could help me with a very important job tomorrow. Do you think you could skip out of work for a couple of hours in the morning?"

"I have a bit on, so I probably shouldn't unless it's important state business. Is it important state business?"

"Extremely," Eddie says.

"Well, then I can give you two hours."

Eddie's eyes crinkle. "That will do nicely."

"So," I say as we're bundling into a car the next morning, "what are we doing?"

"You're helping with an incredibly important diplomatic task. We're shopping for British souvenirs to give to my hosts in Canada."

"Isn't there someone at the palace whose job it is to source gifts for the politicians you visit?"

Eddie chuckles. "Naturally, but they always choose completely dull things like fifteenth-century sculptures. I like to supplement with something a bit more fun."

"What did you have in mind?"

"Hm," he says, scratching his chin. "I'm not entirely sure. I thought we'd go down to the Portobello Road market and find some tacky souvenirs."

"Can we do that? There'll be a million people there!"

"Of course we can. I've organised for some stalls to open an hour early, we've got security with us, and—" he says, digging around in a satchel sitting on the seat beside him, "we've got my secret weapon." He pulls two baseball caps out of the satchel and waves them in the air triumphantly.

My eyebrows shoot up. "Your big plan is for us to go incognito by wearing hats? I suppose you've got oversized sunglasses in there too."

"Naturally," he says, upending the bag to reveal said eyewear.

"You get everyone will still recognise us and take photos, right?"

His eyes crinkle. "Yes, I'm aware of that. The cap and glasses aren't particularly intended as a disguise. They're more of a signal to people that we're not on duty—it usually helps to keep things somewhat under control. Plus, the papers pay barely anything for photos where you can't see my face."

I scratch at my neck. I'm not sure about this. I can barely sit in a chauffeured car right now without photographers literally trying to jump on top of me. Surely going for a walk down a busy street is a recipe for disaster.

"I can see you worrying, Mils."

I sigh. "I've had some pretty scary run-ins with photographers lately. It doesn't feel safe to be out on the street like this."

He laces his fingers through mine. "I understand, but I think you need this. I know you haven't been out in weeks unless it's to go to the office. We can't lock ourselves away behind the palace gates forever. It's time to start getting back out into the world and normalising Edelia for the public—it's the only way things will improve. Besides, if there's so much as a whiff of an issue, security can have us out of there in under twenty seconds. I've timed it."

"Hm, I'll reluctantly agree that you've got some valid points there, but before I do, can we go back to Edelia? Is that *really* the couple name we're going with?"

He pouts. "Have you thought of a better one?"

"Not yet, but it can't be hard. Edelia is pretty awful. What about Edil? Or Miled?"

"Miled?" he says, blanching. "It makes us sound like a hundred-and-three-year-old woman who spends hours telling people about her arthritis and bunions."

"Fine, I'll admit they're also not great options. I'll spend some more time brainstorming, but fair warning, if our names don't work together, we will probably have to break up."

Eddie shrugs. "Makes sense. In the meantime, can we go souvenir shopping?"

"Ugh, okay, but the second I decide it's a bad idea, I want to be back in this car and on my way home. Got it?"

"I'll throw you over my shoulder and carry you to the car myself if I have to."

"I hope it won't be necessary, but I also wouldn't object if it was. If it doesn't come to that, can you carry me out of the car when we get home?"

He reaches across me to grab something and deliberately flexes his arm in front of my face. "That can be arranged."

Be still my heart.

After his little muscle display, we arrive at the top end of Portobello Road and start our shopping spree. It's still early, so stalls are being set up and the crowd is fairly small. I feel a bit stupid walking around in a cap and glasses when its overcast and not even nine in the morning, but it makes me feel kind of hidden and strangely does seem to have the effect of discouraging most people from approaching us. A lot of people are staring and taking photos on their phones, but as we make our way through the antiques section, only a few people wave or call out to us. Maybe people in Notting Hill are too cool to be seen fawning over royalty. Whatever the reason, I'll take it.

Eddie stops abruptly in front of a stall. "Look at this!" he says.

I take off my glasses to examine the table he's pointing to. It's covered in an array of items plastered with the British flag or pictures of Eddie's parents and grandparents. From the looks of it, most of the items are at least fifty years old.

"All original," the man behind the table says. "Collected 'em myself from op shops and old ladies' living rooms."

"When are these from?" Eddie asks, pointing to a set of biscuit tins shaped like postboxes and London buses.

"Early fifties, I'd say," the man says. "No biscuits left, I'm afraid."

Eddie nods. "Now these," he says, "these are fantastic." Eddie picks up an object and hands it to me. It's a heavy glass snow globe with a model of Westminster Abbey inside it. On the abbey steps stand a couple of tiny figures.

"Very special those are," the stallholder says. "Produced for Queen Alice's coronation. That's her and King Richard standing in front of the church there, see?"

"I see," I say, shaking the snow globe and watching the confetti sprinkle down on Westminster.

"I like these," Eddie says decisively. "How many have you got?"

"I've got four of 'em. Had to go to great lengths to collect 'em, see. They've taken me years to find."

Eddie raises an eyebrow. "I take it they're rather expensive then?"

"Oh, yes," the man says. "Couldn't part with 'em for less than two hundred quid a piece."

Eddie frowns as he turns a globe over in his hands. "That's a bit steep."

The stallholder squints at Eddie. "For you, I could do a hundred and eighty each. Special discount because they're part of your family history and all."

"We'll take the four of them."

The stallholder gives a dramatic bow. "Good choice, Your Majesty."

While Eddie pays, the man wraps the trinkets up in bubble wrap, and I hear someone shout.

"Oy! Amelia, give us a smile!"

I turn around and see about a dozen photographers barging down the footpath. Looks like someone tipped them off we were here.

"Hey," Eddie whispers to me, "ignore them. Part of this is about being photographed. We're normalising us, remember?"

I squeeze his hand. "Got it," I whisper back. Secretly, though, I'm super glad we're almost done shopping and can get back in the car in a few minutes.

After our purchases are wrapped up, Eddie insists on stopping briefly to buy some strawberries. He claims it's because they look so good, but I'm pretty sure it's his version of paparazzi-exposure therapy because a growing pack of photographers follows us the whole way. They call out to us, but I grasp Eddie's hand tightly and do my best to block out the noise. Thankfully, after ten minutes, we're back at the car. After I'm bundled into the Range Rover, Eddie turns and gives the photographers a wave before climbing in next to me and pulling the door closed behind him.

"How do you feel?" he asks.

"Good, I think. It was weird being out in public together again, but we were lucky the photographers didn't turn up until the end. People on the street taking photos on their phones was a bit awkward, but I managed to mainly tune it out. It wasn't as bad as I expected."

"That's my girl. I know it's all rather uncomfortable, but I don't want you to feel you can never leave the house. Besides, if we hadn't come out, we never would have found these snow globes. I bet Trudeau would love one. I'm going to keep one for myself as well."

I take one out of our bag and turn it over in my hands. "They are beautiful." I turn it upside down and notice a price sticker. "Hey! These were meant to be fifteen pounds each! He ripped us off!"

Eddie guffaws. "The scoundrel! Looks like the outing wasn't a complete success then."

CHAPTER 25

I'm at work, on the phone to a lawyer at the King's Trust, when there's a rap on my office door. As I look up to check who it is and gesture that I'm on a call, the door swings open and William strides in, scowling. He drops into the chair across from me and starts drumming his fingers on my desk. I get the impression he doesn't want to wait for me to finish this call. "Sorry, Selene," I say, cutting her off mid-sentence, "I've had something come up. Can I call you back? Great, thanks. Speak soon."

I hang up the phone and smile at William. "Hi, William. How are you?"

"Fine, Amelia," he says. "I'm fine." We fall back into silence.

Right, he's in one of those moods then. I suppose expecting him to tell me why he's here and then leave me in peace to get my work done is asking too much. "Are you coming to the planning workshop with Netflix this afternoon? It should be a good session."

He clears his throat. "About that, Amelia . . ."

Did I manage to stumble on the reason for his visit? Amazing. Maybe I'll get him out of my hair faster than I expected. "What about it?"

"I am attending the session, but you won't be."

What is he going on about? "Sorry, I don't follow. Why won't I be going to the meeting?"

"I've decided you shouldn't attend the meeting this afternoon. Or any other meetings, for that matter."

"Can I ask why?"

William splutters, and his face reddens. "Amelia, I'm your CEO. Are you questioning my judgement?"

Ugh. How did I end up with insufferable middle-aged men in charge at home and at work? After seeing Henry walk all over Eddie, I want to give William a piece of my mind, but I know there's no point getting into a fight with him. Deep breath. "No," I say, speaking slowly and deliberately, "I'm not questioning you, William. I'm simply trying to understand where this is coming from."

"You're a distraction," he spits out.

"Sorry?"

"It's all very well for you, being shuttled in and out of the police-secured basement by your security convoy, but the rest of us live in the real world. Have you seen how many people are outside the building? Do you have any clue how many people are trying to force their way into the foyer and the office? Have you heard how many people we meet with who are only interested in asking about you?"

I blink and shake my head. I'm still gathering my thoughts, trying to figure out how to respond when he speaks again.

"As you know, initially I thought we could leverage your association with the king and make it work to our advantage. But frankly, Amelia, it's a liability. You're detracting from what we're trying to do here, and I strongly recommend you consider doing the right thing and step aside."

"Are you firing me? Didn't we have this conversation a few months ago?"

His lip curls into a snarl. "Amelia, let me make myself clear: I am not firing you. I am merely suggesting you consider what is best for you, given your personal situation, and what is best for the foundation as a whole. In the meantime, we're going to have to limit your interface with partners and staff. I don't want you attending any internal or external meetings."

"William, how am I meant to do my job without attending any meetings?"

"We'll adjust your duties as necessary to allow you to work independently."

I force myself not to roll my eyes. There's no use in antagonising him, but damn it, I can't let this go. I've given too much of my life to this place to just disappear quietly. "William, I understand what you're saying, but I don't agree. We've had this conversation before, and I'll keep having it for as long as it takes for it to sink in. I am an excellent lawyer. I add value to this foundation, and I deserve your respect. You can hide me away, but I'm not planning to quit my job. If you want me out, you'll have to fire me."

He shakes his head and stands up. "Amelia, I'm not going to engage with you when you're being hysterical like this. I'd suggest you call your driver and go home."

With that, he turns and walks out before I can respond. It's probably a good thing he left quickly because hot tears are rolling down my cheeks. How do I keep ending up in this situation where my boss is trying to get rid of me? Do I worry that I'm not experienced enough or talented enough to run the legal department for a charity that manages programs worth hundreds of millions of pounds? Of course. *Constantly*. But deep down, I know those worries are me indulging my insecurities. I am good enough. Even so, doubt niggles at me. Something feels different this time, and I don't like it at all.

I wipe my tears away, do a quick make-up fix so it's hopefully not obvious I've been crying—the last thing I need right now is someone in the car park selling a photo of me looking all puffy-eyed to a paper—and collect my PPOs on the way down to the basement. I'm desperate to talk to Eddie about this, but he's hosting a roundtable for European ambassadors this afternoon, so he probably won't be able to check his phone. Given their work situations, Lucy and Emma wouldn't understand this particular issue, and Penny is always supportive but can't relate to the palace side of things. Maybe I should talk to Caroline? She did help me the other day. I dial her number.

"Hello, Amelia, how are you?"

"Hi, Caroline. I'm all right, kind of. Are you around KP? I'm having a bit of a rough day and need someone to talk to."

"Of course! Mummy still won't let me flee back to the country, so I'm at her house. Come over whenever you can."

I breathe a sigh of relief. "Thanks so much. I'm on my way."

I hang up and tap Michael on the shoulder. "Can we please go to 1A instead of home? I'm going to visit Caroline."

"Of course, ma'am."

When the car pulls up outside Apartment 1A at Kensington Palace, I hold my breath. At twenty-plus rooms and four storeys high, describing it as an apartment seems somewhat inadequate. The imposing building had been Albert and Louisa's home for over forty years, since well before Albert became king. When he took the throne, they stayed at Buckingham Palace, but they never had much of a chance to settle in. Louisa was back at 1A less than a day after Albert died. It's where Eddie, Caroline, and Leo grew up, and she insisted it was much more her home than Buckingham Palace would ever be.

As I'm standing outside staring, a PPO appears. "Good afternoon, ma'am. Are you visiting Her Majesty or Princess Caroline?"

"I'm here to see Caroline."

"Very well, ma'am. Please go in. Bertha will show you through."

He holds the door open for me to enter and nods towards

Michael, who takes the sign I've been successfully handed over to the protection of Louisa's PPOs.

In the foyer, I'm greeted by a maid—Bertha, I assume. "Good afternoon, ma'am. Is her Royal Highness expecting you?"

"Yes, I spoke to her on the way over."

"Excellent, come through then. She's in the sitting room."

As I walk along behind Bertha, I gaze around the enormous foyer, trying to calculate how high the ceilings are. They must be at least twenty feet. And the floors! The floors are a spectacular checkerboard of oversized white and black marble tiles, worn down in places by hundreds of years of foot traffic. This apartment is significantly grander than the other palace residences I've visited. It was clearly designed to impress—and probably intimidate—visitors.

As we round a corner, Bertha stops in front of a large mahogany door and knocks. Caroline's voice sails out into the corridor. "Come in!" Bertha opens the door and stands aside for me to pass through into the former king's sitting room. I walk in, and it's . . . not what I expected. I try to keep my expression neutral as I gaze around, drinking it all in. The room, which features a collection of mismatched and fraying floral sofas and chintz armchairs arranged around a television, could kindly be described as cluttered. There are at least seven bookcases and five side tables scattered around the room, all piled high with books, papers, and random knick-knacks. The walls are covered in paintings of horses and wind-whipped English seascapes, which look, to be honest, pretty damn miserable.

Caroline rises from the sofa and comes over to give me a hug. "Hello there. Come and sit down."

I search around for somewhere to sit and see that, other than where Caroline was sitting, all the armchairs and sofas have old newspapers or dog blankets scattered over them. Caroline looks at me, an amused smile playing on her lips. "You haven't been here before, have you?"

"No, I haven't," I say. "It's, uh . . ."

She lets out a peal of laughter. "It's quite something, isn't it? I'm so used to it I sometimes forget. You didn't grow up in houses like these, so I expect you're even more confounded by it." She grabs a stack of newspapers off a sofa, tosses them onto one of the coffee tables, and gestures for me to take a seat. "You see, one of the delightfully odd things about older generations of aristocrats is that most of them are certified hoarders. They've grown up in houses where the spare rooms and attics are packed with hundreds of years' worth of family detritus, so they never throw anything away. They can also be rather cheap. Mummy has lived here for decades and has a state-funded renovation budget, but she would never dream of replacing a perfectly good armchair simply because it doesn't match the other ones. Buying new furniture is terribly gauche if you ask her. It also doesn't help most of the aristos in old houses spend so much money on heating rooms with ludicrously high ceilings and fixing holes in leaky roofs that there's barely any money left for furniture."

"Wow, I had no idea. I assumed all the palace residences were renovated like Ivy Cottage and Eddie's place."

"Oh no, not at all! You can thank Eddie and Em's love of home renovation shows for the improvements to the cottages."

"I'll have to send a thank-you letter to HGTV. I'm not sure I would have been so keen on moving into Wren House if it looked like this. Clutter gives me anxiety."

"Don't worry, give it a few decades, and you'll barely notice it anymore. Perhaps one day you'll even be looking for a copy of a newspaper from 1987 and be glad someone kept it conveniently located on the bookshelf."

"I mean absolutely no offence when I say I really hope that never happens."

Caroline smirks. "We'll see. Anyway, enough about the peculiar interior decor of the British upper classes. What happened today? You sounded rather upset when you called earlier."

My shoulders slump, and the air drains from my lungs. "My boss basically told me I'm a terrible lawyer, a liability to the foundation, and he's going to fire me. Again. We went through this like three months ago."

"My, that is dramatic! Is that, er, exactly what he said?"

I shrug. "No, not exactly. He said he wants me to consider resigning and avoid all meetings in the meantime because I'm a distraction. My being in meetings means all people want to do is gawk and ask questions about Eddie."

"Well, I think that's equally ridiculous. He can't expect you to hide away and not do your work properly. You earned your job, and it's important to you."

"It is important to me. I've worked so hard for years to be a good lawyer and earn the respect of countless men like William who only want to deal with people who look like them. I love what I do, and I'm proud of it. Until I met your brother, my career was the most important thing in my life."

"Right," Caroline says, clapping her hands together. "In that case, you can't go down without a fight. If something is important to you, it's worth annoying a William or two in order to defend."

I nibble my bottom lip. "The problem is, I think he might be right this time. Last time he tried to shift me out of my role into something ceremonial, I fought it because I knew it was unfair. But this time, I'm not so sure. To tell you the truth, I haven't been doing a great job lately—I've been distracted, I've been making mistakes, I haven't been as committed as I should be. I'm not convinced I can manage a life with Eddie and my job."

"I'm sure you're being too harsh on yourself. You've had a bad few weeks. It happens."

"I don't know. It's more than just that I'm struggling at work. It's that I don't feel like myself since Eddie became king and I moved in here. I'm not sure what I want in life anymore."

Caroline clucks sympathetically. "This life can be extremely challenging. I understand that better than most people in the family. But it's not that way for everyone. Some people thrive in this world and find great purpose in it. I can't promise you'll be one of those people, but I think you owe it to yourself to take the time to find out."

"It feels like too much."

"Depending on how things pan out, your current job may be too much. Have you thought about other options? What are you going to do when you and Eddie get married? I don't want to discourage you from trying to make your job work for now if that's what you decide you want to do, but when you get married, you won't be in a position to maintain a nine-to-five."

I let out a puff of air. "I haven't really thought about it. Eddie says he wants to marry me, but everything has been so up in the air, and the idea of actually getting married feels like a pipe dream. I don't want to plan a life around something that may not happen."

"I believe it will happen, dear. I know my brother, and I know he's never been as happy as he is with you. It's a question of when, not if."

"Even if that's true, I wouldn't know how to start planning a life as queen. Henry has made it emphatically clear he wants me to have nothing to do with the kind of palace duties I'm interested in, and as you've said, I won't be able to keep my legal job. I don't know what other options there are."

"Happily, you have some time to figure it out. Perhaps the best way to start would be to think about what you enjoy about your job and what you most want to achieve. Then we can think about ways you can incorporate those things in a job that's more compatible with the life of a full-time royal."

"That's extremely sage advice."

Caroline bows her head to me with a flourish. "Thank you, dear. It's because I've been through it all before. I rather hope you manage to navigate it better than I did."

"Fundamentally, what I love about my job is knowing I'm making a difference. I enjoy the challenge of complicated legal work and the thrill of a negotiation, but the impact of the foundation's work is what motivates me most."

A smile spreads across Caroline's face. "Well, that's rather convenient. This family happens to be in the making-a-difference business, so I'm sure you'll be able to find an opportunity that works quite nicely. It would be better if Henry would get off his high horse and let you assist with family engagements and patronages, but you don't need him—you can do it by yourself." Suddenly her eyes light up. "It's just occurred to me that a friend of mine might be able to help. Can I set up a meeting?"

I bite the inside of my cheek. "Do you mind if I pass for now? Given Eddie and I aren't even engaged, I don't want to make any big changes yet. I feel like I need to refocus on doing a better job at the foundation for the moment."

"Whatever you feel is best, dear. But if you ever want to discuss your options, you know where to find me."

CHAPTER 26

A WEEK LATER, I'm sitting at my desk in Eddie's spare room—sorry, *our* spare room—reading the first sentence of a grant agreement for about the seventh time, when I hear a loud whistle coming from downstairs. At this point, I'll take any form of procrastination, so I jump out of my chair and head to the landing to see where the noise is coming from. Leaning over the railing, I see Lucy and Emma standing in the foyer wearing all-black athleisure outfits I'm certain have never been anywhere near a gym.

"Hey, what are you two doing here? Eddie's not home."

"We're aware of that, darling. We're here to see you," Emma says.

Lucy grins at me, which I'm coming to realise is normally a sign she's about to say or do something completely mad. "We're here on a morale-boosting mission. You've been hideously glum lately, and frankly, it's depressing. We don't need that kind of negative energy circulating."

I slump. "I've been a bit down. Things have been harder than I expected here and at work."

"No need to explain," Lucy says. "Clearly, our dear cousin

doesn't know how to keep a woman happy, so we're going to step in."

"It's not his fault! He's been great. It's every—"

"Shh, shh," Lucy says, cutting in. "I said no need to explain. We understand Eddie has neglected you terribly and been an awful partner. We're all well aware he's an underwhelming human at the best of times. Lord knows why you put up with him."

"Admit it's all his fault, Amelia," Emma says. "And even if it's not, blame him anyway. That always makes me feel better."

I giggle and roll my eyes. "Fine, let's blame Eddie."

Emma claps her hands together. "Excellent! Now we're all agreed on that, let's cheer you up."

"How exactly are you going to do that?"

"Easy," she says, grabbing both my hands. "We're kidnapping you."

I gawk at her and then, out of the corner of my eye, see Lucy walking towards me, brandishing a blindfold. I knew that grin was trouble.

An hour later, I'm bundled out of a Range Rover and led blindly into a building and down a set of stairs.

"We've arrived!" Emma exclaims.

"Great. Can I take this blindfold off, then?"

"I suppose so."

I rip the blindfold off and find myself standing in front of a nondescript wooden door. I whip my head around, trying to figure out where we are. "Are we at Buckingham Palace?"

Lucy throws her arms out and spins around like she's a nun dancing in the Swiss Alps. "The one and only."

"Why did it take us an hour to get here, then? It's barely a ten-minute drive from home."

Lucy gurgles with laughter. "We wanted to throw you off the

scent. Where would the fun have been if you knew where we were going?"

"I was blindfolded! I still wouldn't have known where we were going."

"Details, details."

"The important thing is not where we are or how many times we drove around Hyde Park in a circle to confuse you," Emma says. "The important thing," she continues with a flourish, "is what's behind this door."

I peer around the corridor. I don't recognise it as one I've walked down before. Then I turn my attention to the heavy wooden door, painted white and surrounded by ornate architraves. In other words, it's exactly the same as the other seven hundred doors at Buckingham Palace.

"Okay, I give up. What's so special about this door?"

Emma smiles indulgently at me. "Everything, darling, everything."

Lucy reaches out and opens the door to reveal . . . another door. This one isn't your standard-issue two-hundred-year-old palace door, though. This door is made of sleek metal and has what looks like a fingerprint scanner instead of a door handle. Lucy glances around the corridor before gingerly placing a hand on the panel. Yup, definitely a fingerprint scanner. What on earth is going on? The scanner beeps, and the lock on the door clicks. Emma and Lucy bustle me into the dark room beyond. As the door slams shut, the lights come on, and I'm momentarily startled by light glinting everywhere. Diamonds. We're in a room full of diamonds. "Oh my god. Is this where they keep all the crown jewels?"

"Not *all* the crown jewels. Some of the most expensive bits and pieces are still stored at the Tower of London, but this is where the family's personal collection and all the pieces currently on loan from the crown are kept."

I wander over to a display cabinet against a wall and run my finger along the thin pane of glass separating me from a diamond and sapphire necklace featuring jewels the size of golf balls. "This place is amazing. You two really know how to cheer a girl up. I hope you didn't have any other plans this afternoon, because I'm going to spend hours looking at these beauties."

"Why just look at them when you can try them on?" Emma asks.

My eyes widen. "Can we do that?"

Lucy titters. "Do you see anyone here to stop us?" she asks, gesturing around the room.

"True. Actually, should we even be here? It seems like there should be security here."

Lucy clicks her tongue. "Security, schmurity. If we weren't meant to be in here unaccompanied, why would I be authorised to open the door?"

"I guess you're right . . ."

"Don't listen to her," Emma says. "She shouldn't be able to get in here at all. She used her feminine wiles to convince a security guard to give her access years ago, and he forgot to take it away."

Lucy slaps Emma on the arm. "Em, you weren't meant to tell her that part!"

"It's fine," I say, laughing. "I won't tell on you, mainly because I'm blinded by diamond sparkle."

"Excellent! In that case," Lucy says, with a glint in her eye, "what do you want to try on first?"

Soon, I'm sitting on a red velvet slipper chair in front of a large mirror while Emma lowers a tiara onto my head. The tiara is a stunning platinum band set with hundreds of brilliant cut diamonds and seven emeralds, including one of the biggest jewels I've ever seen, even after an hour of roaming through the vault's display cases. As the tiara settles onto my head, I let out an involuntary gasp. Even in a dirty T-shirt and jeans full of holes—the worn-out-from-having-been-used-for-ten-years kind, not the fashionably ripped kind—the woman in the mirror wearing the tiara, delicate diamond earrings, and a necklace that's heavy with emerald drops doesn't look like me. She looks like someone else entirely.

Emma whistles. "Look at you, lady! You look fantastic."

"She's right," Lucy says, nodding. "You look more than fantastic. You look like a future queen."

There's a tight squeeze in my stomach, and my chest suddenly feels tight. I shake my head—carefully, of course, don't want to dislodge the priceless jewels. "Don't say that."

"Why ever not?"

"Because I'm not . . . we're not . . ." I trail off, not sure how to finish that thought. Not sure I want to finish it.

"I know Eddie's been a bit of a coward, letting his fear of public opinion keep you two from taking the next step, but he loves you and is going to marry you one day."

My throat tightens, and I gulp. I can feel the tears building. "You don't know that. He says that's what he wants, but he seems totally unwilling to do anything about it. Besides, I don't know if it's what I want."

Lucy pats my shoulder. "Buck up, love. I don't want to hear any of this uncertainty from you. I know for a fact Eddie wants nothing more than to grow depressingly old with you, so don't you dare doubt that. I can't tell you what you want, but I think you'd be bonkers to leave. Who else is going to give you these kinds of baubles to play with?"

"And don't forget," Emma says, "marrying Eddie means you get to be related to us. If that's not a selling point, what is?"

I give a small laugh and gaze at the mirror, twirling an emerald in my fingers. Could this really be my life?

Emma claps. "Okay, enough introspection, please. Time to wrap up here."

I pout. "Do we have to put everything back?"

She barks with laughter. "Back? No, no. We're taking these to go." She pulls three canvas tote bags out of her handbag.

My eyebrows shoot up. "We're taking things with us? That definitely feels like something we're not meant to be doing."

"Who's to say what we're 'meant' to do?"

"Uh, the police?" I say, sceptically. "I'm pretty sure taking this jewellery with us would be an actual crime."

"You know what's a crime? Leaving all these lovely jewels down here in the dark. We're giving them a day out."

I realise this is just another ridiculous Emma and Lucy scheme, and I should be the sensible one and tell them to stop. But . . . I do really want to keep wearing this tiara. What's the worst that could happen? Are they really going to throw us in jail? Hmm, they actually might. I'm pretty sure the princesses would find a way to get us out of trouble, though. Surely. Before I can talk myself out of it, I pull out my earrings and drop them into a tote. "Let's do this."

Lucy and Emma squeal with delight and set to work selecting their party favours. Emma walks to a closed cabinet in the corner and opens it up, revealing a selection of tiaras and brooches.

"What are those?"

"Ah," she says, extracting a tiara made of loops of diamonds, "this is the cabinet of jewels-that-must-not-be-named."

I stare at her blankly.

"They're the politically unacceptable pieces," Lucy says, lowering her voice. "You know, gifts from despots and Russian oligarchs who turn out to be heavily involved in organised crime. They're beautiful, but they don't get out much given their history."

"Poor loves, it's not their fault," Emma says, tutting and tucking a tiara into her bag.

A COUPLE of hours later we're at KP, lounging on the sofa and eating cookies left over from one of Eddie's middle-of-the-night baking frenzies and watching *Grand Designs*.

"All right, guesses, please, ladies," Emma says. "How far over budget will they be? I'm saying three hundred thousand pounds."

"No, it has to be at least five hundred," I say. "Underground pools don't come cheap, especially when you're building them under sixteenth-century flour mills."

Lucy is about to weigh in when there's a loud cough. I glance up and see Eddie standing in the doorway.

"You're home!" I jump up and give him a quick kiss. "How was your day?"

Eddie looks at me, brow raised. "Less exciting than yours, by the looks of it."

I wrinkle my nose. "I know you love renovation-themed TV, but I'm not sure I'd describe a *Grand Designs* marathon as super exciting."

He doesn't respond and instead points at my head. I go to rake a hand through my hair and hit something hard. Oops, the tiara. How did I forget about that? "It's not what it looks like."

"Oh, really?" Eddie asks, a small smile tugging at the corner of his mouth. "So while I've been hard at work, the three of you *didn't* break into my vault and steal what looks to be at least fifty million pounds worth of jewellery?"

"Well," I say, my cheeks burning, "when you put it like that, it's pretty much exactly what it looks like."

"Amelia, you're the lawyer here. You're supposed to be above petty crime."

"It was all us, cousin," Emma calls out. "We put her up to it."

Eddie spins to face her. "Don't worry, Em, I assumed that. You're a terrible influence."

"And proud of it," she says. "Also, I take offence to you referring to it as a petty crime. If I'm going to commit a crime, it's jolly well going to be a serious one."

Eddie chuckles. "Striving for excellence as always, I see."

"Always," she says with a wink.

"Well, I think I'll leave you all to your afternoon of debauchery, but I'm going to have to insist on taking the crown jewels with me."

Lucy snorts. "Pretty sure they're attached."

Eddie rolls his eyes and sticks out his hand. "Mind out of the gutter, Lucy. Hand over the diamonds."

"I'll give you the necklaces, but you'll have to pry Anastasia from my cold, dead hands."

"Anastasia?" Eddie asks with a raised eyebrow.

"The Russian tiara a delightful man who ended up having a teensy, tiny murder problem gave Mummy. She's my favourite, and she never gets a day out. Let her live a little!"

"I don't even know where to start with that," Eddie says, shaking his head. "If you don't want it to start with me calling security, though, I'd recommend you hand her over."

She huffs and starts flinging pieces into a bag. "Fine. You're no fun."

"Perils of being the one in charge, I'm afraid."

He takes the bag from Lucy and nods. "A pleasure, as always, ladies. Mils, I'll see you for dinner."

CHAPTER 27

I'M busy proofreading a contract in the office one morning when I get a message from Caroline.

Caroline: *I know you didn't want to speak to anyone about other job options, but I gave my friend Nicole your details anyway. Even if you don't want to make any changes, she'd be a good person for you to know. She may call you today xx*

I barely have the mental space to do my current job, so I'm definitely not in the right headspace to think about new jobs. Then again, going out for coffee with someone would definitely be more fun than this proofreading. I flip through the stack of paper on my desk—almost 200 pages to go. What a day.

When I hit 113 pages to go, my phone rings with a number I don't recognise. I let it go to voicemail and then listen to the message. "Hi, Amelia, it's Nicole Philips from UNICEF here. Caroline gave me your number. I'd love to meet for coffee if you've got time. I'm in London until the day after tomorrow, so call me when you can."

Nicole Philips. The name sounds familiar. Maybe she's been involved in some work with the foundation? I pull out my phone and search for her on LinkedIn. A profile pops up showing a young brunette smiling broadly. Nicole Philips, Programs Manager at UNICEF. Reading her profile, it looks like she runs UNICEF's programs for refugees across Europe and Africa. It's an impressive job for a woman who, based on my stalking of her education and job history, can't be older than thirty-five. I guess it never hurts to have more connections in the industry. Meeting with her doesn't have to mean I'm looking for a new job.

I call her number, and she answers on the second ring.

"Hello, Nicole speaking."

"Hi, Nicole, it's Amelia Glendale from the Prince's Charitable Foundation. I'm returning your call."

"Amelia, hi! Thanks for getting back to me so quickly. As I said in my message, Caroline has told me a lot about you, and I was hoping we could meet."

"I'd love that. When are you free? You said you're in town for a couple of days?"

"Yes, I'm only in London until tomorrow afternoon and then off again to Greece. Is there any chance you can meet today?"

I look down at the 113 pages of dense contract I have left to check for misplaced commas. "Sure, does three o'clock work?"

"Absolutely. I'll send you the address of a café."

"Perfect, I'll see you then."

AN HOUR LATER, I hop into my car and give the driver the address of a coffee shop in Soho. It's your standard cool café—the kind of place where they've spent an eye-watering amount of money to make everything look industrial and slightly run-down. When we arrive, I duck into the café with Michael and PPO Elba trailing a respectful distance behind me. They're in civilian clothes to blend in, but they never quite seem to manage it—there's something about their impeccable posture, stony expressions, and enormous muscles that mean they always stand out in a crowd. They take a seat at a table in the corner as I scan the room for Nicole. I spot her waving to me from a table across the room.

"Amelia!"

I smile and walk over to her. "Hi, you must be Nicole. I shouldn't admit this, but I recognised you from your LinkedIn. I read your profile earlier and am so impressed by what you do."

"Lovely to meet you. And thank you. I feel incredibly fortunate to have landed in this role."

"I'd love to hear more about it."

Over chai lattes, Nicole tells me about the projects under her umbrella and the travel she does visiting refugee camps and communities all over Europe and Africa. It sounds incredible.

"So," she says, after telling me about a project a member of her team is setting up to improve access to clean water in a camp in Greece, "what do you want to do?"

I laugh nervously. "That's the big question. I'm embarrassed to say I haven't figured out the answer yet."

"Perfectly understandable. Caroline told me you've been having some issues juggling your current role with family life. I've never been in your position, but I grew up in the same circles as Caroline and her brothers, so I know what a circus their lives can be."

I sigh. "It's really tough. I want to keep working, but it's been difficult lately. I don't know if I'm interested in changing jobs, though. Any kind of legal job is going to be demanding. At least at the foundation people understand my situation. Well, some of them do."

Nicole stirs her latte thoughtfully. "Have you considered a non-legal role? I have something I think could work well for you."

"Hm," I say, scrunching up my face. "William—our CEO—suggested I move into more of a spokesperson role a while ago, but I'm not keen on taking a job where I'm mainly used for photo ops. I want to do real work, you know?"

"Absolutely. That's not quite the kind of role I'm suggesting. Would you be open to something on the strategic side of project development? I've heard about the work you did on the vaccination clinic program, and I think you could do good work in project development."

"What would that look like? I don't think I'm even remotely qualified for that kind of thing."

"You wouldn't need any formal qualifications. They never hurt, of course, but you've spent time in the not-for-profit industry, and I'm sure you have a lot of knowledge already. I'm envisioning a position where you help with researching opportunities, developing project pitches, and evaluating the outcomes of existing projects. You'd be reporting to me, and you'd be able to do all the research and pitch development work from home. You'd also do the kind of travel I was talking about earlier to go and see your ideas come to life and figure out how to improve operations."

"Wow," I say. "That sounds fantastic. I still don't think I'm qualified, though. I wouldn't even know where to start."

"I'd be willing to bet you're a fast learner. I've heard great things about you from some of my friends who've come across you through the foundation. I'm also fairly certain that being a lawyer will have given you good research skills."

"Hm, true. I probably couldn't commit to full-time hours, though."

Nicole smiles. "That's okay. As I mentioned earlier, I know being in the royal family can be time-consuming. I'd be happy to work around your other commitments. This kind of role would be fairly easy to scale up or down the time commitment by limiting how many projects you're involved in at a time."

This is so tempting. I could have more control over what I was doing, and I'd get to travel more—both things I've been missing in my current job. But I'm scared. I've always liked my job, and maybe more importantly, I'm good at it. The idea of starting an entirely new career where I have to learn how to do everything from scratch is terrifying. Especially if I'm doing it at a time when my life is in flux and I don't know if I'll be able to commit enough time to it to make it work. At least if I stay in my current job, I don't need to prove myself. If you ignore William, everyone at work trusts and respects me. Building a reputation in a new environment takes time and effort, and I'm not at a place in my life where I'd be able to do that.

"Thank you so much for the offer," I say. "But I'm going to have to politely decline. I'm a lawyer, and that's what I know how to do. If you ever need one of those, you know where to find me."

"I understand. Please consider it, though. I think it's a role you could grow into and mould to fit your life if your circumstances change."

If I become queen, she means. It still seems like such a remote possibility, though. I can't make life-changing decisions based on the assumption it's going to happen. Especially with Henry doing his damnedest to get rid of me.

CHAPTER 28

After dinner one evening, Eddie and I are sitting together in front of the fire in our living room when our phones buzz in unison.

Charli: *Just got an advance copy of an article from* The Times. *I recommend you read it.*

Eddie groans. "Good lord, what is it this time? Is someone else claiming Dad was their father? I swear, if he turns out to have as many secret children as Prince Albert over in Monaco, I will dedicate the rest of my existence to finding a way to bring him back to life so I can kill him myself."

"I have no idea what it's about, but if Charli thinks we should both read it, we should probably open it and find out. She knows we've been stressed lately. Maybe it's something to cheer us up—like a listicle of photos of dogs who think they're people, or a 'Which Lindsay Lohan character are you?' quiz."

Eddie raises an eyebrow. "What do you think the chances of puppy photos are?"

"Ugh, not high. I'd probably even say low."

"Just as I suspected."

"Only one way to find out," I say, gritting my teeth. I click on the file transfer link she's sent us and download the document. I read the headline—*Exclusive: Lady Isla Barrington sets the record straight*—and glance at Eddie, who rolls his eyes.

"Do we really need to read more of this drivel?"

"If Charli sent it to us, we probably should. It might not be what you expect."

He gives a joyless smile. "We'll see."

Lady Isla Barrington has finally broken her silence on revelations about her parentage and rumours that have been raging about her intentions to take on the palace. Thirty-two-year-old Lady Barrington sat down exclusively with The Times *to discuss her experience and hopes for the future.*

"I was shocked and utterly devastated when I first heard about King Albert's relationship with my mother and my parentage. I found it incredibly difficult to process and, for a time, couldn't quite believe it," Lady Barrington said. But over time, she came to accept that King Albert had been her biological father. Despite the revelation, Lady Barrington is adamant her family and identity haven't changed. "Whatever happens, I'm still the same person and the man who raised me is still my father."

The initial news of King Albert and Lady Sumner-Jones's affair was met with shock around the world. The revelations were quickly followed by reports that Lady Barrington was planning to sue the royal family for the right to be known as a princess and a place in the order of succession. The unprecedented lawsuit would, if successful, lead to her being installed as heir to the throne and potentially change the course of the nation's history forever. However, it is an outcome that will never come to pass—Lady Barrington has no intention of taking any legal action against the palace. She commented, "I would like to take the opportunity to set the record straight and put all wild speculation to bed. The rumours about me suing the palace are both unfounded and extremely hurtful. I have absolutely no desire to be a princess. I cherish my privacy and quiet life."

Of her reportedly icy reception from King Edmund and other royals,

Lady Barrington said, "I have had a long association with the royal family, and no member of the family has ever been anything but courteous and kind to me. I wish them well and would never want to cause them any undue stress."

...

I look up from my phone and see Eddie hunched over, reading with his brow furrowed. I wait until he gets to the end of the article and watch in silence as he scrolls up and reads it again. He places his phone in his lap and rubs his temples. "Did you know she was going to do this?"

"No, I haven't spoken to her since the dinner debacle. When I met with her a while ago, I did tell her you were stressed about the rumours and the palace was stopping you from making a statement, though. Looks like you won't have to now."

"This will take much more pressure off us than me making a statement would have. She's the only one who can say with any authority that she won't be suing us. Why would she do it, though? I don't understand her motivation. Other than my failed attempt to contact her, we haven't done much to earn her loyalty with the way we've been treating her."

I cock my head to the side. "Well, call me crazy . . . but it might be she genuinely doesn't want anything from you and thought she could help you and the rest of the family by putting the rumours to bed."

"You may be right." He lolls his head back and closes his eyes. "What should I do?"

"I'm not going to tell you how to deal with the situation—not again. But if you're asking me what I'd do if I were you, I'd reach out to her again. She's done a good thing here. I'm sure she'd like to know you appreciate it."

"How am I going to do that, though? You saw how Henry reacted last time."

"Can you talk to him again? The statement might change things."

I can see the gears turning as he sits and considers things. "You know what? You're right. Surely in light of this, Henry will be able to see Isla isn't a threat to anyone."

~

ON SATURDAY NIGHT, I'm sitting at the kitchen island, eating cheese and crackers while I watch Eddie make dinner. "Mm, dinner smells delicious."

"It should do," he says, wiping his brow with the back of his hand. "This meal has been a labour of love. Do you realise how complicated boeuf bourguignon is to make?"

"I'll have you know I've seen *Julie and Julia* at least three times, so yes, I do. But I can also barely make toast, so any kind of actual cooking seems pretty difficult to me." I spread a layer of eggplant dip on a cracker and top it with a wedge of double brie. "I make a mean charcuterie board, though, so if you ever want to switch to a diet entirely made up of cheese and quince pastes, I'll be happy to take over dinner preparation responsibilities."

"Thanks, Mils, I'll keep that in mind. Although I'm fairly certain that's the kind of diet that killed off Henry the Eighth, so perhaps I should retain control of the kitchen for now."

"Please yourself," I say, popping a slice of salami into my mouth. As I do, the doorbell rings. "I'll get it!"

I bound to the door and fling it open to find Lucy, Emma, and Caroline standing outside.

"Movie night!" squeals Lucy, holding a cocktail aloft.

I shake my head. "There are drinks here, you know."

"Oh, I know, darling. This was one for the road."

"Lucy, you live fifty-three steps from here. I've counted."

"Amelia dear, if you've counted how many steps there are between our houses, you clearly need a drink even more than I do."

"Touché," I say, throwing my hands up in surrender. "Anyway, come in. Eddie's making something unnecessarily complicated for dinner and did more stress baking overnight, so there's a four-layer hummingbird cake in the kitchen that looks incredible. Meanwhile, all I've done is stick some cheese on a plate."

As we walk into the foyer, Emma's stomach rumbles. "It smells amazing. Goes to show that he's good for something, even if he is a bloody useless king. Did you know he's had the top job for months now and hasn't had so much as a single one of my speeding fines withdrawn? I tell you, useless."

Caroline rolls her eyes. "Em, have you ever actually paid a speeding fine? I'm utterly convinced you collect them."

"Look," Emma says, shrugging, "I've never been one for finances. I leave all of that to someone else, but I assume they get taken care of somehow. And for your information, I haven't got a single ticket this week. Other than the one on Tuesday."

"Impressive," Caroline deadpans.

In the kitchen, we all gather around the island.

"Hello, everyone," Eddie says from in front of the stove where he's standing watch over a large cast-iron pot.

"Evening, cousin dear," Lucy says. "Food smells divine. But this," she says, gesturing to my charcuterie board, "this is the highlight. Outstanding cured meat selection."

Emma fans herself, and Caroline cheers, "Hear, hear! Perhaps a perfect prosciutto-to-salami ratio. Quite an achievement."

Eddie groans. "Did Amelia put you lot up to this?"

"Whatever do you mean?" Lucy asks, before throwing me a wink. "I merely tell things as I see them. And as I see it, this platter is clearly the culinary highlight of the night."

"Why do I even bother cooking for you ingrates?"

Caroline walks around the island to give Eddie a hug. "Because you love us."

"Sadly, I do. I expect life would be much easier if I didn't," he says.

"Ah," Emma says, wagging a finger at him, "easier perhaps, but infinitely duller. You're lucky to have each and every one of us. *Especially* me."

Lucy plucks a slice of cheese from the platter. "As they say, family is one of life's greatest gifts. Speaking of, how does everyone feel about the statement?"

"I thought it was a jolly decent thing for her to do," Caroline says. "She's a good egg, really. Always has been."

"I must admit, it has taken a lot of pressure off us," Eddie says. "The more ridiculous news stories have dried up, and approval ratings are bouncing back nicely. Charli and Cornelius are thrilled."

"Have you considered talking to her?" Caroline asks.

"I would like to speak to her, to thank her for issuing the statement, but I'm not sure Henry would be too keen on it. I tried to call her once before, and when Henry found out, he was apoplectic. I'm hoping the statement has changed his position, so I'm going to try to convince him."

Emma scoffs. "Oh, come on, Ed! Don't try to convince him. We all know it won't work. Just *tell* him you're going to reach out to her. Or, even better, do it without telling him! She's done us all a favour here. Even if you're not ready to have any kind of ongoing relationship with her, she deserves a thank you."

"We've respected your wishes and not spoken to her ourselves," Lucy says. "But it feels wrong for none of us to even acknowledge what she's done. I'm with Emma. You should talk to her without telling Henry, better to ask for forgiveness and all that."

"Besides," says Emma, "as I keep trying to remind you, you're the boss here, cousin. You don't even need to ask for forgiveness."

She's absolutely right. Eddie needs to get past his subservience to Henry and start doing what he thinks is right. But given how things went last time I encouraged him to go behind Henry's back, I'm going to stay right out of this.

Eddie rubs his jaw. "I'll consider it, but he gave me the

tongue-lashing of the century last time I tried. No, if I'm going to speak to her, I'll need Henry's blessing. I'll talk to him tomorrow." He turns to me. "Will you come with me, Mils? You can help me convince him."

Well, there goes my plan to stay out of it. "Of course. Whatever you need."

AT TEN THE NEXT MORNING, I'm walking along the State Rooms corridor towards Henry's office. I knock on the mahogany door, and Henry's assistant answers the door and looks down her nose over her glasses at me. "Good morning, ma'am. Do you have an appointment?"

"Yes, His Majesty asked me to join him here. He might already be in with Henry?"

"Hm," she says, narrowing her eyes. "My schedule doesn't have you listed as attending this meeting. Please wait here while I check."

Right, I'll stand here, loitering in the hallway, then, I guess. I feel like telling her I can't stand Henry and the last thing I'd ever want to do is try to sneak into an extra meeting with him, but I'm not sure it would help my cause.

A few minutes later, she returns and gestures for me to enter the office. "Please come in."

I walk through the antechamber and into Henry's large office, where Eddie is sitting across from the desk. As I walk in, he turns towards the door and his face lights up. "Hey," I whisper. He pats the chair next to him, and when I sit there, he takes my hand and weaves his fingers through mine. Henry's lip curls, and he can barely conceal his sneer.

"As I was saying, sir, we will have a draft of your speech to parliament ready for your review by tomorrow morning. I'll need you to review it carefully to ensure it is ready for the opening ceremony in the new year."

Eddie nods. "Noted, thanks." He clears his throat. "Now, I have an item that wasn't on our agenda I'd like to discuss."

"Is that why we have a guest with us, sir?" he asks, giving me an appraising look.

"Yes, Amelia has something of an interest in the topic, so I asked her to join us."

Henry's eyes flick between Eddie and me before landing back on our clasped hands. "Sir, I trust this conversation isn't about a potential engagement—as we've discussed previously, my firm recommendation is that you not take any steps at this stage. As you are aware, if you insist on maintaining this relationship, my very strong view is that there should be no talk of an engagement for several years. At an absolute minimum, you must wait until after the coronation next year. But as we've discussed, announcing another engagement so soon will be seen as rash and cause significant issues. I won't let you lose any of the ground you've been gaining after Lady Barrington's statement."

If he insists on maintaining this relationship? Well, that's a slap in the face. Also, since when has Eddie been discussing our relationship with him? I'm trying to come up with a response that won't result in him calling security on me when Eddie speaks.

"Don't worry, Henry, I'm well aware of your position on Amelia's and my future." He squeezes my hand and mouths "Sorry" to me. "Funny you should mention the Isla situation, though, because that's actually what I wanted to speak to you about."

A cloud of confusion passes over Henry before he rearranges his face into a neutral expression. "What about it, sir? I don't believe there is anything further to discuss on the topic."

"Well, I've been reflecting on it, and since Isla took one for the team as it were and set the record straight with the media, I believe I owe her an apology. We here at the palace haven't treated her well at all, and I'd like to make amends."

Henry shakes his head violently. "Absolutely not. After your last attempt at reconciliation, you know full well where I stand on the issue."

"Henry, surely you can see she's trying to help us. Doesn't she deserve some thanks for that?"

"She doesn't *deserve* anything from you or this family. And what would you stand to gain from speaking to her? She's already addressed the media issues, and your approval ratings are recovering. You don't need anything else from her."

"I'm not trying to get anything from her," Eddie says, exasperated. "I want to apologise."

"Well, that's hardly a good enough reason to risk further media exposure. Regardless, if you engage with her, you may well be simply playing into her hands. Who knows what she was trying to achieve with her stunt. Perhaps it was all an attempt to lure you into approaching her."

Eddie scoffs. "You think she was using the statement to lure me into approaching her? To what end, Henry? What would that achieve?"

"We can't be sure, sir. It could be something as simple as her hoping to make some quick money off an association with you or something as sinister as her hoping to obtain more information from the family before bringing an action against you."

I grip the arm of the chair I'm sitting in, trying not to roll my eyes. Of course, it's part of Henry's job to worry about anyone who might cause an issue for the palace, but this is getting ridiculous. Clearly Isla was only trying to help. She's not so much as sent a single text to anyone in the family since the article came out. If she was trying to use it to get close to the family, she's doing a terrible job of it.

"Come on, Henry. Be reasonable here," Eddie says. "She's solved all the issues you were concerned about. I can't believe it was all part of some sinister plan. It's certainly not about money, since she's got plenty of that as is. She just inherited millions of pounds. I'm not proposing we move her into KP and buy matching Christmas pyjamas. All I'm suggesting is a phone call."

"Absolutely not, sir. It would be a mistake, and I won't allow it."

"You won't allow it?"

"No, sir, I won't. As I've said before, you don't appreciate all the potential implications of you making contact with Lady Barrington. It is simply not an option."

Eddie fixes his gaze on Henry. "You're being entirely unreasonable here, and I don't appreciate your tone. Let's keep things civil here so this conversation doesn't end up like the last one we had about Isla."

Henry bangs his fist on the desk with a thump. A vein in his neck twitches as he starts to yell. "You have so much to learn. You may be the king, but that's nothing more than luck. You would do well to remember which one of us got here based on skill and experience. I will not be disrespected!"

Eddie's jaw goes slack, and a shocked silence hangs in the air. How dare he speak to his boss like that? Eddie isn't normally an angry person, but I don't think this is going to end well for Henry. Eddie smacks his lips, and I brace myself for what comes next—is it going to be loud, explosive anger or a cold, calculating fury? After last time, there's no way he's going to sit back and take this kind of disrespect from Henry. Once he might get away with, but twice? Twice is too much.

"You're quite right, of course. Consider the issue dropped."

I'm sorry, what? I'm so confused by what has just happened. I turn to Eddie, and he gives a small, crooked smile. "It's time for us to go, Amelia."

"Uh, okay."

Eddie tugs at my hand, and we stand to leave. As we approach the door, he turns around. "Thank you for your time, Henry."

Henry simply nods. We walk in silence down the hallway to Eddie's office.

Once we're inside, he flops onto the sofa and groans. "Well, that didn't go quite the way I'd hoped."

Try to stay neutral here, Amelia, don't insert yourself in other people's fights. "Mm-hm."

He leans his head back over the arm of the sofa. "I might leave it for a few weeks and then try to raise it again."

Don't get involved, don't get involved.

"It seems highly unlikely he'll be receptive to the idea, though, so I'll probably have to drop it."

Okay, I can't do it. "Why should you have to drop something you care about? Henry isn't the king, you are! I don't get why you keep letting him walk all over you again and again."

He shoots up and frowns. "I don't let him walk all over me. He's my adviser—I take his advice. I couldn't do any of this without him. I'd be at an utter loss."

"Honestly, Eddie? You let him railroad you. I realise you're going through a big adjustment, and you're leaning heavily on your team because you're second-guessing yourself and your decisions. But guess what? Henry knows that too, and he's taking advantage of it. He has absolutely no respect for you. None."

"Come on, that's not fair. He's trying to help me navigate some incredibly sticky issues."

"I don't care what he's trying to do. Can you imagine your father ever letting his private secretary tell him who he was or wasn't allowed to speak to privately? Would you father have let an adviser get away with tapping his phone?"

"Of course not, but Father wasn't exactly one to take orders."

"Maybe you shouldn't be either. You're smart and capable and can make your own decisions if you start believing in yourself. I'm not going to demand you fire him, but I do need to know one thing."

"Anything."

Deep breath, in and out. "Is he the reason we're not engaged?"

Eddie pulls at his collar. "Well . . ." he says, and then trails off.

"Is he?"

"It's not as simple as that. But, yes, essentially I have accepted his advice that I shouldn't propose until after my coronation." He clears his throat. "Possibly until some years after it."

Years? This is unbelievable. I shake my head. "His advice? You've taken Henry's advice about our relationship? Great. Tell me this, Eddie, do you even want to marry me?"

"Of course I do!" he yells before looking at me, eyes full of pleading. "You know I do."

"So why don't you make it happen? There's nothing stopping us from getting married right now. You're the freaking head of the Church of England. I'm pretty sure you could get a priest here faster than I could change my outfit."

"Trust me," he says, clutching his head, "I would love to. But I can't break my word to Henry and put my desires ahead of the interests of the palace."

Welp, there it is. He loves me, but not enough to annoy an employee. Hot tears prick at the corner of my eyes. "Thanks for clarifying, Edmund. It's good to know where I stand."

He reaches for my hand, but I pull it away. "Oh, Amelia, don't be like that. I'm sorry about all of this, I truly am. But you must have known coming into this relationship things wouldn't be easy, and I don't always have the luxury of putting myself first."

"Sure, in theory I knew things would be complicated. But, Eddie, when we got back together and when I moved in with you, I thought I had your support. I didn't realise that I'd feel like I'm facing all of the challenges of palace life on my own or that I'd basically have to put my life on hold to be with you. Being the king's girlfriend is not at all the same as being a prince's girlfriend—I have so much more attention on me and so much less freedom. I'm stuck in a holding pattern where I can't keep living my old life, but the palace won't let me take on a new role as your partner either."

He hangs his head. "You're right. I was selfish when I asked you to move in here. I knew that Henry and the others weren't going to make your transition to this life easy, but I needed you here. Becoming part of this family comes with a steep learning curve and significant lifestyle adjustments. Before Dad went and flew his helicopter into the side of a mountain, I told myself we'd have years to live a relatively private life, and we could deal with everything else later. But as it turns out, later is now. "

"It is," I say with a nod. "So we're going to have to figure out how to deal with it. If we're going to make a go of this—if our relationship is going to work, and you're going to be the leader I know you can be—things are going to have to change. You need to trust yourself and take charge of your own direction. I'm not saying you can never take advice, but you can't blindly let other people control what you do. I sure as hell won't be letting Henry control my life."

"I can't just take control like that."

"Why not?"

"Because I'm *terrified.* Terrified I'll get things wrong, that people won't like me, that I'll be the one who brings down hundreds of years of tradition. I try to make decisions, and I just . . . freeze."

I can absolutely relate to the fear he's experiencing. It's exactly how I feel about making a move and taking a different path in my career at the moment. But he can't continue like this. "I know being too scared to take a risk feels awful. But the feeling isn't going to go away if you keep avoiding the issue by letting other people make all your decisions for you. The good thing is you're never on your own—you've got a whole palace full of specialist advisers. And you've got your family."

He drops his head and groans.

"Look," I say. "All I'm saying is you've got so many great

people behind you, even if you do fail, you won't be doing it alone. So maybe you could let go of a little bit of the pressure you put on yourself."

"I suppose I could try."

"I hope you do. While we're talking about things to let go of, you've got to get rid of Henry. I know you think he's trying to help, but he doesn't respect you, and I'm not going to sit back and watch him treat you like a naughty schoolboy. He speaks down to you and doesn't value your opinion at all."

"I can't do that. Firing people because you don't like them isn't exactly the way things are done around here."

"It's not only that I don't like him, it's that he's holding you back. He's never going to give you the freedom to rule in the way you want to."

"I'm not ready to make that kind of change."

"You said you want to marry me, but how is that ever going to happen if you keep working with Henry who has made it clear that he's vehemently against the idea?"

"That's not fair. Henry is happy for us to get married at the appropriate time."

I raise my eyebrow. "Really? That's not the impression I got."

"All right, 'happy' may be overstating it a tad. But he has said he will accept it as long as we wait long enough and ensure the timing doesn't clash with any campaigns or cause any optical issues."

"Eddie," I say with a sigh, "you could drive a train through the loopholes in that so-called approval. You don't need to be a lawyer to see he's clearly setting himself up to be able to change his mind later and say no."

"I'm sure he wouldn't do that. We'd just need to negotiate timing."

"I don't *want* to negotiate the timing of my relationship with public servants. I love you, and I want to marry you at a time *we* choose. And, being completely open with you, I'd prefer it be sooner rather than later. Do you know what being the king's girlfriend is like? I'm living in limbo. I feel like I have no real place here."

"Of course you have a place here. You're my greatest support. I couldn't do any of this without your support."

I scoff. "That's all very nice for you, but where's my support? I've been doing everything I can to support you—including going along with decisions I don't agree with—and feel like I'm getting nothing in return. I'm on your team, but are you on mine?"

He tries to pull me in towards him, but I push away. "Of course I am! Always."

"Then why is it always my opinions and goals that end up being sacrificed? It seems like when you say you want me on your team, what you mean is you want me to silently stand by or tell you that you're right. I won't do that. If this is going to work, it needs to be a real partnership. I'll always tell you the truth and have *your* best interests at heart—not your interests as king, or the interests of the country, but your interests as a person. But in return, you need to genuinely value to my input, and you need to make sure I have the support and respect of the palace."

"I wish I could give you that."

"You can! If we got married, I could take on a new position that legitimises me and gives me opportunities to do meaningful work myself."

Pain tears through his eyes. "I'm sorry, Amelia, but I can't."

Can't or won't? I sigh. "So, where does that leave us?"

"It leaves us exactly where we are now," he says. "We still have each other. Nothing has to change."

From where I'm sitting, it seems like everything has to change. For as long as Eddie and I are simply dating, I'll be under constant media and palace scrutiny. My life will be put on hold. The attention and need to be there for Eddie mean I can't maintain my current job or life, but the lack of an official place within the palace means I have no role here either. "That doesn't work for me, Eddie. I can't live this half-life anymore. Look, you're flying to Canada tomorrow. Why don't I stay with Penny while you're away? It would give us both a chance to decide where we want to go from here."

"I don't like the sound of that at all. I'd rather you stay here."

I shake my head. "I don't want to. I need to take some time away from the KP bubble to figure things out."

Eddie groans. "I won't stop you, but I'm begging you, please be here when I get home. I need you."

"Eddie, I love you. But if you can't promise to put me first, I can't promise to come back." I feel like my insides have been hollowed out. I don't want this to be the end for us, but things can't continue like this. I need a partner who is going to prioritise me, and Eddie may never be able to do that.

CHAPTER 29

BACK AT HOME, I pack some bags and haul them down the stairs. As I'm transferring them to the car parked outside the door, Caroline strolls around the corner.

"Hello there," she says, waving. "Going somewhere fun? Oh, did Ed finally invite you to go along on the Canadian tour?"

"No. Henry told him it wouldn't be appropriate for me to go, given the 'impermanence of our relationship.' I'm actually going to stay with a friend while he's away."

Her face falls. "Oh no! Do you not like staying here by yourself? You should have said something. I could have come by to keep you company. You're always welcome at Mummy's too."

"Thanks for the offer, Caroline, but it's not that. I need some space."

"Hm," she says, her brow knitting together. "Space to order too much pizza without the security guards who vet deliveries judging you for it or space from my brother?"

"The latter. Well, it's not about him as such, it's everything that comes with him. And a little about how he's dealing with it all. I need to step back a little and reassess."

She wraps her arms around me and gives me a tight squeeze.

"I understand. Do what you need to do, but please come back. It's not just Edmund who needs you here. Call me anytime if you want to talk. I'm normally far too British to voluntarily hug people, yet here I am draped all over you, so it's clearly a genuine offer."

"Thanks. I'll remind you of this if I end up calling in tears at three in the morning."

"I prefer to take calls during business hours, but for you, I'd answer anytime. Take care of yourself. If my clueless oaf of a brother doesn't fix whatever the issue is, I'll be ropeable."

If I can't make this royal life work for me, I'm going to miss having such good friends here at KP. I smile sadly at Caroline and pick up one of the bags sitting on the footpath. "I'd best be off. We'll talk, though."

"Have a good break. And make sure you come back soon." With that, Caroline nods primly and continues on her way down the path.

As I reach out to open the boot of the car, Michael appears to open it for me. He glances at the stack of bags sitting next to the car and back at me, but he says nothing. Instead, he opens the door and waits for me to climb into the car before wordlessly loading my luggage into the back. Settled behind the dark tinted windows, I feel a pang of homesickness. The thought of potentially losing my chosen family here makes me miss my family back home even more. I unlock my phone and send a quick message to my sister.

Me: *Hey, I know it's after midnight there so you won't be awake, but wanted to say I miss you. FaceTime soon?*

While I'm thinking of it, there's someone else I should send a message to—Isla. Eddie may be too scared to do anything that isn't approved by Henry, but she deserves for someone to acknowledge what she's done for the family.

Me: *Hi Isla, I wanted to reach out and say thank you for the statement you made. Edmund isn't in a position to be able to speak to you himself, but I wanted to make sure you know how much we all appreciate what you did.*

Isla: *Thank you, Amelia. I'm glad to be able to help the family in any way I can. Take care xx*

There. Eddie may not be doing the right thing, but at least I've done my bit.

Half an hour later, we pull up outside my old flat in Camden, and Michael jumps out of the car to check for crazed anti-monarchists and whatever other security threats he's paid to monitor. He quickly gives the all-clear signal and opens the car door for me. I know the routine well enough now that by the time he opens the door, I'm ready to climb out and make a quick dash to the flat. I slip the key I refused to return to Penny into the lock and let myself in. "Hello! Anyone home?" No answer. It's only three in the afternoon, and given Penny is a productive member of society, she'll probably be at work for another few hours still. Like I should be. Six months ago, I would've been horrified by how often I just don't turn up to the office these days. That reminds me, I've got approximately one million emails I need to reply to. I should probably do that while I wait.

I'm lying with my legs dangling over the edge of the sofa when the door opens, and the room fills with an ear-piercing scream. The noise makes me jump in shock, and as I try to twist around to figure out what's going on, I fall off the sofa and land on the floor with a thud.

"Amelia! You scared me! What are you doing here?"

"Catching up on emails. I'm down to thirteen unread. It's basically a miracle."

"Well, congratulations, that is an achievement. Is there a reason you're achieving it in my flat, though?"

"Oh, what am I doing here? Right. Well . . ."

Penny casts her eyes around the room and sucks in a sharp breath as her eyes land on the pile of bags.

"Say, Mils . . . I know you don't always pack light, but this looks like a whole lotta luggage for an afternoon drop-in."

"Ah, yes. Well, I was hoping I could come and stay for a little while. You haven't rented out my room, have you?"

"You insisted on keeping up with your share of the rent while you're living rent-free at KP, so no, I haven't."

"Perfect."

Penny looks at me like I'm a weirdly shaped Bronze Age tool in a museum display, clearly trying to make sense of what's going on and coming up short. To be fair, I probably look slightly weird given I'm still lying where I fell on the floor.

"Edmund is going on tour in Canada this week, isn't he?" she asks eventually.

"Yes, heading off tonight."

"Right." She narrows her eyes at me.

I should tell her why I'm here, but I've had such a surprisingly productive couple of hours, I'm not going to get dragged back down into the muck. Not yet. "Well," I say, picking myself up, "I'm going to unpack. Should we order Thai food for dinner?" Before she can answer, I grab a couple of bags and bound down the hall towards my old bedroom.

A couple of hours later, we're curled up on the sofa watching a made-for-Netflix Christmas movie. There's something perennially comforting about Christmas movies. Warm and fuzzy ones anyway, not the depressing kind where you spend an hour and a half watching a love story and then find out the love interest is actually some kind of ghost-slash-hallucination and the main character will in fact likely be alone forever. I'm looking at you, *Last Christmas*.

As the couple in the movie climb up onto a stage, ready to sing what I'm sure will be a supposedly improvised duet after realising it's up to them to save a Christmas charity concert, Penny turns to me. "So," she says, checking her watch, "by my count, I've given you a full three-hour grace period. Are you going to tell me what's going on? There's a limit to my patience, and as it turns out, the limit is three hours."

"Eddie's away, so I thought I'd come and get a refresher on what real life is like."

"Real life?"

"You know, life in a place where there aren't staff running around everywhere and where I don't sleep on sheets that cost more than a second-hand car. Although I probably should have brought some sheets with me. They're definitely better than a car."

"Okay, two things. First, right now there are two security guards outside the front door and one in the courtyard, so coming here hasn't solved your staff issue. Second, I've been your best friend for five years now—do you think jokes about sheets are going to distract me from finding out what's really going on?"

I cringe. "I hoped they might?"

"Well, too bad. You're going to need to give me a better explanation. Are you and Edmund having problems?"

"There are issues," I say, hanging my head.

"'You guys are done, and I'm going to have to readjust to having a full-time roommate' kind of issues, or 'you need a little break and will have a loved-up, not-safe-for-work reunion when he comes back in a couple of weeks' kind of issues?"

"I'm not sure. I love him so much—I've never had a relationship like this before. We just click, and he makes everything so much fun. But his life makes things so difficult. He's being completely controlled by this ogre of an adviser, Henry, who's been at the palace for about a million years. All he cares about are appearances and approval ratings. He works for Eddie, but Eddie is so worried about messing things up that he won't overrule him on anything. Henry knows it, and he's taking total advantage of it."

Penny regards me thoughtfully. "What kinds of things are we talking about? If he's been around the palace for a while, I could understand why Edmund would take his opinion seriously. He's probably just a responsible guy, trying to do his job."

"If it were only decisions about which events to attend or who to invite to a state dinner, it'd be fine. But it's more than that, it's personal stuff. He's the reason Eddie hasn't spoken to Isla, even though he wants to, especially after what she did with her interview."

"That seems like a bit of an overreach, but it has been a pretty hot media topic, so I can see why he'd be worried about it."

"Mm," I say, pursing my lips. "There's more. He's also told Eddie we can't get engaged or married for at least another few years. Turns out he was going to propose back in Kenya, but now he won't. He claims he still wants to get married, but he's scared to go against what Henry says."

"Okay, I take everything back. Henry is a monster. How dare he stop me from being maid of honour at a royal wedding? What does he look like? Maybe I can make him disappear. I have no idea where to find a hitman, but I'm sure I could figure it out. That's what the dark web is for, right?"

"Of course. Make sure you use a burner phone and a VPN, though. I can't have you ending up in jail."

"Amelia, I'm insulted you don't think I'd be able to get away with murder. I've listened to so many true crime podcasts, I could plan a perfect murder in my sleep."

"Sorry. I'm sure you'd make an excellent criminal."

Penny takes a bow. "Thank you, I would."

"To be clear, even though you would definitely never get caught, please don't murder or hire anyone to murder Henry. Things are messy enough already."

Penny grumbles and rolls her eyes. "Fine, I won't. But can I at least give him a piece of my mind or throw a glass of water at him or something? I'm not okay with him stopping you from marrying your dream guy. Although, with all due respect to said dream guy, I'm also not exactly okay with Edmund letting someone else make the decision either."

"Trust me, neither am I, Pen. We've talked about it, and he's so insecure at the moment. He doesn't trust himself to make decisions."

"But surely when it comes to your relationship, he can grow a backbone and tell Henry to keep out of it? Give him an ultimatum."

"I tried to convince him to fire Henry recently, and it didn't go anywhere. I haven't decided if I want to try again."

Penny's eyes widen. "Why not? Don't you want to marry him?"

"I do. I think. Maybe."

"Where's this doubt coming from, Mils?"

I pull a blanket tight around my shoulders. "I just . . . I haven't been happy lately. I feel like I have all the drawbacks of royal family life and none of the positives."

"None of the positives? What happened to those sheets you were raving about earlier?"

"Okay, that was harsh. Obviously, I enjoy living at the palace and being with Eddie. Things have been hard, though. I can't do anything without worrying about how it would look to a photographer, I can't go for a walk without a security team, and I can't focus on my job."

"Mils, I know the attention and security and everything must be a lot to get used to, but I'm sure you're still doing a good job." She reaches out and pats my knee. "You're always too hard on yourself."

"I'm not sure that's true. Did I tell you William wants to fire me again? And you know what? He probably should. I've been making mistakes and falling behind with work. I can't juggle everything."

"All right, so you quit your job then. Everyone would understand."

"That's not what I want to do, though. I like working and helping people. It's who I am. I don't feel like myself when I'm not working."

"I know you're an A-type overachiever and have your whole identity wrapped up in work, but you're more than your work. You're a complete person with or without it. A pretty cool person actually. Sure, you can't cook to save yourself, but I love you anyway. And so does Edmund."

"I don't know what I'd do without my job."

"So, what *are* you going to do? You don't want to leave your job or leave Edmund, but you can't do your job and be with him."

"I don't want to break up with him, but *something* has to change. In the meantime, I'm going to be sitting here on your sofa watching Hallmark movies and trying not to cry."

CHAPTER 30

I WAKE up the next morning and rub my puffy, dry eyes. Clearly the whole not crying thing didn't go so well. In fact, you could say it went badly. I'm propped up on a stack of pillows, scouring the internet for news stories about Eddie's arrival in Vancouver when there's a knock on the door. Before I can say anything, the door handle turns and Penny barges into the room.

"Hope you're not doing anything embarrassing because I'm coming in!"

"Do you have any boundaries?" I ask.

"Boundaries are for people you're hiding something from. You're reading about yourself online, aren't you?" She puts her hands up. "No, wait! You're reading stories about Eddie."

I flop back onto my bed and pull the blanket up over my face. I can't get away with anything in this house. "Don't judge me."

Penny lands with a thump on the bed next to me. "I'm your best friend, Mils—I'm not judging you. I'm worried about you."

I pull the blanket down a fraction and peek out at Penny. "Promise?"

"Of course. It's only natural you want to see what he's up to when you're not with him. You're not going to break up with him again, are you?"

"Ugh, I don't know. I don't want to, but no matter how much I think about it, I can't figure out a way to take control of my life again if I stay with him."

"Obviously I'll support you whatever you decide, but I want it on the record that I think you're barking mad to even consider that this life might be better than life as a royal girlfriend. You remember the hot water in this flat lasts for a maximum of four minutes, right? Bet limited hot water supply isn't an issue at KP."

"You're right, it's not. Living in happy obscurity might be worth the short showers, though."

Penny looks at me sceptically. "Let's agree to disagree on that one. I'm also not sure you'll ever be able to go back to a life of obscurity again after everything that's happened."

"It would take some time, but I think I could. No one cares what most of Leo's ex-girlfriends are doing now."

"True, but he's dated half of London, and none of his exes have ever lived at the palace or been accused of breaking him up from his fiancée. Twice."

"Sure, so it might take me a little longer for the interest in me to fade, but it would. Let's be honest, I'm a really boring person. Basically, all I ever do is work and go to the supermarket."

Penny rolls her eyes at me. "When you put it that way, you might be right."

"Speaking of work, given Eddie isn't here, I should probably drag my butt into the office."

AFTER A LONG AND frustrating day of work, I jump into my car to head home. On the way, I check Eddie's schedule for the day on a Canadian news website. One advantage of Eddie being on tour is his days are planned down to the minute, and the plans are very easy to find. You don't even have to venture into the live-tweet feeds—at least three newspapers have "King trackers" on their websites. I can see he's visiting a school in Vancouver in the morning, followed by a trip to the Granville Island market, then a walk about in the city, a tour of a sports stadium, and finally a dinner reception at City Hall. With the time difference, the only chance to speak to him will be after dinner. Luckily, he has a rule of leaving official dinners no later than ten o'clock to give himself time to prepare for the next day, so I should be able to call a little after six in the morning tomorrow London time. Why do the people I love insist on being in such inconvenient time zones?

Me: *Morning, hope you have a great day. Can't say I'm sorry to miss the sports thing, but the market looks great. Can you talk after your dinner tonight—half past ten your time?*

I'm not expecting a reply—Henry normally confiscates his phone during engagements—but before we reach Camden, my phone buzzes.

Eddie: *Caught me just in time, managed to hide my phone from Henry this morning, but I'm sure he'll find it before we make it to our first stop for the day. I'm looking forward to the market. I'm sure the pastries aren't as good as mine, but I'll sample some to make sure. We should come here together on holiday one day soon, I think you'd love it. Sleep well, we'll talk later.*

Before I finish reading the message, another one pops up.

Eddie: *I'm so glad you want to talk. I've missed you.*

I miss him too, but I miss being happy and feeling like I'm in control of my life more. It's time to figure out once and for all if we can make this relationship work for both of us because I can't be the best version of myself if things continue the way they've been going.

I distract myself by doing some research for work until around nine and then decide the best way to deal with my inner turmoil is to sleep it off. The nerves don't go away, though, and I end up lying in bed, staring at the dingy, water-stained ceiling until after one in the morning. I try reading a book and listening to meditation tracks, but nothing can calm the jittery energy that's keeping me awake. Eventually I fall asleep, only to be woken up by my alarm what seems like about three minutes later.

You can do this, Amelia. You deserve to be supported and having a fulfilling life. If Eddie can find a way to make that happen at the palace, that's fantastic. If he can't, then being together was never going to work out anyway. If that's the case, it's better to rip the Band-Aid off and end things now than to spend years together and find nothing changes. Right? I'm still mid–pep talk when my phone rings. "Hey, Eddie. How's the tour going?"

"Fantastic. Utterly exhausting, but such a thrill. I've obviously been on loads of overseas tours before, but never as king. There's something special about seeing how much support I have from total strangers halfway across the world. It's been incredibly invigorating."

My heart swells. Hearing the pride and excitement in his voice is so nice. He sounds like he's rediscovering some of the passion he had for his role before everything went slightly off the rails. "That's great. I'm so happy it's going well."

"It really is. I wish you were here. Then it would be perfect."

"Mm, Henry made sure that didn't happen, though, didn't he?" Oops, I didn't want to drag Henry into this so soon, but I couldn't help myself.

Eddie scoffs. "Let's not get into this again, shall we? I've had such a good day. Please don't ruin it."

"I don't want to ruin your day, but we need to talk about things."

"I'm exhausted. Can we leave this for another day? I'm fairly certain I know your views on Henry already."

My stomach churns. "I'm sorry," I say. "But I don't think it can wait. Eddie, this situation isn't working for me."

There's a choking sound on the other end of the line. "Pardon?"

"Please don't make me say it again, Eddie. This isn't easy for me."

"Are you telling me you don't love me? Is this all about Henry?"

"Eddie," I say, with a huff. "We've been through this. Of course I love you, but it's not that easy. Being with you is hard work, and I can't do it on my own. Lately, it feels like all we do is fight about what the palace says we can or can't do. It's angst-city around here, and I won't put myself through it unless I know you're going to be on my side every time. I'm not an ultimatum kind of girl, but I'm at the end of what I can handle. If you choose to keep working with a man who constantly undermines me and tries to minimise our relationship, I'm out. I have too much self-respect to keep living like this. To use your words, we need to be a team, and that can't happen while he's calling the shots."

Silence. After what feels like days, there's a deep sigh. Eddie starts to speak, and then stops.

"Still there?" I ask.

Silence for another beat. "Yes, I'm here. Amelia, you know I can't do what you're asking me to. Even though I wasn't king yet when we met, you always knew my duty above everything is to the British people. If there's a choice between me being happy and me being a good king, my personal interest will lose every time. I don't have the luxury of doing what is best for me when I have millions of other people to think of."

"I get that you're never going to do anything that jeopardises your family or their reputation. But, Eddie, let's be real here. I'm not asking you to spit on children in the street or set fire to a soup kitchen. I'm not even asking you to stop any of the work you're doing. All I'm asking is you stand up for yourself and replace one person in your staff of hundreds. I understand the monarchy is bigger than you and you can't always do what you want, but you know what? It's bigger than Henry too. I guarantee if he left tomorrow, everything would keep going."

"You're probably right, Amelia, but I can't risk losing the trust of my team. I'm sorry."

"So that's it. You're choosing him over me?"

"I reject the premise of the question. I'm choosing to believe this is not an either-or situation. We can be together, *and* I can avoid creating unnecessary turmoil at the palace. Let me find a way to deal with the issues you're facing without firing anyone."

I try not to scream. He's not going to budge, is he? "I wish it were that easy, but it's not." Tears start sliding down my cheeks. "It breaks my heart to say this, but we need to stop seeing each other. It might not be forever, but it's going to be until you're in a place where you can give me and our relationship as much respect as you give your advisers."

"Mils," he says, his voice breaking. "Don't do this. I'm begging you."

"I'm sorry, Eddie, but I have to. We broke up once before because I felt like I was losing myself in your world and wanted more out of life than just being someone's girlfriend. So much has happened since then, but somehow I've found myself stuck in exactly the same position—being with you has taken over my life, and I don't know who I am anymore. Nothing changes unless you make a change, and it doesn't look like you're ever going to, so I'm doing it myself."

In the background, there's a knocking and muffled voice calling to Eddie.

"I hate to end this conversation, but apparently there's a call I need to take urgently. Can we talk about this when I get home next week?"

"We can, but you should know I'm not going to change my mind."

He sighs. "I love you, Amelia."

"I love you too. I wish it was enough." Before he can say anything else, I hang up and burst into ugly, body-racking tears. This isn't how things were meant to end. I think it's the right choice, but I feel sick to my stomach and utterly deflated. Should making the right choice feel this awful?

AT SOME POINT I must have cried myself to sleep because when Penny shakes me awake, I check the time, and it's been four hours since I spoke to Eddie.

"Hey, love, are you okay?"

I grab a tissue from the coffee table and swipe at my nose. "Yeah, I'm fine."

"Are you sure?" Penny asks, giving me a pointed look. "Because I found you curled up in the foetal position with huge streams of tears running down your face, and it's not even midday. Call me crazy, but I think something happened."

"Fine, I called Eddie and told him it was me or Henry."

"I take it you didn't win that particular *Hunger Games* matchup?"

I blow my nose again. "I did not." My lip quivers, and I blink, vainly trying to stop the growing well of tears from breaking. "I ended things."

Penny nudges me across the sofa and then plops down in the space next to me and starts rubbing my back. "I'm so sorry. I know how much he means to you. You probably don't want to hear this right now, but I still think you can work it out. You guys are too good together for it to end this way."

"You're right, I don't want to hear that right now."

"Got it," she says, pointing at me. "Course correcting—he's

been totally spineless, and you deserve more because you are awesome. Better?"

"Much better, thank you. Top marks in supportive friend school."

She gives me a big squeeze. "Excellent. All right, now to help me support you, can you tell me, is this a 'going out drinking to forget about everything' kind of melancholy or are we in more of 'a tub of Häagen-Dazs on the sofa' type of situation? I'll happily enable either."

I laugh weakly. "I definitely don't want to go out. I want to stay curled up in a ball under a blanket for as long as humanly possible."

"Got it," Penny says, clapping her hands together. "Ball mode it is. You stay here and build yourself a cocoon. I'll fetch the wallowing supplies."

Three hours, a litre of ice cream, and an embarrassing number of dark chocolate Lindt balls later, things are starting to feel ever so slightly better. Sure, I still have an enormous black hole in my chest where my heart should be, and I will never be happy again, but I am now pretty confident the earth isn't going to open up and swallow me whole. Who knows, I might even be able to get out of bed one day. Gotta dream big.

I turn to Penny, who is snuggled up next to me in bed, watching TV on my iPad. "How is it that my boyfriend told me today he'd rather keep a fifty-year-old man happy than be with me, and yet somehow the *Gossip Girl* reboot is still the most disappointing part of my week?"

She lets out a delighted peal of laughter. "That's my girl. Not even a day into a break-up and here you are, bringing the gags. I was worried there for a hot minute, but you're a fighter. You'll be okay."

"One day, maybe."

"Not maybe. Definitely. You've got to take it one day at a time. Whatever you need, I'll be here."

I may not have a boyfriend anymore or have my family here, but at least I can always count on my best friend. "Thanks, Pen, you're the best. I don't know what I'd do without you. Probably take the train out to Heathrow and jump on the first flight back to Melbourne."

"I am the best, aren't I? Lucky I didn't sublet your bedroom."

CHAPTER 31

A couple of days later, when I've managed to emerge from my ball, I'm eating breakfast in the kitchen when Penny walks in. "Morning!"

"Good morning to you too, Miss Amelia. You're looking particularly well dressed for someone planning to spend another day wallowing in bed."

I pick some invisible lint off my skirt. "Thank you for noticing. I've actually got different plans for today. Today, I'm sorting out my career. It's step three in my four-step plan to reclaim my life."

"What were steps one and two?"

"Step one was to reclaim my bedroom. Step two was to fix my relationship situation. That step obviously didn't go quite to plan, but it is what it is, so we're moving right along to step three anyway."

"Right. What's step four, then?"

"Step four is to get rid of the car and security detail who are lurking outside. I'm putting that one off for as long as possible, though, because having a driver in London is actually one of the greatest things I've ever experienced. I haven't been on the Tube in months, Pen, *months*. I'm not sure I can go back."

She shudders at the mention of the Tube as if she's a PTSD-sufferer experiencing a flashback. "Can you keep the car? I'm still pressed up against strangers on the daily, and I do not recommend it. It would still be your life, just with better transport."

"I'll think about it. Not sure my salary would stretch to a driver unless we took in at least another couple of flatmates, though."

"Back on the train for you then, missy!"

I smirk. "That's what I thought. Anyway, I'm trying to get to work early to start catching up on everything I've neglected, so I'd better get into that car while I've got it."

"You should. Before you do, though, have you considered sorting out your career by quitting your job?"

I let out an exasperated sigh. "Pen, we've been through this—I'm trying to avoid getting fired, not quit."

"I know what you said," she says, rolling her eyes. "But are you sure? Even with Eddie out of the picture, you haven't been excited about work lately—which for most people would be normal, but for you is a sign something is deeply wrong. Maybe it's time to try doing something different."

She's got a point. I haven't been excited about anything at work in a long time. Some of the work issues I've been having were because of the other demands on my time, but not all of them. I think back to all the times over the last few months where I've spent hours procrastinating, the times where I've jumped at any excuse to leave the office early, the times where I couldn't be bothered with any of it. I haven't wanted to admit it to myself, but Eddie or no Eddie, I'm not passionate about my job anymore. It doesn't feel like what I should be doing with my life. But what am I going to do, go back to a corporate law firm? No thanks.

"I wouldn't even know what else to do."

"That's not a very good reason to stay. You could always take some time off to figure out what you want to do next—you're boring and responsible, so unlike me, you've got savings you could live off. I don't think you'd need them, though. You'll probably be able to get a different kind of job at a not-for-profit in about fifteen seconds."

"Actually, someone from UNICEF did kind of offer me a project development job a while ago."

Penny's eyes widen. "That's amazing! Why didn't you take it?"

"Because it's not what I do. I'm a lawyer, I don't know how to do anything else."

She rolls her eyes at me. "Please. That's not a reason, that's fear."

I don't care what she says, sticking with what I know is the sensible choice—and if I'm anything, I'm sensible. And fine, also terrified of trying something new and failing. But what if Penny and Nicole are right? What if I could do more? I don't know if taking the job with UNICEF would work out, but I do know staying where I am isn't fulfilling anymore. I've been telling Eddie he needs to back himself and make bold choices. Maybe it's time I take some of my own advice.

"How did you get so wise, Penny?"

She shrugs nonchalantly. "I may be a complete mess, but I'm great at telling other people how to fix their lives. It's a special skill."

I MAKE it into the near-empty office by eight in the morning, bunker down at my desk, and scan through my emails. As I do, my resolve strengthens. I don't want to be doing any of this work, I want to be doing something different, something tangible where I can see the outcomes and know I'm making a difference. I'm going to do it. I'm going to take the job with Nicole. Not because it would work better with a palace schedule—since that's not an issue anymore—but because I truly believe it would be more satisfying and challenge me to grow in ways that working as a lawyer never will.

I close my door and dial Nicole's number.

"Hello, Nicole Philips speaking."

"Hi, Nicole. It's Amelia Glendale from the Prince's Charitable Foundation."

"Amelia, how are you? I hope that you're calling because you've reconsidered coming to work with us."

I laugh. "Actually, I am. If the offer is still open, I'd love to join your team."

I can hear her clapping over the phone. "That's fantastic news, I'm so pleased. Let me sort through the details with HR and I'll send you a formal offer letter and contract."

"Thank you, I'm incredibly excited about the opportunity. Don't get me wrong, I'm still super nervous about it too, but I think it's going to be great."

"Trust me, Amelia, it will be. I have to run to a meeting, but someone from HR will be in touch later today. Welcome aboard."

When I hang up, I feel like I'm sitting at the beach with the wind in my hair and sun on my face. I'd almost forgotten what it felt like to be excited about the future. It's exhilarating.

After taking some time to bask in the feeling, I'm figuring out the best way to resign. I look up and see Daisy walking past. "Daisy! Come in," I call, gesturing enthusiastically for her to enter.

The door opens, and she walks in. "Hi, Amelia, good to see you." She smiles, but it doesn't reach her weary eyes.

"Good to see you too, Daisy. Sit down."

She sits down in the chair opposite my desk. "What can I help with?" she asks, pulling out a notepad and pen. "Is there a meeting you need me to cover?"

"No, nothing like that. I wanted to apologise."

She looks at me, her face clouded with confusion. "Oh! What for?"

"For the way I've been treating you lately. Things have been a bit, uh, busy in my personal life recently, and I've been relying on you too much. You've been doing your job and at least half of my job for months now. You must be exhausted."

Her shoulders slump, and her politely neutral expression breaks. "I'm so tired! I love working with you, and I'm always happy to help you out, but there's been so much to do. You haven't been around, so I've had to deal with quite a lot on my own. I'm not at all ready for that level of responsibility."

"Don't talk yourself down. You've done an amazing job and kept everything running super smoothly. But you shouldn't have had to, and I'm sorry. While you're here, I want to let you know I've decided to resign."

Her face crumples. "Are you sure? What am I going to do without you?"

"I'm going to miss working with you, but I have to move on. I'm not going to leave you in the lurch, though—I'll stay until we can find someone great to replace me."

She breathes a sigh of relief. "I wish you weren't leaving, but I understand. Thank you for your help and mentorship over the last few years."

"It's been an absolute pleasure. I've loved seeing you grow and develop. It sounds super cheesy, but I'm *so* proud of you. Now, I need to go talk to William before I lose my nerve."

Her cheeks redden, and she gives a small nod before standing and leaving the room.

Time to make this official. I'm as ready as I'll ever be. I pick up my desk phone and call William's secretary, Cheryl.

"Hello there, Amelia. I haven't heard from you in a while."

"Hi, Cheryl, yes, it's been a while. Is William around this afternoon?"

"He is, but he's extremely busy."

"I'm sure he is, but I'd really like to have a quick chat with him. It's important."

She tuts. "Hm, I could give you fifteen minutes at four thirty. He has a hard stop at quarter to five, though. He has a *very* high-profile dinner to get to."

I clench my jaw. I'm sure he does; half his job seems to be attending dinners. You could do a lot of good in the world by donating the price of his gala tickets. I force myself to smile, hoping I'll sound cheerful over the phone. "Four thirty would be great. I'll see him then."

Five minutes before my allotted meeting time, I'm pacing up and down the corridor just out of eyeshot of William's office. He's incredibly pedantic about people being on time to meet with him, so it's always best to be a few minutes early. He also gets anxious and annoyed if he can see people waiting outside his office, so everyone goes through this ridiculous game of arriving five minutes early and hiding around the corner where they can't be seen. The things we do to keep difficult men happy.

At exactly four thirty, I step in front of William's door and knock. He looks up from his desk and gestures to me through the glass to enter.

"Good afternoon, Amelia. I'm rather surprised to see you here. Your attendance at the office recently has been somewhat sporadic."

Right in there with the insults, I see. Classic William. "Yes, as you're aware, I've had some issues to attend to at home. With the king." I stare straight at him, waiting for the response.

He splutters and shakes his head. "Yes, I'm well aware of your situation, Amelia. Now, don't just stand there lurching over me. Take a seat, girl."

I grit my teeth and sit down. Telling William to go jump isn't part of my plan—I'm trying to be professional here so I don't burn any bridges—but with every word he says, it becomes more and more tempting.

"Are you here to talk about resigning from the foundation as we'd discussed?"

I dig my fingernails into my knee and count to three as I take a slow breath. "Actually, I am. But not for the reasons you think."

"So he's left you, then?"

Don't snap, don't snap. "No, that's not what happened. But the details aren't important. What's important is I've decided to pursue a different opportunity."

"What kind of opportunity? I hope you're not planning to join a competitor."

"With all due respect, William," I say, when obviously what I mean is with no respect at all, "we work in the not-for-profit sector. We're not in competition with anyone. Or we shouldn't be anyway."

He looks me up and down with his beady eyes. Why did I ever want to keep working for him? One of the best things about moving on from the foundation may be that I never have to pretend to be nice to this man again.

Finally, he speaks. "Very well. Sort out the details with HR."

"Thank you, William, I will. I'd better leave you to it. I believe you've got an event to go to this evening."

"Quite right. See that you don't slack off on work because you're leaving, I expect you to work at full capacity through your notice period."

I stand and walk out of the room at lightning speed. Ugh, he makes my skin crawl. I may have an Eddie-sized hole in my heart, but I feel like I've won the jackpot getting away from both William and Henry in one week.

CHAPTER 32

A WEEK LATER, it's my birthday and, thanks to the break-up, it's a bit of a depressing affair. Eddie sends a happy birthday message in the morning, and I almost respond but instead write out a reply and delete it three times in a row. Penny and I host a small lunch in our flat with Jane from upstairs and then spend the afternoon watching *Bring It On* movies. Yes, movies, plural. Who knew there were *six* of them? There really shouldn't have been. The first is a classic, obviously, but after that, things go downhill fast. It's never a good sign when not a single actor returns for a sequel. It also makes me wonder if there is an age limit on watching TV shows and movies about high schoolers. I hope not because I'm pretty sure I'll be fifty and still watching *Clueless* at least once a year. Maybe it's okay if you're watching movies where the teens were played by twenty-five-year-olds.

"Another round of desserts?" Penny asks as the credits roll on *Bring It On: Worldwide #Cheersmack*—a true insult to the film industry and humanity in general.

"Why not?"

After I finish the bowl of cake Penny served me—my third for the day—I'm lying on the sofa in a food coma when a FaceTime call pops up on my phone. It's my mum, and I squeal a little when I answer it and see she's there with my dad and my sister, Grace.

"Ah! You're all there!"

"Happy birthday, sweetheart," Mum says.

"Wait, what time is it there? It looks like it's still dark."

"It's just after six in the morning."

My sister rubs her eyes and groans. "Mum made us all get up early to call you in case you had dinner plans tonight. Thanks for that, Mum."

Mum glares at Grace. "Grace, don't be rude. It's Amelia's birthday, and she's sad and alone in a foreign country with no family and no boyfriend. The least we can do is call and say hello."

Ouch. To echo Grace, thanks for that, Mum. "Thanks for calling. It's great to talk to you all. Don't worry too much about me, though. I'm having a great day with my friends here."

"Hi, Mrs Glendale!" yells Penny in the background.

"Hello, Penny," Mum clucks. "I'm glad to hear you're having a good day. Are you keeping your spirits up? Must be hard to go through a break-up and then see his face every time you take a banknote out of your wallet."

"Actually, they haven't started printing the new banknotes yet, but he is definitely hard to avoid. I'm holding up all right. I wish we could all be together for my birthday, though."

"We wish we could be there with you too, love. Don't we, Harold? Harold?" Mum pokes Dad.

"Eh, what was that?" he asks. Typical Dad.

"We wish we could see Amelia, don't we?"

"Oh, sure. Yes, we all miss you, pet."

"Might be time for you to think about moving home?" Mum asks hopefully.

I mumble something non-committal. "Anyway, I should let you all go—I'm sure you've got things to do. Have a great day."

"I'm going back to bed," Grace says. "Next time you move overseas, choose somewhere closer, please."

"Don't listen to her," Mum says. "Enjoy your night. We love you. Take care of her for us, please, Penelope."

Penny leans over to insert herself into the camera frame. "Will do, Mrs Glendale. She's a disaster. She needs all the help she can get!"

I hang up and hurl a cushion at Penny. "Penny! You're meant to tell them I'm a highly functional adult with no issues at all."

She snorts. "Please, I couldn't keep a straight face through a lie like that if I tried. Here, why don't you binge-eat some more cookie dough?" Penny turns the TV back on, and an image of Eddie flashes up on the screen. He looks so good. Why does he have to look so good? It's the jaw that does it. No jaw should be that chiselled without surgical intervention. The effortless way his sandy hair flops in just the right way is icing on the cake. Penny peers at me as I study the screen, looking for any kind of secret sign he's changed his ways and we could make things work. She clears her throat. "Ahem, should I turn this off?"

"No, I'm going to allow myself one news report. Can you turn the volume up?"

Penny looks at me sceptically. "If you say so. I'm going to remind you that you asked for this if it makes you cry, though."

"Deal," I say, nodding. "I'm not going to cry."

Footage of Eddie walking along the street, shaking hands with well-wishers and waving to the crowds plays while the newsreader speaks.

"Yesterday, His Majesty King Edmund completed his tour of Canada before returning to Kensington Palace to continue preparations for his coronation. The tour was a triumph for the young king who was previously known for his austere manner."

The image changes to Eddie inspecting a display of cakes at some kind of county fair.

"On the last day of the three-week tour, the king delighted

young fans in a children's hospital in British Columbia by making an unofficial early morning stop at the facility. Press photographers caught the king entering the hospital through a service door at seven o'clock in the morning and leaving almost three hours later. No photographers were allowed inside, but it's understood His Majesty spent time reading and playing with the children."

A freckled girl and little boy with missing front teeth pop up on the screen. The girl speaks. "He was so nice, I showed him all the pictures I've drawn, and he helped me draw a train. It was really tricky."

The boy bounces up and down. "It was so cool! I never thought I'd beat a king at *Mario Kart*!" he says.

"Hey," Penny says, poking me. "You said you weren't going to cry."

"I'm not crying! I swear. You should probably turn it off before I see any more, though."

The TV clicks off, and I hug my knees to my chest. I am almost crying, but they're not sad tears. They're proud tears. Are proud tears a thing? I think they must be. He looked like he was doing so well over there—he looked warm and engaging and totally comfortable. I love that he went to the hospital by himself too. He would have been so thrilled to be able to play with the kids without people watching. I can't believe Henry let him shut out the photographers and lose such a great photo opportunity. Maybe he's started standing up for himself more after all.

THE NEXT COUPLE of weeks pass in a blur. I spend my days beavering away doing handover at work and my nights doing research for a new aid project for UNICEF that I'm really excited about and hoping to pitch to my new boss, Nicole, soon. Also crying, there's still a lot of crying. Every day since I moved back in with Penny, Eddie has been sending me a message when he wakes up in the morning and a message before he goes to bed. The ones since our fight the other week have been full of grovelling apologies and professions of love, which, if I'm honest, are definitely making me question my decision. So far, I haven't replied to any, but I have been spending far too much time sitting in bed at night reading them over and over again.

I try to avoid being photographed coming and going from the flat so people don't start questioning why I'm here instead of with Eddie at KP. I'm lucky that after he got home from the tour he decamped to Balmoral for a break, so the press attention is focused up there. Despite the inconvenience of trying to keep the paparazzi off my tail, I feel like I'm finding a bit of a rhythm in life again.

On my official last day at the foundation, I go into the office in the morning to clear out my desk. Lucky I've still got a car to cart all my pen holders and spare shoes home in.

I've sorted through all the papers in my office and decided almost all of them can be tossed. It's so freeing to get rid of it all. It really makes it feel like I'm getting a new start. I'm dumping another pile into an enormous recycling bin when there's a knock on my door. I look out and see Leo standing outside. What is he doing here? Without thinking, I duck behind the bin.

"Amelia, I know you're in there. I can see your feet."

Well, that's embarrassing. I climb up and open the door. "Hi, Leo. It's been a while. I was just, uh, picking something up off the floor."

"I don't believe you."

I roll my eyes. "Fine, if you must know, I was hiding from you."

"I can't imagine why. I'm a joy to be around. Everyone says so."

I'm not sure I want to take that bait. I think this is definitely a "if you don't have anything nice to say" situation. Leo chuckles. "Lighten up, Amelia. It was a joke."

I laugh nervously. It may have been a joke, but based on the outbursts I've seen from him recently, I don't want to push my luck by finding it too funny.

"Anyway," he says, "I heard you're leaving."

"Yes, I've decided to move on. I've taken more of a strategic role with UNICEF."

He smirks. "Sounds like the kind of thing a do-gooder like you would enjoy."

Again, not quite sure how to respond to that. "I'm looking forward to it."

"Listen," he says, plopping down on the edge of my desk, "I hope you didn't leave because of me. I know we've had a few fracas lately, but I know you're a good lawyer. I might have threatened to have you fired a few times, but I would never have followed through."

"Thanks for saying that, Leo, but it's not about you. I need a new challenge."

"I've no idea why you'd want a challenge instead of a nice token job that doesn't involve any actual work, but I respect it."

Wow. That may be the nicest thing Leo has ever said to me.

"Between you and me, I'm also leaving because William is a bit of a dick."

He laughs heartily and looks at me with a soft smile. "Have you spoken to Eddie lately?"

I bite my lip. "No, I haven't. Have you?"

"I have. Decided it was time to patch things up. I felt bloody awful about the Kayla debacle. Despite what some people think, I don't intentionally set out to destroy the family."

"No one thinks that. Eddie and the others know how much you love them."

"I'm not sure that's accurate, but I appreciate you saying it. I'm not going to stick my nose in your relationship, but maybe you should speak to Eddie too. I know you probably think I don't approve of you—and don't get me wrong, a lot of the time I don't—but the truth is, you're good for him. He needs someone who isn't blinded by the whole king malarky and will stand up to him when he's wrong. I can't be the only one calling him out when he's being a complete idiot."

My throat thickens. After feeling like Leo had such a huge problem with me, it's overwhelming to suddenly feel like I have his support. Shame it's too late.

He regards me appraisingly. "It takes a brave woman to dump a king twice. Well"—he shrugs—"either brave or stupid."

I chuckle. There's the Leo I know and barely tolerate. "Thanks, Leo. Let's go with brave."

He winks. "Done."

"I appreciate you saying all of this, but Eddie and I are over. I don't think there's any coming back from it this time. There are issues he's not willing to address."

"I wouldn't be so sure," he says. "I think you two crazy kids can probably work it out. Unless you're selling stories about him to tabloids, of course. Apparently, that's a capital offence in this family."

I wish he were right. I've been so excited about my new job and all the possibilities it opens up for the future, but it's not the same without Eddie to share it with. I smile sadly. "We'll see."

"Well," he says, clapping his hands together. "Good chat. I need to keep moving. I've got a meeting with William and then two dates this afternoon. Kayla was holding me back. I would never have met that company of Russian ballerinas if she were still around."

I laugh. "Enjoy."

"Oh, don't worry," he says with a smirk, "I definitely will."

A FEW DAYS LATER, I'm sitting at our tiny kitchen table after dinner, reading a report about comparative living conditions in different refugee camps, when Penny makes a strange, high-pitched squealing noise. "What happened? Did you see a mouse again? Actually, don't tell me if you did. I'd rather not know."

"No, it wasn't a mouse, thank god! Did I ever tell you the same day I saw that mouse in here I was walking along Oxford Street and a car drove through a puddle next to me as I was talking to someone and I got puddle water in my mouth? In. My. Mouth."

I gag a little. "That's so gross."

"It really was—I don't think I'll ever forget the taste. Between the mouse and the street juice, that was the only day since I moved to London where I seriously considered packing up and leaving. I probably would have if I hadn't just spent all my money on a weekend in Portugal."

"Well, I'm glad you were too broke to flee. But back to my question. Why are you shrieking today?"

"Oh, that? Nothing," she says, tucking her phone into her pocket.

I raise an eyebrow. "Nothing, eh? I don't believe you. You may be completely eccentric sometimes, but you don't usually go around screaming for the sake of it."

"It's a new meditation technique. Gwyneth Paltrow swears by it."

"She also recommended steaming your vagina and putting some kind of crystal egg up there, so, you know, I'm not sure I trust her."

"Fair point."

"What's really going on? Don't think you can distract me by getting me to think about all of Gwyneth's ridiculous lady-part-related products."

Penny looks at me sheepishly. "Fine," she says, fishing around in her pocket. "You should probably read this." She thrusts her phone out towards me. Ugh, what is it this time? Things were starting to feel somewhat normal—I can't handle another scandal throwing my world upside down. I walk over and tentatively take the phone.

"Do I want to read it?"

"Maybe not," she says, "but you should. You'll probably hear about it anyway."

I take a deep breath and brace myself. As long as it's not a story about Eddie moving on with a twenty-year-old model with legs for days, everything will be okay. I really hope it's not that—that would cause a major regression in my attempt to act like a mature adult about the whole "dating the king" thing not working out. I glance down at the screen.

Struggling king abandoned by right-hand man

In breaking news, The Telegraph *can confirm that King Edmund's most senior adviser, Henry Deleney, has resigned. A statement released by Deleney this morning confirmed he has left the king's office and taken up a position with the Duke of Sheffield, the king's second cousin and up-and-coming politician. Deleney, who served in senior roles in Queen Alice's advisory team for over two decades, has been working as King Edmund's private secretary for the past five years. He was reportedly hand-chosen by Queen Alice to work for then-Prince Edmund, tasked by her with teaching the prince the ropes and providing a steady, guiding hand as his role in the monarchy grew.*

While the statement issued by Deleney sheds no light on the reason for the sudden change, reports are rife that he had lost all faith in the king following long-rumoured issues with his mental stability. If true, it is likely Deleney's departure will be only the first in a string of high-profile departures from the palace. Regardless of the reason, the defection will only add fuel to the fire regarding the young king's suitability for the top job.

. . .

So let me get this straight: Eddie refused to fire Henry for me, and then he quits anyway? Well, that stings. I can't believe he'd choose an employee over me without even knowing if the guy was committed enough to his job to hang around for more than three minutes.

Penny speaks, breaking my rage spiral. "What do you think is going on? Do you think Edmund fired him after all and Henry is just trying to save face?"

I shake my head. "No, I don't think so. He was so convinced he couldn't get rid of him I can't imagine he magically changed his mind in the last couple of weeks."

"Do you think he'll try to win you back now Henry is gone?"

"I don't know, he might. He has still been texting me every day. I don't know if I'd be ready to take him back, though. Sure, Henry will be gone, but not because Eddie listened to my concerns or stood up for me. What happens when he's replaced with someone equally controlling?"

Penny winces. "Good point. I guess Edmund didn't actually do anything to fix the situation." She clicks her tongue. "It all seems so weird."

"It is. I don't fully understand what's happened, but I don't see that it changes anything. I needed Eddie to fight for me, and he didn't. End of story."

Still, a small part of me—all right, an extremely large part of me—hopes something actually has changed. What if Eddie did fire him and the statement is Henry trying to get ahead of the story and write his own narrative? It might change everything. Caroline and I are still on good terms, I wonder if she has some inside intel.

Me: *Hey, have you heard anything about Henry quitting?*

A few seconds later, my phone buzzes in my hand.

Caroline: *No clue what's going on, but it's causing enormous drama here. Good old Sheffield isn't taking any of our calls and Mummy is furious. Will keep you posted x*

A WEEK GOES by without so much as a text from Eddie—his messages seemed to magically dry up after the news about Henry broke. I have no idea what that means, but it can't be anything good. To avoid thinking about it too much, I throw myself into work. Now that I've officially finished at the foundation and started at UNICEF, I've got a new lease on life and am feeling so invigorated. For now I'm spending most of my time on a proposal for the new project I've been researching, an initiative aimed at providing more education opportunities in European refugee camps. It's right within Nicole's wheelhouse and a great opportunity to build better futures for children who have been displaced. I thought about suggesting to Eddie that we partner with the King's Trust on it because I know he'd love it, but the trust has a much more domestic focus, so it wouldn't fit there. Conveniently, it also means I don't have to find the courage to talk to him.

One afternoon, I'm preparing for my pitch meeting with Nicole when my phone rings. I'm about to answer when I see it's Eddie calling. I drop the phone like it's burning my hand. I've done such a good job of trying to push my feelings about the whole break-up situation into a tiny little locked box. There's no way I'm going to risk letting them out by hearing his voice.

Rattled by the call, I decide to take a break and go for a walk down by the river. I'm only just out of the office foyer when my phone rings again. Ugh, I should have left my phone on my desk. I'm about to reject the call when I notice that it's Caroline. That's a weird coincidence. I know I said I wanted to clear my head, but I also desperately want to know if she's found out anything more about Henry.

"Hi, Caroline, how are you?"

"I'm fine, darling, just fine. It's been quite a wild week around here, but that seems to be the way of the world at the moment."

"Have you heard any more about what happened with Henry?" I ask, making my way down towards a bench overlooking the river, two plain-clothes security officers trailing a respectful distance behind me.

"Not a word, sorry."

I let out a puff of air. "That's okay."

"What's wrong, love? You sound disappointed."

"I guess I was still holding out hope Eddie had realised he didn't need Henry and had let him go."

"Mm. Tell you what, would a girls' night cheer you up? That's the other reason I was calling. Lucy, Emma, and I miss you dearly. Will you come for dinner and facials tonight? Mummy is doing much better lately, so I'll be heading home tomorrow and probably won't be back in town for quite a while."

I tap my foot on the ground. I do miss them all, and hanging out with them always makes me feel better, but I'm not sure I want to go to the palace. "I don't know, Caroline. I'd love to see you before you go, but I don't think I can come over there. I've been avoiding Eddie and don't want to risk running into him."

"Don't worry, he's still up at Balmoral. No risk at all."

"You promise he won't be there? He's the last person I want to see right now."

"I promise."

This feels like a bad idea, but I am desperate for a girls' night, and no one does pamper sessions like the princesses. "Can I bring Penny?"

"Of course, she's always welcome. Can you come over now?"

"Hm, I have a few things to finish up at work this afternoon, but I can probably leave here around five."

"We'll see you soon then."

CHAPTER 33

After work, Michael collects me from my new office and signals for my daytime security detail that their shift is over. "Good evening, ma'am. Where to?"

"Hey, Michael. Can we head to KP, please?"

He looks at me, his expression inscrutable.

"I'm going to Ivy Cottage," I rush to add. He nods and closes the door behind me.

On the way, I get a text from Penny.

Penny: *FYI, I'm at Ivy already. Are you on your way?*

Me: *Have just left the office now, will be there in twenty mins.*

Penny: *See you soon!*

As we make our way down the drive at KP past Wren House, I try not to look, but I can't help myself. My heart rate shoots through the roof, and I quickly glance away when I notice there are lights on inside. I know Caroline said he's away, and it's probably someone cleaning up, but I can't handle the idea of seeing Eddie right now. When we pull up at Ivy Cottage, I scope out the path before ducking up to the front door. I don't even get a chance to ring the bell before Lucy opens the door and greets me in her typical style: holding a bottle of champagne.

"Amelia! It's so good to see you. It feels like you haven't been here in years!"

"Lucy, it's only been three weeks, and we FaceTimed while we were watching *Emily in Paris*, like, four days ago."

"Details, darling," she says, waving her non-champagne-carrying hand. "Come in, come in. We're having a fab time."

I follow her through the foyer into the living room and am confronted by the sight of far more people than I was expecting. I thought this was a quiet night in, not a party. But when I take a second look around, I notice the extra people aren't guests—they're staff. Some of the furniture has been moved, and there are massage, manicure, make-up, and hair stations set up around the room. Emma is lying on a bed by the window, a woman massaging serums into her face. When she hears me walk into the room, she shoots up. "Amelia! I'm so glad you're here."

"I've missed you too, Em."

"Welcome to girls' night. Get a drink and then come and have your face done. I recommend having a massage, then moving on to nails and make-up. We need to get started right away. We're on a tight timetable tonight."

I giggle. "We have a pressing movie schedule to attend to, do we?"

A strange look passes between Emma and Lucy before Emma speaks again. "Yes, something like that." Oh, I don't like the sound of that at all. There's something sneaky going on here. Before I can think too much about what it is, a woman approaches me with a warm towel and a drink.

I catch Penny's eye across the room. She shrugs. "Just go with it," she says. All right, I guess I'm going with it. An hour later, I'm having finishing touches put on my make-up. "Wow, this looks amazing, but it's, uh, a lot more make-up than I'm used to wearing for a Friday night at home."

The make-up artist glances at Emma, who says, "It's fine, darling. We're having a glam night."

I raise an eyebrow. "Right." This is getting more and more suspect. "Em, can I talk to you in private for a sec?"

"Of course, but can we talk in"—she checks her watch —"twelve minutes?"

"Oddly specific, but sure."

"Here," she says, pouring a drink and handing it to me. "Have this in the meantime."

I accept the drink and take a sip. I'm going with it, I'm just going with it. Approximately eleven minutes later, the doorbell rings.

"I'll get it," Caroline says, jumping up. A few moments later, Lucy, Emma, and Penny stop chatting, and the room falls into silence. I glance up, and my breath catches as I catch sight of him. Eddie is standing in the doorway, looking heartbreakingly good in a tuxedo. My heart flutters. Say what you will about his taste in staff, but the man can wear a suit.

"Eddie . . ."

"I have to check on something in the kitchen," Lucy says.

Emma flies to the door. "Me too."

"I'll help," Caroline adds. For her part, Penny just scuttles out of the room with the beauticians. Traitors.

"Hi, Amelia."

"Hey," I whisper. "They all set me up, didn't they?"

He nods. "I'm afraid they did."

"This is why you should never date someone with more influence than you. Things can go terribly wrong."

"Did they, though? Go terribly wrong, I mean. From where I'm standing, everything looks like it went rather well until a few weeks ago." He takes a step forward into the room and gazes at me with his lopsided grin and puppy-dog eyes. "Can we sit?"

"Why not?" I say. "We're here now." We each take a seat on the sofa, leaving a safe distance between us. "So tell me, Eddie, why are we here?"

He sits, twisting his cufflinks around. "Well, Amelia, I was hoping we could talk."

"I think you'll find that we already are."

"Very funny," he says, rolling his eyes. "I was hoping we could talk about us. I'm not sure if you received any of my three hundred apology messages?"

"Eddie, I appreciate the grand gesture, but I don't think there's anything to talk about. And yes, I got the messages."

"Did you read them?"

I roll my eyes. "Yes, I read them." Many, many times, but he doesn't need to know that part.

"Well, then you know how dreadfully sorry I am. Over the past few months, you've done nothing but support me, and I haven't reciprocated. Your life has been in flux as much as mine has, but you don't have the help I do. I should have been there for you, and I should have pushed harder to make sure you had the respect and assistance you needed to be happy. All this time, you've been facing exactly the same challenges as me, and I've been too blind to see it. Please give me a chance to do better."

This may be exactly what I want to hear, but it doesn't change anything that's happened. "You're right, I needed more from you. I would love to give it another shot, but nothing has changed. Henry is gone, but that doesn't change the fact that you had a chance to stand up for me—for us—and you didn't take it."

His face falls. "I know, and I feel ghastly about it, I do. But you're wrong about one thing—things have changed. I fired Henry."

My jaw drops. "You did?"

"Yes, I did. He tried to spin it so people would think he resigned, but he didn't. My time in Canada opened my eyes. It reminded me what I love about my life, and it gave me the confidence boost I so desperately needed. I realised I may not have the answer in every situation, but I have good instincts and good people around me. I don't need Henry or anyone else here trying to control me or insisting on things being done in exactly the same way they've always been done. Sometimes, the old way of doing things isn't the best way—for me, or for the country. I may be the figurehead of this ancient institution, but I'm still a person, and I need to fulfil my role in a way that's true to me and my values. From now on, I'm going to trust my instincts and make my own traditions."

Wow. Where has this Eddie been for the last few months? "I'm so proud of you. It seems like you've really found your confidence and grown into the role."

"Everything in my life feels like it's coming together. The only thing I don't have is you."

I suck in a sharp breath, and he moves imperceptibly closer to me. I should move away, but it's so hard to think straight and stick to my guns when I've got those warm hazel eyes staring at me and his chiselled jaw is close enough to touch—close enough to kiss. No, snap out of it, Amelia. Things haven't been magically fixed just because he comes in with his smooth speech and intoxicating, woodsy smell. "You make things sound so easy, but they're not. Henry is gone, but will that really change anything? What if whoever you replace him with doesn't like me either? What will you do then?"

He reaches across and takes my hand in his. "I'll fire them. I'll fire anyone who disrespects my wife."

My eyes shoot up and meet his. "Your wife?"

"Yes," he says, sliding himself off the sofa and onto one knee on the floor in front of me. He puts a hand in his pocket and emerges with a small black velvet box. "Amelia Marie Glendale, you are the smartest, funniest, most passionate woman I've ever met. I should have asked you to marry me that night in Kenya, and I should have asked you every day since. Can you overlook my utter stupidity and marry me anyway?"

"But what about my job and the approval ratings and everything else?"

"You can do whatever you like for work. You can keep your job, and I'll put a team around you here to make sure you have enough time to devote to it, you can leave and take on patronages and a traditional working royal role, or you can think of something entirely different to do. You are brilliant. I will support whatever path you choose and do whatever it takes to make it work."

"Okay, but what about the approval ratings? You heard what a disaster it would be if we got married any time this century."

He shakes his head. "To hell with the approval ratings. I don't care about them anymore. The only things I care about are doing the best job I can do and being happy with you. If people don't approve of that, that's their prerogative."

I open my mouth and shut it again. I'm running out of arguments.

"Amelia, you said we couldn't be together because we're still in the same position we were when we first broke up, but we're not. We've both grown and changed an incredible amount over the last few months. We're both more confident in ourselves now than we've ever been. It's exactly like RuPaul says—if you don't love yourself, how in the hell are you going to love somebody else? We're both in a place now where we can do that and be our best selves for each other, I'm sure of it. I'm not saying things will be perfect, but I'm saying we can deal with them together."

"You really want to do this?"

He looks down and flips open the velvet box to reveal an oval-cut emerald the size of a marble, surrounded by a thick halo of diamonds. "More than anything."

This is it—this is when I have to decide. If I say no now, I probably won't get another chance. Do I want a life of love where we work together to figure everything else out, or do I want stability? Is it better to take the leap for love or play it safe?

As much as I've been frustrated by Eddie not standing up for himself and being decisive enough, I have to admit maybe I was too rash in deciding to end things. Taking more time and trying to work through the challenges together would have been the riskier choice, but that doesn't mean it would have been the wrong choice.

I gaze into his eyes, and my heart skips a beat. I know deep down that I can't choose a life without him. I don't want to be sitting here in forty years' time like Soph, with nothing more than a box of old knick-knacks to show for having loved Eddie. He may have taken longer to understand what he had to do than I would have liked, but I can't hold that against him. He's only human after all.

"So, what do you say?" he asks, hope shining in his eyes.

"Yes. I say yes."

Eddie breaks into a grin that lights up his eyes and puts his dimple on full display. I'd forgotten how much I love his dimple. He slips the ring on my finger, and I pull him up to sit next to me before I run my hand along his jaw. "I love you, Edmund Louis Albert George Huntington. I love you, and I'd prove it to the world by marrying you today if I could."

He tangles his hands through my hair and kisses me deeply. When we break apart, his face is plastered with a goofy grin. "I was hoping you might say that."

"Uh, why?"

"You may or may not remember that a little while ago you pointed out that as the head of the Church of England, I could probably arrange for a priest to appear in less time than it took you to change your clothes."

I narrow my eyes. "Yes, I remember."

"Well," he says, "it turns out you were right."

I give a bark of laughter. "Have you got a priest stashed away in a cupboard somewhere? Is he going to jump out and yell surprise?"

"Not exactly," he says, with a glint in his eye. "But there is one waiting in the courtyard at home. I hoped if you said yes, you'd agree to marry me tonight. I can't stand the thought of spending another day without you as my wife."

Wow. I wasn't prepared for this at all when I came over for drinks and TV. It's crazy! There's no way I can get married tonight. I've been at work all day, and I'm a total mess! Wait . . . no, I'm not. Those sneaky little traitors and their glow-up night. They knew! I look at Eddie, biting my lip.

"Don't worry," he says. "There's no pressure at all. I don't want to rush you into anything. I wanted to have the option available to show you how serious I am about this—about you."

"I don't have anything to wear."

I hear someone cough in the foyer. I turn around and spot four heads poking through the doorway. "I think we can help with that," says Lucy.

"Oh, you've got a makeshift bridal salon set up in your bedroom, have you?"

Lucy guffaws. "Of course not. It's in my dressing room, obviously."

I flick my eyes back to Eddie. "Are we really doing this?"

"That's in your hands. You say the word, and we get married tonight. You say no, and we have a fabulous engagement party tonight and get married whenever you like."

I look across the room at Penny, and she shrugs again. "Just go with it."

A wide grin breaks across my face. I'm going to do it. I'm going to marry my prince—sorry, my king. So, for the second time tonight, I say yes.

I SPRINT up the stairs to Lucy's dressing room. She wasn't kidding—it has been set up like a full-on bridal salon. I feel like I'm having an out-of-body experience, running my hand through racks of tulle and lace gowns. As I gaze around in wonder, Penny and Lucy get to work selecting a shortlist. Soon a dressmaker appears from nowhere to help me into the first gown.

The first gown does nothing for me, but I tell you, Penny is good, because the second dress is perfection. As soon as I see myself in the mirror, I know. I'm floating.

I twirl and watch the skirt move in the mirror. It's a confection of blush tulle with a sweetheart neckline and deep-V back. The bodice and skirt are adorned with exquisitely embroidered ferns and roses that cascade down the dress and pool in the train. It's not a traditional royal wedding dress at all, but it feels like me.

"Excellent choice," the dressmaker says. "Hermione de Paula, one of a kind."

"It's beautiful," I whisper.

Emma looks at me and wipes a tear from her eye. "*You're* beautiful. We've done a fantastic job."

"And with so little to work with," Lucy adds.

"Oh, stop it," Caroline chides, swatting at Lucy's arm. "You, Amelia, look like a queen."

I gaze around the room and beam. A queen. I'm going to be a *queen*. That's going to take time to get used to, but I'm sure with Eddie and this motley crew by my side, I'll get there.

Soon a hairdresser appears to fix my hair, and then I'm done and walking down the path to Wren House. My house. Light glows from the windows as I approach, and music floats out into the cool night air. I'm about to walk inside when I see someone walking down the path towards me.

"Amelia! You look divine."

I do a double take as the figure gets closer. "Isla? What are you doing here? We're a bit busy right now, so it might not be the best time to visit."

Isla lets out a tinkling laugh. "Don't worry, Eddie invited me."

My eyebrows shoot up. "He did? Does that mean you've spoken to him?"

"I have. He reached out to me not long after he arrived in Canada. We've been talking quite a lot since then actually. It's been lovely."

A hand grasps my shoulder, and I turn to see Eddie has appeared behind me.

"Isla," he says, "I'm so glad you could make it. This is a very important night for me, and I want to share it with my family."

Isla glows. "I wouldn't miss my brother's wedding for anything."

I turn to Eddie, shocked. "You told her you were going to ambush me with a wedding?"

"I did," he says, grinning. "You were right, as usual—it's nice to have someone else I trust and can talk to." He turns to Isla. "I've said it before, but I want to take this opportunity to apologise in person for how I treated you. I should never have held Dad's infidelity against you. I've been under an immense amount of pressure, and I took it out on you. I'm not proud of it, but I hope that, in time, you can forgive me for it."

"Thank you for the apology. It was a very difficult time for all of us. Luckily we have a lifetime to process it all together."

He nods. "We do. Now, I have something else I was waiting until we saw each other in person to discuss."

"Oh?" she asks, her eyebrow raised.

Eddie looks down and kicks at the ground like a shy toddler. "Well, I was wondering whether you would like me to make the orders so you can officially be known as Princess Isla? It was Dad's last wish after all, and I want to show you I'm committed to making you part of our family."

Isla bursts into a fit of laughter.

"What's so amusing?" Eddie asks.

She doubles over and clutches her sides, then straightens out and wipes an invisible tear from her eye. "Sorry, Edmund. I wasn't laughing at you—I was laughing at the irony of the situation. To be perfectly frank, I've never wanted to be a princess.

Not even as a young girl. I always thought the whole business sounded like a terrible bore. I appreciate the gesture more than you know, but I am going to respectfully decline. I'd much rather have a standing dinner invitation."

Eddie's dimple flashes as he breaks into a radiant grin. "You're always welcome."

I fan myself with my hand. "You guys! You're going to make me cry and ruin my make-up."

"Well," Eddie says, hooking his arm through mine, "we can't have that."

"Don't worry, you look gorgeous," Isla says.

Eddie strokes my hair. "Are you ready?"

"As ready as I'm ever going to be," I say. "I wish my family could be here, though. Can we call them? It's coming up to seven in the morning for them. My parents might even be awake already."

He smiles softly. "I'm sure we can get hold of them."

As if in a dream, I let him lead me through the foyer and kitchen and out into the courtyard. When I step outside, my heart grows three sizes. The scene before me is beautiful: there's a canopy covering the whole courtyard, and hundreds of fairy lights have been strung from the enormous oak tree to the surrounding walls. I laugh when I realise the string quartet in the corner is playing an instrumental version of an NSYNC song. Poppy is running around in the corner, chasing her tail, wearing a miniature veil and sparkly rain boots. It's perfect. Most stunning of all, though, is the people—I immediately start to cry when I scan the courtyard. I see Lucy, Emma, and Penny have been joined by Queen Louisa, Princess Helena, Leo, my parents, my sister, and even Penny's boyfriend, Josh, and my upstairs neighbours Jane and Steph from the flat in Camden. I turn to Eddie. "I don't even care that I'm ruining my make-up anymore. I'm so happy everyone is here. You brought our family."

"Of course I did. A very smart woman told me recently that family is everything, and it turns out she was right."

"Wow. Whoever she is, you should really listen to her more often."

"Don't worry," he says, leaning down to kiss my temple, "I plan to."

EPILOGUE

Six months later

"Are Your Majesties willing to take the Oath?"

Eddie and I look at each other, hands clasped. "We are."

"Will you solemnly promise and swear to govern the Peoples of the United Kingdom of Great Britain and Northern Ireland and all countries and territories of the Commonwealth, according to their respective laws and customers?"

"We solemnly promise so to do."

As we bow, the archbishop places a crown on each of our heads.

"God save King Edmund. God save Queen Amelia."

The sound of the crowd cheering fills the room, and I flip off the TV and spin around to face Eddie. "Can you believe we did that with a billion people watching?"

He chuckles. "I can't. I'm genuinely not entirely sure it actually happened. I remember walking into Westminster Abbey, but I have no memory at all of anything after that. Perhaps I blacked out?"

"Well, I can remember it all, and I promise you it happened. We've got the crowns to prove it."

"Speaking of," Eddie says, "can you believe Emma wore that blasted Russian tiara to the coronation?"

I shake my head. "Poor Anastasia, she never gets to go out! Emma just wanted her to live a little."

"She'll certainly never get to go out again now. I've revoked everyone's vault access. No one gets in or out without my fingerprint. Even you."

I poke Eddie's stomach. "You're no fun. If that's the approach you take, you may well end up with one of your cousins trying to cut off a finger while you sleep."

"I'd like to see them try," he scoffs. "My security team is top-notch."

"We'll see. Lucy and Emma can be distracting for security guards sometimes."

He throws his hands up in surrender. "If they can get through multiple Scotland Yard–trained protection officers and aren't too squeamish to remove a finger, they're welcome to the diamonds."

"Very generous of you."

"I thought so," he says, nodding. "Speaking of generosity, how's your new education project going? I was so glad we could use the coronation celebrations to raise money for the initiative."

I beam. "*So* well. We've confirmed our launch date, and there'll be boots on the ground starting construction and sorting out supply chains in the next few days. It's been so great to see it come together. I'm flying out to do a site visit next week. I can't wait to see it in person."

"That's fantastic. I'm so proud of you. Aren't you glad you made the move into a strategic role?"

"You know what? I am. I was so scared at the time that it wasn't going to be the right choice and I wasn't going to be any good at it. But stepping out of my comfort zone and away from the day-to-day legal work has given me an amazing opportunity to focus on new ideas. Nicole has been a fantastic boss and so accommodating of my schedule. I love that I've been able to keep working on stand-alone projects there while I figure out what I'm doing long-term. Which reminds me, I think I've finally decided on the charities I'd like to become patron of as well."

Eddie claps his hands together. "Oh, do tell. Which ones did you choose?"

"Working on my project for UNICEF made me realise I want to focus on education for now. My education has taken me so many places. I want to help make that happen for other people too. So I've chosen a not-for-profit that runs schools overseas and then a couple of domestic charities focused on early childhood education. I want to keep the number of organisations I'm involved in limited so I can really dig in."

Eddie leans in and kisses me. "Seems like everything worked out."

"Seems that way," I say, smiling.

Outside, a bird chirps and sunlight filters through the leaves of the oak tree, leaving sun-dappled patterns on the grass. "Let's go outside. I want to make the most of the sun while it lasts. I swear it's winter eleven months of the year here."

"Hey, be nice. That's your kingdom you're talking about there, Queen Amelia."

I flick my eyes up to the ceiling. "I'm sorry, Britain, I love you."

He smiles approvingly. "Much better. I'm sure the country forgives you."

Eddie grabs a large tartan picnic blanket sitting next to the door, and we walk out to the back garden. He spreads the blanket out on the grass under the tree and flops to the ground. I lie down and rest my head on his chest. He twirls his fingers through my hair, and the sun warms my cheeks as I watch the branches swaying in the breeze above me. I close my eyes and sigh. "This is it, isn't it?"

"This is what?" he asks lazily.

"Our happily ever after."

He leans down and kisses me slowly. "You know what? I believe it is."

THE END

THANK you so much for reading *God Save the King*. I hope you enjoyed reading this story as much as I enjoyed writing it. If you did, I'd love for you to let me know by either leaving a review on Amazon or getting in touch at Facebook or Instagram.

The series will continue with Caroline's story in 2023. To be the first to hear when it is available to order, join my mailing list.

ACKNOWLEDGMENTS

For me and many others, 2021 was a roller coaster in so many ways. The process of writing this book was no different.

I started writing it at the start of the year, full of enthusiasm and excited for a productive, pandemic-free year. Obviously that didn't work out so well. Through the year I struggled through lockdowns, work issues, stressed children and writer's block. There were times when I stopped writing for extended periods and didn't know if I'd ever be able to start again. Luckily for me, the encouragement of some special people and my love for Eddie, Amelia and their ragtag crew kept me going.

I'd like to thank my earliest readers and biggest supporters - Emma, Lucy, Josh and Stef. Without your comments and support, Eddie and Amelia wouldn't be where they are today.

I would also like to thank all my other friends and colleagues who have read *The Other Prince* and generally supported my writing journey. It means more than you know.

To my family—Mum, Dad, Clare, Caitlyn, Joe, Julia, Dette, Scott, Peter, Concetta and Lawrence—thank you for always being there.

As invaluable as support from friends and family has been, this story couldn't have been brought to life without the help of my amazing editor, Sarah. Thank you.

Last, but far from least, a huge thanks as always to my husband, Gerard. Without you I'd just be curled up in a ball somewhere, hiding from the world.

Here's to a better 2022 for everyone.

ABOUT THE AUTHOR

Hi! I'm Alice. I'm so glad you're here.

I write funny stories about people falling in love. Mainly. Princes and princesses because I'm a bit of a royal family tragic. Also because writing about royalty is the closest I'll ever come to wearing a tiara that isn't made of plastic.

I live in Australia with my husband and three small humans. In my seventeen seconds of free time each day I love reading romantic comedies, watching cheesy Netflix movies and baking cakes which I absolutely do not eat most of myself.

To be the first to hear about new releases, join my mailing list.

Printed in Great Britain
by Amazon

43885905R00179